DANGEROUS MEMORIES

A LUCKY TOWN NOVEL
BOOK 2

AMANDA SIEGRIST

McCord Family Novel

Protecting You

Trust in Love

Deserving You

Always Kind of Love

Finding You

Dare You to Love

Mona & Mason

The Paranormal Chronicles, Volume I

Perfect For You Novel

The Wrong Brother

The Right Time

The Easy Part

The Hard Choice

Psychic Love Novel

Exploding Love

Captured Love

Slaying Love Novel

Won't Let You Go

Doomed Love

Deadly Crazy

Evidence of Sin

Finding Redemption

Obsessed Hope

Short Stories

Paint By Murder

Follow Me, Sweet Darling

Sleighville Novel

Dashing Through the Fear

Here Comes Chaos

The Last Noel

Standalone Novel

The Danger with Love

———

Conquering Fear Novel

CO-WRITTEN WITH JANE BLYTHE

Drowning in You

Out of the Darkness

Closing In

HAS THE NIGHTMARE RETURNED OR IS THIS A DARKER THREAT?

1

A STRONG GUST of air nearly knocked her over. Or perhaps it was the breath that left her mouth as the door closed in her face, like a punch to the gut.

"Damn jerk."

Kat shuffled her purse and duffle bag on her shoulder as best as she could while juggling the empty boxes in her hands.

This trip was supposed to be relaxing. A way for her to get away. Some time to herself. To heal a little.

Or a lot.

Oh, and to help Aubrey pack up her apartment, which was the main reason she came all the way to Tampa, Florida.

Every time her brother Logan talked to Aubrey about taking a trip to Florida, she saw the fear enter Aubrey's eyes. So much fear.

She was always telling Aubrey to face her fears. Don't hide from it. Just this once she decided to let Aubrey have her way.

Because she wanted to get away.

Of course, Aubrey and Logan didn't need to know that. Although, they probably had an inkling—especially Aubrey. They talked about anything and everything.

Since the moment Aubrey stumbled upon their family cabin after she escaped being held captive, they had been good friends. It also helped that Aubrey fell head-over-heels for her brother.

It hadn't been an easy road to recovery. No memory of what happened to her, only horrible nightmares. She had clung to Logan in almost an unhealthy way, but nobody tried to stop her. Not even Logan, who had fallen just as hard for her. The pressure, the stress he dealt with had been tremendous. As the sheriff, it had been his duty to find the people responsible for hurting Aubrey, and the way he felt about her made him that much more determined.

Now, Aubrey remembered it all, the memories ten times worse than the nightmares. Kat wasn't positive, but she imagined the nights were the worst for Aubrey. She couldn't stand the dark or being away from Logan when the sun dipped below the horizon. Two months later, after her brother and the FBI caught the man who hurt Aubrey, she still couldn't stand the thought of being away from Logan.

It had been a slow recovery. Most days, Aubrey did well. And some days...some days it broke Kat's heart to watch her friend in so much pain.

Maybe that's why she said yes to Derek when he asked her out. Maybe that's why she thought she'd give him a chance.

It didn't explain why she broke his heart.

"Not gonna think about it. Not gonna think about him."

"Normally when a person talks to themselves, it

concerns me. But a beautiful woman, it sort of intrigues me," a soft, velvety voice said from behind her.

Kat jumped from the intrusion, nearly dropping all the boxes. A man, quite attractive to her annoying heart, stood very close. Light blonde hair, slightly shaggy, yet framed his face well. Deep blue eyes and a smile that probably made most women swoon at the sight. And clean-cut. Not an inch of scruff on his face. She always had a thing for clean-cut men.

So, why not Derek? He was the epitome of clean-cut.

Raising a brow, a slight pursing of her lips, she almost dropped the boxes to prop a hand to her hip to add to the look she was trying to portray. Damn this stranger for frightening her and making her continue to think about the one person she didn't want to. "Does it intrigue you to scare women?"

The man chuckled, a deep throaty laugh that almost made her want to smile. Almost. She'd had enough of men lately. She wasn't about to let another one in her life so soon.

Placing a hand on his chest in an innocent gesture, his lips curled into a sweet smile. "It wasn't my intention to scare you. My apologies. I saw you shout to the guy to hold the door and he clearly ignored you. Do you need help?"

Despite him initially scaring her, he was already an improvement to the jerk who refused to hold the door for her. That made her want to smile.

"Please. I have to grab my key. Could you hold these boxes for me?" Kat held out the boxes with the sweetest smile she could manage, which wasn't much to talk about lately.

He snatched the boxes with ease, holding them with one arm as if it were nothing, and produced a key in his other hand. "Let me get the door for you." He swiped the key against the electronic keypad and opened the door, then gestured her ahead of him.

Kat nodded in thanks and walked through. Turning around, she held out her hands. "I can take those now. Thank you."

He hesitated, then held out his hand instead of the boxes. "I haven't seen you around before. Did you just move in? I'm Erik."

She eyed his hand and decided to play nice, but what she really wanted to do was escape to the apartment and enjoy the peace and quiet for once. Just her. No one to pester her. To ask how she was feeling. To ask questions she didn't want to answer.

"Nice to meet you, Erik. I'm Kat with a K."

"Well, Kat with a K, it's a pleasure to meet you. What does Kat stand for? Or is that your actual name?"

Raising her brow again, she was thankful he held the boxes for her because her hands immediately went to her hips. "For now, it's Kat."

Maybe it was growing up with a brother who worked in law enforcement. Maybe it was the horror Aubrey lived through. Maybe it was being in a new town where she didn't know anybody. Back in Lucky, Minnesota, she knew everybody.

Here, she didn't know a soul. She wasn't about to tell him her full name was Katrina. Not that anybody called her that. She couldn't recall the last time someone called her by her full name. Perhaps her father when he was still alive and she did something she wasn't supposed to do.

He laughed. "Ah, more intrigue. You make it hard to resist that, Kat."

"Please. Resist." She chuckled, trying to lighten her rejection. She didn't want a man to flirt with her when she had barely been in Florida for less than three hours. Holding out her hands, she smiled. "Thanks again, Erik. I'll take the boxes."

"I can carry them to your place."

"That's very kind of you, but I've held you up long enough."

Nodding with a smile, he handed her the boxes. "I hope I see you again, Kat with a K."

"Have a nice day, Erik." Beaming her smile up a notch, she was surprised when he winked and turned around without another word.

Part of her had expected him to ask her for her number or at least try to keep the conversation going. She wasn't used to a man getting her hints, very obvious hints, that she wasn't interested. Or maybe most men got the hint except one.

Not gonna think about it.

A gust of wind slipped in as Erik walked outside. A shiver rushed over her as she met his gaze. Then her eyes caught the look of the man next to him. The shivers increased.

Dressed all in black, from head to toe, the man right away gave her the heebie-jeebies. Not many people could manage to make her uneasy. Not much frightened her.

He had black oily-wavy hair that peeked out from underneath the black knit hat he wore, almost covering his eyes, giving him a beady eye look. He grinned at her, appearing more like a sneer. Her eyes then pinned to the black gloves covering his hands. It was over eighty degrees outside. Why was he wearing gloves? And black. What was with all the black?

Erik waved, nudged the guy next to him, and walked away.

Kat pushed the two men from her mind and continued to Aubrey's apartment. Not her problem, or concern, why the man wore all black and gloves on such a blistering hot day. Neither was Erik her concern. She had enough of men. It never worked out for her. Not even with a good man.

It didn't take her long to ride the elevator five floors and walk down the corridor to the very end of the hallway. Setting the boxes down, she shuffled through her purse for the key.

With a quick flick of her wrist, she unlocked the door and shoved it open. Too lazy, or more like exhausted from the day, she kicked the boxes into the apartment. Wearily, she tossed her purse and bag to the floor, closed the door, and leaned her forehead against it.

"Don't think about it, Kat. Just don't."

A LOUD, persistent knock echoed throughout the house. Resisting the urge to slam her glass down, she took a sip first. The cool rich wine slid down her throat loosening her up.

Another knock sounded.

Ignoring it wouldn't do any good. She knew exactly who it was.

Deputy Derek Graham. Best friend to her brother. Great friend to her. A man who deserved the best woman. A woman she clearly wasn't.

He knocked again. He'd continue to do so until he had his say. She knew this. She had anticipated it.

With a quick jerk, she opened the door. "Hi, Derek."

"Can I come in, Kat?" He looked tired. So sad and tired.

She put that sadness there, and she was about to add more. Not that she wanted to, but she couldn't help how she felt.

"Sure. Do you want something to drink? I'm having a glass of wine." *Heading back to the kitchen, his heavy footsteps trailed.*

"You stood me up. Why?"

Grabbing her wineglass, she took a sip. How did she answer that? She still had no answer for herself.

"I'm sorry. I tried to call, but my cell had no service. You know how spotty the service can get."

His eyebrows puckered as his frown dipped further. "That's the best excuse you can give me. These past few weeks have been great, and then suddenly, you stand me up. I felt foolish waiting at the cabin for you."

Yeah, and she felt foolish for accepting the suggestion for a weekend getaway at her family's cabin to begin with. Derek was such a good man. The perfect man when she thought about it. It hurt her that she couldn't like him the way he liked her. Maybe even loved her. She saw the way he looked at her. He wasn't good at hiding his emotions, even if he thought he was good at it.

"I'm sorry, Derek."

Leaning against the counter, his lips thinned. "Sorry for what exactly? You're normally up-front and honest about everything. I get the feeling you're holding something back."

Gripping the wineglass a little harder, she took a deep breath. So true. She was honest to a fault. Always speaking her mind when she should keep her mouth shut sometimes. But to speak honestly now would break his heart. That was the last thing she wanted to do.

He slammed his hand to the counter. "Damn it, Kat! Say it. I should've never asked you out. You don't like me the way I like you. That's it, isn't it? I just never thought you'd stand me up like that."

Refusing to look away, she kept eye contact. "I'm sorry, Derek. I just want to be friends. We're better as friends."

Derek's expression softened, a small smile lit up his face. "We could be even better as lovers, Kat. Give me the chance to show you."

He closed the distance between them, the earnest hope etched across his face. She cupped his cheek. So smooth. So soft. Such great attributes to describe the man himself. "I can't, Derek. I thought I could date you, but I'd rather be friends. I truly think we're better as friends. I can't give you what you want."

Her hand fell as he backed away. "Then you should've never said yes. You felt like this from the beginning, didn't you? What was it? Pity?"

"Don't belittle yourself. I would never date you out of pity."

His eyes swerved to her hip where she had planted her hand again. "There's the Kat I know. The sassy one. The tough one. Whatever the hell that was before, stop acting that way. Stick to who you are. Say what you really think."

Taking a step forward, her wine sloshed over the rim. She poked him in the chest. "The truth? I'll give you some truth. We've known each other for a long time. I never gave you the impression I liked you as more than a friend. Sure, we liked to tease each other, but that's it. When you asked me out, I saw you in a new light. So I said yes to see where it could go. Well, I'm sorry, Derek, but it's not going any further. We're better as friends. It was never pity, so don't make me look like some no-good bitch."

Leaning in, his face became hard. "Well, gee, Kat, I think you earned that title when you stood me up."

"Get out, Derek." She turned around and walked away, afraid she would slap him for saying such a thing.

Sure, she should've tried harder to get a hold of him, but she didn't deserve to be called a bitch. She had no clue what to say to *him. How to break it gently that she didn't want to keep dating him. Did that make her a bitch?*

The door slammed, the loud sound echoed throughout the house, piercing her straight to the heart. Yeah, maybe she was a bitch.

She hurt a good man.

―――――

KAT JERKED AWAY from the door when the handle rattled.

Who could be at the door?

Ugh. Preoccupied with Derek on her mind since she fled Minnesota, she hadn't paid much attention to her surroundings. Dumb. So utterly dumb. She knew better, especially after what happened to Aubrey. Not to mention Logan made sure from a young age she knew how to protect herself.

Did Erik follow her up here? She never ignored the vibes from people, and while he appeared innocent enough, there was something about him that gave her cause for concern. Or perhaps it was his friend that gave her cause for concern.

They were trying to break in.

Maybe Derek followed her here. Perhaps to convince her again they could be good together. Or to apologize. As much as she would like an apology for the way he spoke to her, she sort of deserved it. She stood him up.

No, it couldn't be Derek. He would knock.

The sound of the lock clicked open. Kat took a few steps back.

"Get your shit together, Kat. You don't back down from anything."

Pep talk firmly done, she attempted to rush to the door to block the intruder from entering, but the door swung open. Groaning at the sight of her visitor, she jerked in place before she ran right into his arms.

"Ah, hell. I don't want to deal with you right now. What the hell do you want?"

"What would you say if I said you?" He arched a brow as a silky smile lit up his face.

DANNY SMOTHERED HIS LAUGH, making sure to keep his smile firmly in place. Laughing at this woman would do him no good. But damn, she looked gorgeous when she got all fired up. His words had definitely fired her up and confused her a little.

Confused him, too.

He had no idea where those words came from. They sort of slipped out when she spoke. He hadn't realized how much he missed her.

Missed her? How could he have possibly missed this woman? She aggravated him more than anyone else. Yet, she managed to make him smile when he rarely did anymore. Even Deke told him he needed to lighten up and have some fun.

"I'm shocked. I have rendered the all-mighty Kat speechless."

"Wipe that grin off your face. Quit jerking me around. We both know how much we like each other. We're barely civil, and only for Aubrey's sake."

Danny straightened up and finally wiped the smirk off his face. Aubrey. His sister. Damn, he missed her. "Where is my sister?" He pushed past Kat, ignoring her irritated groan, and looked around his sister's apartment. It looked the same as the last time he visited.

Unlived-in. Empty. Hollow. Sort of like his heart.

"She called you. I know she did. You know damn well she's not here."

He turned around. "Why the hell are you here? Did the sheriff—"

Kat advanced on him, poking him hard in the chest. "Don't you dare say one nasty word about my brother. Not one word. You know Aubrey is still recovering. She has good days, and she has bad days. Can you try calling Logan by his name instead of *the sheriff*?"

Danny shrugged and took a step back. Standing so close to her wasn't a good idea. The reason behind that, well, he didn't want to look too deep into it. She was right. They barely got along. He had only been teasing her when he said he wanted her. Only teasing.

"He is the sheriff."

"You know it upsets Aubrey when you call him that. She loves him. He loves her. Why can't you be happy for them?"

"Aubrey's not here, and unless you're going to go crying to her..." He arched a brow as he let that sink in. Kat lifted a brow right back like he knew she would. "She sounded better on the phone. She said she was coming to pack up her apartment and to visit me."

To his surprise, Kat stepped closer and laid a hand on his chest. This time he couldn't find the energy to back away. Not when her touch instantly calmed the raging pain inside.

"Danny, she is getting better. She wanted to come, she really did. Yet, I could see the fear in her eyes, hear it in her voice."

"But why? She's safe now. That bastard is behind bars. This is her home." God, he sounded pathetic and desperate, even to his own ears. He hated thinking about how his sister was hurt. He should've killed the bastard, Wayne, who hurt

his sister when he had the chance. He expected the Chee-
tahs, the gang Wayne fled from, to kill him the minute he hit
the prison. Surprisingly, they didn't. He heard he got a rough
beating, though, that nearly took his life. He wouldn't be sad
the day Wayne died. He wouldn't care if it happened today,
not after what Wayne did to his sister.

"She didn't say she was scared to come. She wouldn't.
Aubrey is one of the toughest women I know, which I'm sure
she gets from you." Kat smiled, drawing out another small
smile from him. "She needs a little more time. It's almost
Christmas. Why don't you celebrate it with us? Bring Deke."

At the mention of his best friend and partner's name, he
backed away from her. The minute her hand fell away, the
pain scorched his heart like a hot iron poker.

Why would he need to bring Deke? Sure, he was like a
brother to Aubrey. But it was probably more like he'd keep
the peace between him and the Caldwell family. Kat knew
that. She obviously wanted a buffer so he wouldn't cause
problems. It's not like he wanted to cause problems. He
wanted to fix them. He wanted to help Aubrey recover.
"Maybe."

She rolled her eyes and walked around him. "Why are
you here again? I know Aubrey called you. I don't need a
babysitter to pack her stuff, and I certainly don't need help. I
can handle this."

He followed her to the kitchen, attempting to keep his
eyes off her ass. It was a pretty useless attempt. No matter
how hard he tried, he could never keep his eyes off this
woman. He never understood it either. They rarely got
along. Fighting and arguing over what was best for his sister.
That's what they were good at.

He knew Kat's brother loved his sister, but damn if he
still wanted to hate the man for taking his sister away from

him. She should've come home to Florida with him. He should be the one helping her to heal, to take care of her. He screwed up taking care of her, letting her get kidnapped. He had to redeem himself somehow.

But no. The damn Caldwell family was helping his sister to heal, and he wanted to hate them all. Right now, he wanted to hate Kat the most because she stood right in front of him.

"She did call me. She asked me to check on her apartment but somehow failed to mention you'd be in it."

Kat whipped around. Her long blonde hair, tied up in a ponytail, swung in a graceful arc, reminding him of an Amazon goddess.

An Amazon goddess? Really? What did one of those look like anyway? Beautiful. Strong. Tough.

Why did he have to think of Kat as anything other than a nuisance?

Not the way he wanted his mind to trail. He hated this family. He needed to.

Kat slammed her hands to her hips. "She wouldn't. You're jerking me around again. She had to tell you I was coming to pack her things up."

He smiled. Wow, for the third time. That had to be a record. "Are you sure? Perhaps you don't know my sister as well as you thought. She's a troublemaker."

"Aubrey's a sweetheart."

His smile grew. "When she wants to be. Need I remind you that I raised my sister during her formidable teenage years? Complete troublemaker. Somehow, I picture you the same way."

Kat closed the distance between them and poked his chest. "You know nothing about me. I'd like you to leave now. You know why I'm here, so let me do my thing."

His eyes grazed down to where her finger was still pressed against his chest. He didn't like it when she touched him. It made him want to touch her all over. That was the last thing he should do or even think about.

"Have I ever told you that you're beautiful when you get angry?"

Her eyes grew wide, then simmered with heat. Yeah, she remembered all right. He *had* said that to her before. It shocked the hell out of him the first time he said it, just as it shocked him now. He couldn't seem to keep his words in check. She did things to him he didn't understand.

"Get—"

Grabbing her around the waist, his lips stopped whatever nonsense she was about to holler. He couldn't resist pulling her closer. She tasted more heavenly than the sweetest candy in the world. Her taste was intoxicating. Like an addictive drug, he couldn't get enough of.

That was the last thing he needed. He didn't even like her. Why was he kissing her?

He pulled away. Confusion covered her features, with a hint of pleasure mingled in.

"Why did you do that?" she asked breathlessly.

"To shut you up. You talk too much."

She shoved him away, an adorable angry look adorning her face. He loved it way too much when she got angry. "Get out, Danny. Stay away from me. I don't need another man to cause problems in my life."

Shit. Who was causing her problems? What kind of problems?

Not his concern. He refused to make it his concern. Acting like a jerk had the desired effect. She shoved him away and told him to leave.

Because that's what he needed to do. Leave. If he didn't,

he might do more than kiss her. He could never do more with her. Not even kiss her again. Hell, he couldn't figure out why he kissed her to begin with.

She was nothing but trouble.

He'd let her pack up Aubrey's things without interfering. No good would come from him hanging around.

"Tell the sheriff I blame him for my sister not coming." With those parting words, he walked out.

2
_____

YEAH, like she was about to tell her brother that Danny blamed him for Aubrey not coming. Logan already felt guilty enough. He knew how much Danny loved his sister. How much he wanted her to come home. Family was everything. Logan would never want to keep Aubrey away from her family.

Danny was just too dumb and arrogant to realize it.

The pain. Maybe it was the pain of his sister getting kidnapped that warped his thinking. He felt responsible. Kat saw that clearly every time he talked about Aubrey. It wasn't his fault. Not even Aubrey blamed him.

Oh, boy, he and Logan were more alike than those two probably realized. Logan would blame himself if anything happened to her, and it wouldn't even matter if she hurt herself while in Florida. Which was ridiculous, she wasn't anywhere near him, he couldn't possibly keep her safe. She was a grown woman. She could take care of herself.

Kat brushed her fingertips across her lips.

He kissed her.

Why did he kiss her?

Did he think she'd believe his excuse that she talked too much? Although, she did have a difficult time holding her tongue, especially when it came to him. She never held back her thoughts to Danny. When she first met him, waltzing in like some big hotshot FBI agent, she had let him and his partner Deke know exactly how the investigation would go. She didn't work for the sheriff's department, but she didn't like that Logan called in help.

Of course, she hadn't realized Aubrey was his sister. She thought he was an annoying FBI agent trying to come in and take over.

Why did he kiss her? Why did he keep saying she was beautiful in one breath and treat her like crap the next? Why did she like that he kissed her?

"No way, Kat. You do not like that man. No more kissing him. But it wouldn't hurt to be more civil. For Aubrey."

Aubrey. Yeah, time to give Aubrey a little piece of her mind.

Digging through her purse, she found her phone and then dialed Aubrey's number.

"Did you make it? Do you like Florida? How was the flight? Any problems? You know, we need to talk."

Kat chuckled at Aubrey's nonstop barrage of questions. "I made it. Florida's hot. Flight was good. No problems... unless you want to count your brother. And I'd say this is us talking."

"Oh, did Danny stop by?"

"Girl, don't act innocent. He said you asked him to check on the apartment. Why didn't you tell him I was coming? We were both surprised."

"I'm sure I did." Aubrey hesitated. "You know my memory..."

"Your memory is back to tip-top shape. Don't try to play me, Aubs. What's going on?"

"Nothing. I swear. I guess it slipped my mind. I...I had a bad night last night, Kat. I'm sorry."

The pain and sadness. Kat hated hearing that in her voice. Even though she knew Aubrey was up to something mischievous, she couldn't ignore the pain that filtered out. "No, I'm sorry, Aubs. Do you want to talk about it?"

"No. Logan made me already."

"Talking is good. It'll help."

"Yeah, yeah, I know. Face your fears. Let's talk now."

Kat chuckled again. "We are."

"You know what I'm talking about."

Derek.

Did he stop by their house? Did he say something to Logan? Logan and Aubrey didn't keep secrets. She loved the relationship her brother had with Aubrey. She wanted the same for herself. Just not with Derek. Would he go to her brother to talk about what happened between them? They were best friends, but Logan was also her brother. Talk about awkward.

"Kat..." She sighed. "Your silence, which never happens, tells me a lot. What happened?"

"I hurt him, Aubrey. I didn't mean to. I should've never dated him."

"Tell me what happened. Logan said he's been acting funny, but Derek won't talk about it."

So he didn't talk to Logan. She wanted to feel thankful, yet, she only felt more and more like she deserved being called a bitch. Derek couldn't even go to his best friend and share his pain. That was her fault, too.

"You have a ton of crap to pack up, Aubs. We'll talk

later." Kat laughed, although it sounded fake, as she glanced around the apartment.

She hadn't toured the place yet, but by the looks of the living room and kitchen, she'd be busy for the next few days. With a quick glance at the bookshelves against one of the living room walls, she knew she'd be busy all day sorting through Aubrey's books.

"You know we will. Danny can help you. I only want what was on the list I gave you. Everything else I want you to get rid of."

"I don't need help."

"I love you, Kat. Stop being so stubborn. You tell me to face my fears all the time. You need to start letting in the help."

They talked for a few more minutes, then said their goodbyes. Kat hung up with Aubrey, letting her words sink in.

Help. No, she didn't need help with this task. She didn't want it. She wanted to be alone. She wanted to enjoy the peace. She really wanted everyone to stop asking her questions.

And if she wanted help, it wouldn't be in the form of one sexy man she shouldn't even think was sexy.

Oh, but he was. His light brown hair, short and styled to perfection, always made her want to run her hands through it and mess it up a little. Never a hair out of place. For such a volatile man, she wanted his hair to be a bit messier, to fit his personality.

His smile. On the rare occasion he decided to grace her with one, brightened his features so much it almost made her weak in the knees.

His five o'clock shadow. She did prefer a clean-cut man,

but something about Danny's rough stubble made him irre-sistible.

His eyes. Such deep brown eyes that held so much depth. So much pain. She honestly hated seeing that pain. At times, it almost mirrored Aubrey's pain. She wanted to take it away. From both of them. Just in different ways. Thinking about how she could take Danny's pain away wasn't wise to contemplate.

No. She wouldn't be accepting any help from Danny O'Rourke. He was nothing but trouble.

Glancing around the apartment, she sighed happily. Neat. Clean. Very organized. This shouldn't be too much trouble to pack. Plus, the list Aubrey gave her was short. Clothes. A few sentimental trinkets. Her photos. The rest, well, she didn't care what Kat did with the rest. That would probably be the hardest part. She had a lot of stuff.

Kat looked at the three boxes she grabbed on her way from the airport and sighed. She'd need more boxes. She had been paying careful attention to the GPS while making her way to Aubrey's place, but when the boxes caught her attention, lying on the side of the road, she didn't hesitate to grab them. Now she wished she could've grabbed more because then she'd have one less thing to worry about.

No worries. She had to keep reminding herself of that.

This trip was for Aubrey but also for herself. For some peace—and maybe a little fun. She wanted to hit the beach before she left. Back home in Minnesota, the cold and potential for snow awaited her. She wanted to take advan-tage of the heat and sun while she had the chance.

Making a mental list of what needed to be completed, Kat started with the first thing on her list. Food. The apart-ment had absolutely nothing, and she was getting hungry, then she could start the task of packing things up.

As long as everyone left her alone, this would be the best trip. And by everyone, she meant Danny.

Seeing him again would be nothing but trouble.

"Oh, look. You left with a gloomy face, and you're returning with one as well. Good to know things don't change."

"Shut up, Deke. What do we have?" Danny needed to focus on work. Not on the woman that got under his skin since the moment he met her.

He could still remember staring at his sister for the first time after he finally found her, hoping for the recognition, the excitement of seeing him again. Except nothing. She stood staring at him like she had no clue who the hell he was. And she hadn't known. She had lost her memory for a short period of time. Everything wiped clean, including her own name.

Then Kat spoke. The feisty attitude. An air of confidence. A sweet, strong voice that touched something inside of him. She made him laugh. He hadn't laughed in all the days his sister had been missing. It still shocked the hell out of him the way Kat affected him.

"Another dead woman. This time close to home." Deke raised a brow. "What's with the funny expression? Aubs asked you to check on her apartment. Everything okay?"

Danny froze, then hit the button to go up on the elevator. "Kat's here. She's packing up Aubrey's things. She didn't come with."

Deke sighed. Danny knew what that sigh meant. It was the last thing he wanted. Turning around, he held up his hand. "Don't. Don't say anything. She's not ready to come back. I totally understand." They both entered the elevator. Danny hit the button for the third floor.

"I know you were looking forward to a little time with her. I'm sorry she didn't come."

"That's exactly what I didn't want to hear. Let's focus on the case."

A few seconds later, the elevator door swished open. Danny stepped out immediately, wanting to flee as far as he could from Deke. He hoped Deke dropped the conversation.

"Does Kat need help? We could—"

He jerked to a stop. Deke almost ran into him. He glanced at his longtime friend and partner. "She made it very clear she doesn't want any help. So, we'll leave her alone."

A smirk emerged. "*We* will leave her alone? I can't even help her?"

Danny's lips drew into a thin line. "That's right. The damn woman doesn't want any help. From anyone."

"You got it, buddy."

"What the hell does that mean?"

Deke shrugged, the wily smirk still on his face. "Nothing. I hear you loud and clear."

"Shut up, Deke." Danny wasn't in the mood to have this conversation. He knew what Deke was trying to imply and it wasn't true. He didn't like Kat. Not even a little.

That kiss meant absolutely nothing.

"That's twice now you told me to shut up." Deke's smile didn't waver. "I guess I won't try for a third. The victim's name is Sheila Crowler. From the call I got from local PD, it sounds like our first two victims."

"Great. This guy is hopping around the state. First Miami, then Fort Lauderdale, and now Tampa."

"That's what serial killers do." Deke stopped next to

Danny outside Sheila's apartment and introduced themselves to the officer standing outside the door.

"Detective Larson's inside." The officer gave a short nod. Not one friendly smile punctured his face.

"I love being welcomed with open arms," Danny said dryly.

"Detective Larson sounded very nice."

Danny stopped right outside the doorway to the bedroom and glanced at Deke. "Yeah, I can see why Detective Larson sounded so nice to you."

Deke peered into the room and produced a devilish grin. Detective Larson was a very tall, very attractive woman. Her black hair was pulled back into a tight bun, glasses perched perfectly on her nose, and a poise to her stance that said she probably wouldn't tolerate any nonsense, especially from Deke. But he never let that hold him back. She had almost a naughty teacher look going on, not that she probably intended to be perceived that way, but that's exactly how Deke would see her.

Deke leaned closer. "You know what your problem is? You need to get laid. I think it would help your crabbiness."

"I get the feeling you don't mean with the beautiful woman in front of us."

"You got that right. You know who I mean." Deke walked into the room. "Detective Larson, it's a pleasure to meet you in person. We talked on the phone. I'm Agent Sumnter, and this is my partner, Agent O'Rourke."

Detective Larson looked away from the woman on the bed and gave them one sharp nod. "This is Dr. Mallery," she pointed to the older woman examining the body, who barely glanced in their direction, "she's almost done. There doesn't appear to be any defensive wounds on her body. She was tied up, probably right away."

"Cause of death?" Danny asked, even though he knew the answer.

"Can't say for sure until I've done an autopsy." Dr. Mallery waved a hand toward the woman's neck. "As you can see, bruises indicate she was strangled." Then she waved a hand toward the woman's chest. "And she was also repeatedly stabbed. I can't be sure how she died yet."

Danny wanted to look away. He didn't want to envision what this woman endured before she died. But he did, anyway.

Completely naked, her hands and legs were spread wide on the bed. The bruises around her wrists and ankles indicated she was tied up; however, there wasn't a distinctive pattern to the bruises to suggest what the killer used to tie her up. The killer removed whatever they used and took everything before they left. Her chest and torso were covered with stab wounds. Danny didn't even need to count. He knew there'd be exactly twelve. Just like the other two women.

Her neck held the same bruising as the first two. He also had a bad inkling about what she endured before the repeated stabbing and strangulation.

"She was raped as well?" He could see heavy bruising between her legs. He still liked confirmation.

"It appears that way." Dr. Mallery stood up and closed the evidence bag she was holding. "How many women were killed before her?"

"Two. They looked exactly like this. Autopsies indicated they died of strangulation. The stab wounds, each stabbed twelve times, never hit any vital organs and it showed they bled a while, but not enough to bleed to death." Deke hammered everything out like it was nothing new.

For them, it wasn't. They dealt with violent crimes every

day. New day, same shit. They had to remove themselves emotionally or they'd never survive dealing with things like this all the time.

"What did you find?" Danny asked as Dr. Mallery placed an evidence bag in the kit on the floor.

"A small piece of trace evidence that was on her neck. Maybe from whatever he used to strangle her with. I'll let you know when the crime lab finishes with it."

"Unless, of course, your department is going to take it from us," Detective Larson piped in.

"Is this an us versus them thing now?" Deke asked with a sultry smile.

Danny wanted to laugh. Not many women could resist those devastating smiles. Detective Larson didn't appear to be any different. Her stiff posture relaxed a little as she tossed a small smile back his way.

"Of course not. I assumed you'd..."

"Jump right in and take over. Agent O'Rourke and I love working with local law enforcement. The more, the merrier. I want this sicko off the streets. Don't you, Detective Larson?"

"I do. Why don't we go over what you already have on the first two cases and go from there." Her smile became even wider. Not a hint of her standoffishness present any longer.

"Great idea." Deke smiled and gestured for her to lead the way out of the room.

Just like that, Danny knew Deke would probably get laid. Oddly, it pissed him off. Not the fact he wanted the detective for himself because he didn't. No way. She gave in to Deke's charm way too easily. He liked—well, damn, he didn't want to think about what he liked. Because when he did, all the qualities he conjured up only made him think of one person.

The one person he shouldn't think about.

Kat.

She didn't want his help. She didn't even like him much. He didn't like her either.

Yet, as he followed them out of the room, he knew he was lying to himself. He did like her. That's what scared the hell out of him.

3

SHE CLUNG a little too tightly to him, obviously not ready for him to leave for the day. She reacted this way any time she had a bad night. And last night had been difficult to get through. Two nights in a row now.

"Are you going to be okay today, honey? I can take the day off."

Aubrey finally pulled away and smiled. "It's Bolt's first day back. You have to go. I'm fine. You know how much I like hugging you."

Logan pulled her closer and kissed the top of her head. "You're a horrible liar. I know you like hugging me, but that's not why you haven't let go yet."

"I'm worried about Kat. Have you talked to her recently? Have you talked to Derek?"

In typical fashion, she wanted to ignore it, the nightmares that plagued her. He didn't want to ignore it or let her do it either. But it *was* Bolt's first day back after being shot two months ago. He wanted to be there for his deputy. He should've never been shot to begin with. If he had figured out who hurt Aubrey sooner, Bolt would've never gotten hurt. No matter how many times people said it wasn't his fault, it still felt like it.

"Derek's not saying much, and you know Kat when it comes to her feelings, her lips are zipped. They'll figure their issues out. I'm going to let you ignore your issue right now, but tonight we talk. You can't leave it inside. It's not healthy, Aubrey."

She cringed and sighed heavily. "I always feel like I'm in trouble when you call me by my name. Call me honey."

Logan kissed her tenderly. "I love you. You know I worry."

"I know you do. You have nothing to worry about. I'm fine. I have a busy day at work today. Teaching a rambunctious group of preschoolers takes a lot of energy. I have a great project planned for the day. I guess I should get ready."

"Have fun. Call me if you need me." Logan kissed her one more time and left for work.

Every morning, he kissed her goodbye and worried needlessly about her. She had made great progress since escaping from being held captive and recovering from memory loss. But nights like last night always concerned him she would take a step back in her progress. The things she would say in her sleep—he knew what happened to her was horrible. He hated hearing every whispered word as she rolled around in her sleep, but she needed to talk about it for her to fully recover. She refused to see a professional. That put it all on his shoulders to be the best listener he could be. He hated it, but he loved her so much he needed the pain to go away. If listening to her horror helped that, then that's what he'd do.

Walking into the building, Logan smiled at Charlotte,

the queen of keeping the sheriff's department running as smoothly as it did.

"I hope that smile stays on your face, Logie."

At those words, his smile dipped, and not because she called him the nickname he didn't care for. "What problem do we have?"

"Derek's waiting for you in your office. It looked serious. Is he okay? I get this feeling something happened between him and Kat." She looked concerned.

He was concerned himself, but talking to Kat elicited no results. Same with Derek. Something obviously happened, but neither wanted to share with him.

"I'll talk to him."

"So something did happen?" Her brow lifted, patiently waiting for him to spill the beans.

"I have no idea. I'm sure nothing serious."

"Bolt's coming back today. I made him cupcakes. His favorite. Chocolate with chocolate frosting and blue sprinkles. Do you think he'll like that?"

Logan smiled, hoping that would make Charlotte's sudden nervousness disappear. She rarely got nervous about anything. "He'll love it. He doesn't hate you, Char-Char."

"He also hasn't forgiven me for thinking he was a suspect in Aubrey's disappearance. I feel bad." Her face crinkled in unease.

Such an unusual look for her. She was always confident. Logan hated to see her doubt herself. But Bolt *had* taken it personally. Logan honestly couldn't be sure how he felt now, but Bolt wasn't known for holding a grudge.

"He'll love the cupcakes. I'll be in my office. I should go talk to Derek now."

Charlotte smiled, then produced a stern look. "The cupcakes are in the break room. No touching them until Bolt's had one. I mean it."

"Scout's honor." Logan held up the symbol he learned long ago when he was a boy scout.

Laughing at her stern smirk, he walked to his office with a little too much anticipation. He wasn't sure what to make about Derek wanting to talk to him. Charlotte made it sound so serious. Since, whatever happened between him and Kat, they hadn't talked as they normally did.

Logan had known for the longest time that Derek liked his sister. He also knew that Kat never shared the same sentiment toward Derek. It surprised him when Derek asked her out, and Kat said yes. Only because he never thought Derek would actually go through with it and that Kat would say yes. He had been happy, of course. One of his best friends asking out his sister, who he knew would treat his sister right, had been a great thing.

It also made it awkward. He wanted to protect his sister and wanted to be on her side with whatever happened between them. Yet, Derek was his best friend, and he wanted to be there for him as well. Talk about a rock and a hard place.

"Hey, Derek. Charlotte said you wanted to talk." Logan gave him an encouraging smile as he hung up his jacket on the coat rack near the door, then sat down at his desk.

Derek looked tense sitting in the chair across from him, not to mention tired and worn out. Deep, dark circles rounded his eyes. His hair looked as if he had been running his hand through it so much it couldn't lay flat if he wanted it to. And the worst part was the five o'clock shadow marring his face. Derek always shaved. Always.

"I need some time off, Logan. Starting today." His voice came out toneless.

"It's Bolt's first day back. What's going on, Derek? Talk to me." Logan leaned forward, hating the hurt etched in his eyes.

"There's nothing to talk about. I haven't had a vacation in a long time and I have two weeks saved up. I'd like to use them."

"The whole two weeks?" Logan didn't try to hide the shock in his voice.

"Yes. I never ask for time off. It shouldn't be difficult to say yes. You and Bolt can hold the fort without a problem." Derek's face went from tired to annoyed.

"What happened with Kat?" Derek might want to ignore the problem, but Logan wasn't going to any longer.

Derek stood up. "Are you denying my request?"

Logan held Derek's severe gaze, wondering what he should say. He wanted Derek to talk to him about Kat, but the longer he stood there, he knew Derek wasn't going to say a word until he gave the okay for his vacation.

"Enjoy your time off, Derek. We should talk, though."

Derek turned around and started for the door. Right before walking out, he glanced at Logan. "Thanks for the time. We have nothing to talk about. I appreciate your concern, but I'm okay." He walked away without waiting for Logan to reply.

Well, that didn't go as Logan had planned. Whatever happened with Kat had to be serious. Derek never acted this way, especially with him.

Neither did Kat. She had jumped on the chance to pack Aubrey's apartment, insisting it was okay that Aubrey didn't go. If anyone was adamant that Aubrey face her memories, it was Kat. For her to let Aubrey off the hook so easily, Logan knew that she was hurting as well. Going to Florida had been an escape. She ran. Plain and simple. His sister never ran from anything.

What the hell happened between them?

Logan glanced at the clock hanging above the doorway. Seven-thirty. There was an hour time difference with Florida. Kat was always an early riser. She'd be awake. It was eight-thirty in Florida.

Grabbing his phone, he dialed her number. He knew she was getting annoyed with him bothering her, but the worry swimming through his veins wouldn't disappear.

Worrying about everything.

He needed a damn vacation. Christmas was coming soon. Perhaps he'd suggest going to the cabin for a few days with Aubrey. He knew she needed a breather and the cabin always offered her a sense of peace.

"Damn it, Kat." Logan tossed his phone onto his desk after hearing nothing but ringing.

She was either busy this early in the morning, which wouldn't surprise him, or she was ignoring his phone call. That wouldn't surprise him either.

"I have too much to worry about. I don't want to have to worry about you, too, Kat." He eyed his phone like a bomb waiting to go off, the seconds ticking down. "Just do it, Logan."

Snatching the phone before he could change his mind, he dialed the last person who probably wanted to speak to him.

KAT ROLLED over to the other side of the bed, grateful the phone had stopped ringing. Apparently, Logan got the idea she didn't want to talk. It didn't mean he wouldn't try calling again later. How many states away and her family and friends were still bugging her. She couldn't truly escape like she had hoped.

Snuggling under the covers, she sighed. She never slept in. Her body never wanted to, always demanding she get up and start the day. Back home, she always rolled out of bed around six, had a quick cup of tea, and then a short run around the block. Running wasn't her favorite activity, but she liked the fresh morning air, the beauty of nature as she ran. It always helped to put her in a good mood. Keeping in shape was also a plus.

Here, she couldn't find the energy—eight-thirty in the morning—it was so unlike her to lounge in bed like this.

Ugh. She was feeling sorry for herself. Completely unacceptable.

Forcing herself to get out of bed, she used the bathroom and then started a pot of coffee. She didn't particularly like coffee, but Aubrey didn't have a teapot, and she didn't want to buy one for the short time she'd be here. So coffee it would be. She needed some sort of pick-me-up in the mornings. Tomorrow would be better. She'd get up at her usual time even if she had to set a damn alarm. No way would she allow any problems with a man make her feel sorry for herself.

She probably wouldn't go running here, unfamiliar with the territory and all, but doing a few exercises in the apartment would work out just fine.

After having two cups of coffee, the brew going down rather easily to her surprise, she did a small set of exercises and then jumped in the shower. Feeling more alive and refreshed for the day, Kat decided to tackle the list Aubrey gave her. Grabbing some boxes, having a good supply today after picking more up yesterday when she went grocery shopping, she started in Aubrey's room.

Opening the closet, she laughed. "Wow, Aubs, we have totally different styles."

Kat would describe herself as the T-shirt and jeans kind of girl. In the winter, she loved comfortable buttoned-styled shirts. Compared to other women, she was a simple girl when it came to clothes. She rarely dressed up, especially in a dress.

Apparently, before Aubrey went missing, she was more into style. Her closet was full of dresses, some looking quite skimpy to Kat. Her shirts were rather expensive looking, some tight and low cut. A few jeans lingered on one side, but not many 'simple' looking clothes hung in the closet.

Staring at all the clothes, Kat honestly couldn't imagine Aubrey wearing any of this. Maybe it's because she now wore half of Kat's clothes. She had graciously given Aubrey a whole suitcase full of clothes when Logan first found her. Kat might have simple tastes, but she owned a lot of clothes. She hated passing up on good deals when she saw one.

Even though it had been two months already, Aubrey never once asked to go shopping for new clothes. She still wore everything Kat had given her.

Would she honestly wear these clothes?

Kat ran a hand down a black dress that appeared to have no back. The front looked a lot more revealing than what she was used to seeing in her small town. Some women like to show off their assets, but not too many. And this dress. Whew! Talk about cleavage. The front cut so low and angular, she wasn't sure a bra could be worn with it.

"Okay, so my brother might enjoy seeing her in this." She chuckled and kept skimming through the clothes.

Her hand stopped on a red dress that still had a price tag on it. "Three hundred dollars. Geez, Aubs, how much money did you make as a school teacher here?"

Her fingers lingered on the dress. So beautiful. The dress was one of those 'off-the-shoulder' dresses, with a cute little ruffle outlining the top. It looked short, but not too short where she'd insist on pulling it down constantly. The back of the dress didn't look outrageous, indicating it wouldn't show tons of skin. Kat wasn't self-conscious with her body, but she also didn't attempt to show off her assets. A little mystery for a man was a good thing. Or so she thought, anyway.

"We are the same size..."

Turning around, she grabbed a box. "Forget it. I'm not trying on the dress. It's not even mine."

Setting the box near the closet, she started to take the clothes down one by one, carefully folding each item before placing it in the box.

A distant ringing sounded.

Now who wanted to bother her?

Walking fast to her bedroom, the spare room, because she felt awkward sleeping in Aubrey's room, she smiled when she saw who was calling.

"Aubs, you never told me you had a wild side. Girl, your clothes are something else."

A soft chuckle lifted her sour mood from earlier. "I'm so used to wearing your clothes now, I completely forgot I used to wear dresses all the time. It gets hot in Florida."

"Yeah, you also liked to dress in *hot* things." Kat laughed.

Aubrey laughed harder. "It's so good to hear you laugh. I was worried about you."

Kat rolled her eyes, thankful she couldn't see the action. She wanted—no, needed—everyone to stop worrying about her. "There's nothing to worry about. Now I'm worried, though."

Aubrey's breath hitched. "Why?"

"When my brother sees you wearing one of these dresses... oh, boy, watch out."

Kat started giggling like crazy when Aubrey's laughter filled the phone once again.

"I don't think I'm brave enough to wear one of those in front of him. Some of them are pretty revealing. I had a sense of adventure and recklessness before...you know."

"You still have a sense of adventure, Aubrey. Are you okay? Shouldn't you be in school right now?"

Kat hated when Aubrey doubted herself. She must've had a bad night again. That was the only time she put herself down.

"I'm in school. I took a small break to call you. I told you, I'm worried about you." Aubrey paused. "Have some fun down there. We're the same size. Wear one of the dresses. Go enjoy yourself."

Kat's mind filtered to the red dress. It had never been worn if the price tag still attached was any indication. "Yeah, maybe. I'm okay. Quit worrying about me. You totally ignored my question. You had a bad night, didn't you?"

"I'm fine. Oh, I gotta go. Mrs. Wilkens is motioning me back into the room. I'll call you later."

Aubrey hung up before Kat could argue with her. She definitely had a bad night. Maybe that's why Logan called her earlier.

Her finger hovered over his number. At the last second, she decided not to call him. No doubt he'd try calling her again, as would Aubrey.

She wished people would stop doing that. So much for peace and quiet.

Heading back to the bedroom, she tossed her phone on the bed and then eyed the red dress.

Have a little fun Aubrey said.

The dress came off the hanger with one quick swipe.

Now if only she didn't want to have a little fun with one man she absolutely shouldn't.

4

TWISTING the key in the lock, he swung the door open and suppressed the laugh that wanted to escape. Damn, this woman always made him want to laugh. A refreshing feeling. One he wasn't used to.

"Seriously, Danny, don't you know how to knock. This isn't your apartment."

Danny closed the door to his sister's apartment and smirked at Kat. She looked cute and delectable in a pair of yoga pants and a T-shirt. Her hair was fashioned in a ponytail, tiny tendrils of hair hanging out, framing her face.

He didn't want to think about her looking cute, looking beautiful, looking like the most gorgeous woman he had ever seen.

He did, anyway.

"My sister's name is on the lease, but I've been paying the rent the last few months, so technically it's like my apartment."

She stood up. Her shirt was slightly loose, yet as she stood, it tightened across her chest giving him a nice vision.

A vision so tempting, he wanted to remove her shirt altogether.

"You could knock. It's rude to just walk in. Give me the key."

"It's my key."

Kat took a few steps toward him. "Not while I'm here. Give it to me. Why are you here? I thought we agreed you'd leave me alone."

They did, somewhat. He had every intention of leaving her alone, especially when every time he saw her he wanted to kiss her like he had the last time. It was wrong to want to kiss her.

Then Logan called him.

"Did we agree on that? I don't remember. I'm not giving you my key."

"Oh, selective memory loss, uh? Get out, Danny. And give me the key before you leave."

Should he tell her that her brother called him worried about her? When his phone rang, Logan's number flashing before him, he hesitated to answer. His first thought had been something terrible had happened to Aubrey. They didn't have the kind of relationship where they randomly called each other for no reason.

Concern for Aubrey had him answering, his heart pounding right out of his chest. Then Logan said he was worried about Kat. He didn't give much of a reason, but said he was concerned and asked if he would go check on her. Keep an eye on her while she was in Florida. For some reason, his heart never stopped pounding.

Without hesitating, Danny agreed. He told himself it was because he owed Logan. He had kept Aubrey safe. He could do the same for Kat. It wasn't because he was dying to see Kat.

"The key, Danny. Standing there and staring at me with that annoying look of yours isn't going to intimidate me. I want the key."

Yeah, he wasn't in the mood to bring Logan into this conversation. She was on the verge of getting fired up. That was never a good thing. His body reacted in the wrong way.

Maybe it was wrong, but it felt good. Too good.

"If you want the key, you'll have to dig it out of my pocket because I'm not giving it to you. Like I said, it's my apartment, and I can walk in here anytime I want. Got something to hide that you don't want me walking in on, Kat?"

"How about I want some peace and you're disrupting it. Don't think I won't take that key from you." Her eyes zoomed to his left pocket.

She must've seen him put it there. Very observant of her.

He should leave. He should hand over the key and not come back. But a part of him wanted her to get the key from him.

He loved her feisty attitude.

Hell, as insane as it was, he ached for any reason to get her hands on him. What did that make him? An asshole, probably.

"Try your best, Kat. I am a trained federal agent. I doubt you'll get it from me."

Challenge officially issued. He could see the fire in her eyes. She wanted the key, and she was going to go for it.

"Oh, I'm going to love putting you in your place, Special Agent O'Rourke." Kat smiled as the fervor in her eyes intensified.

Shit. Her brother was in law enforcement. How well did she know how to defend herself? Too late now. He issued a challenge, and he couldn't wait to see how she enacted it.

"Bring it on, sweetheart."

Her eyes flashed with what he thought was desire at the endearment, something he hadn't meant to say. Then, without blinking, she took two steps and swiped her leg in one smooth motion toward his legs, knocking him off balance.

Unprepared for her quick attack, he almost fell flat on his ass but managed to straighten up before she tried attacking him again, this time, pushing him with a lot more strength than he realized she had.

He would never hit a woman, even in this situation where she didn't hesitate to knock him down. He had no such problem grabbing for her, though.

As she pushed him, he grabbed her arms, both of them falling. Swinging his body to avoid the floor, they fell on the couch instead. Kat's warm, soft body settled underneath him perfectly. Boxing her in, he leaned close to her mouth.

"You're a lot stronger than I imagined. Still looks like I won, though."

"Get off me, Danny. You haven't won yet."

He didn't want to move. She felt way too good beneath him. He could see by the desire lighting her eyes, she didn't want him to move either, even though she voiced it.

"It feels like I won."

"You're a jerk, you know that."

"Yep. I do."

Rolling her eyes, a slow smirk started to form. "You're gonna regret not moving soon."

He didn't doubt that for one second. He already regretted not moving because at any moment he was going to kiss her again.

Kat raised her head, her smirk even wider.

Or perhaps she was going to initiate the kiss this time.

Her mouth clamped down on his shoulder and bit down.

Nope. Definitely not a kiss.

Moaning from the pain, he quickly jumped off her. "Damn! Seriously, Kat, you just bit me." Rubbing his shoulder, he forgot the pain immediately as she dangled his key in front of him. He never felt her dig into his pocket—smart, devious woman.

"I also won. I warned you that you'd regret it. I never lie, Danny."

"Keep the damn key. Clearly, you're okay."

Her brows dipped. "Of course I am. Why would you think otherwise?"

Not in the mood for another fight, or whatever he wanted to call what happened between them, he ignored her question. "I can't believe you bit me."

"Oh, man up. Are you telling me you've never been bitten before?"

Kat paused as she walked around the opposite side of the couch and glanced at him.

Her question hung in the air.

He initiated the kiss yesterday. He even caused the little fight they just had. Now, she created a little sexual tension with that question.

He actually had never been bitten before. He wasn't into any hardcore sex. Biting seemed a little hardcore to him. Yet, the thought of Kat nibbling her teeth anywhere on his body had his libido rising quickly.

"You'd be the first woman to bite me, Kat. Do you enjoy biting men?"

Her cheeks turned a deep red. "You'd be the first man

I've ever bitten. You deserved it." She glanced away. "But I don't need flowers again."

His brows dipped as he chuckled. "Again? What the hell are you talking about?"

"You sent flowers." She pointed behind him.

Danny turned around to the dining room table where a vase of red roses stood brightly. "What makes you think I sent those?"

Because he sure in the hell didn't send her any flowers. And she didn't want any more flowers. Did that mean she didn't like flowers? Or she didn't like flowers from him?

"The card said, "Please forgive me." And yesterday..."

He looked at her after she stopped speaking. "Yesterday, what? What do you think I'm sorry about?"

"You didn't send them?"

"Was my name on the card?"

"You are so obtuse. Why can't you simply answer a question?"

He grinned, which further irritated her. He knew it did when her hands immediately went to her hips. A gesture she often did when she got annoyed. "I think I've mentioned it before, but you're very beautiful when you get angry."

"So what, you purposely try to make me angry?" She rolled her eyes. "Did you send the dumb flowers or not?"

"No, Kat, I didn't send you flowers. Not sure what you think I should be sorry for. If it was the kiss..." He hesitated, yet refused to look away. "I wasn't sorry about that."

"No, I imagine you weren't. That was you being an arrogant jerk like always. Never mind, I know who sent them now."

Danny walked over to the table and grabbed the card lying near the vase. It seemed better to walk in the opposite direction from her because he knew damn well why he kissed her yesterday.

He'd been dying to kiss her for the longest time. She tempted him way too much. Tempted him right this minute to kiss her again.

Pulling the card out of the envelope, he tried to keep his voice calm. "Computer-generated message. No name on it. Who do you think sent these?"

She said yesterday she had man troubles. Curiosity took over. What kind of man troubles? If some jerk, besides him, was pestering her, he wouldn't hesitate to take care of the situation.

Because, of course, Logan asked him to watch out for her. That was his reason. The only reason.

He refused to dwell on any other reasons floating around his mind.

"It doesn't matter."

Danny turned toward her. For the first time, he saw a bit of sadness in her eyes. He didn't like the look on her at all. "It matters to me. I don't mean to come off as a jerk, Kat. Because I know Aubrey would hate it if she found out. I'm sorry I didn't hand over the key. I admit, I like to irritate you because...I have no good reason, actually. Your first thought was that I sent these because I wasn't that nice yesterday. It wasn't me. You're thinking of someone else now, aren't you? Who else upset you? I can be very tenacious. I'm not leaving until you tell me."

TALKING to Danny about Derek was not high on her list. But if Danny didn't send the flowers, then it had to be Derek.

When a knock sounded on her door with a delivery for

flowers, her mind, for whatever reason, immediately thought Danny had sent them.

And no, not because of the kiss, but for his parting comment about blaming Logan that Aubrey didn't come. She honestly thought he felt bad about that.

Apparently not. Danny only felt terrible about bad-mouthing her family if Aubrey found out. Otherwise, he didn't care at all.

Part of her wanted the flowers to be from him.

Not something she should think—or want. Her and Danny, well, it would never happen. He even admitted to purposely making her angry. And for no good reason.

Well, he did admit to one reason. He thought she was beautiful.

Why couldn't they get along?

"Kat, the silent treatment isn't going to work with me. Aubrey always thought it would, too, but I always won. Start talking before I do something you might not like."

Nobody told her what to do, especially a guy like Danny. "And what would that be? Try me, Danny. Who won the last fight we just had?"

He glanced at the couch, then back at her. He had a predatory gleam in his eyes. Perhaps she shouldn't have said that. She almost didn't win the last fight. The entire time his body was pressed against hers, she swore he would've felt her digging in his pocket and attempt to stop her. When he didn't, she thought he enjoyed it and wanted to kiss her. Kissing Danny was bad.

One of the reasons she bit him. She knew he would back away.

Teasing with him was fun. She feared they both enjoyed it a little too much. The sexual tension was swarming around them like bees to a hive. How could they feel like this? They barely liked each other.

He started walking toward her.

"Are we about to spar again?"

He didn't respond, yet his eyes blazed with heat. Not the angry kind of heat either. The angry kind would be so much better.

"Danny, does it matter who I think sent the flowers? Stop being—"

He cut her words off with a kiss. Wrapping his arms around her body, he pulled her closer as his tongue dipped inside her mouth. The tangoing fusion melted her senses. He was kissing her again. But why?

Because he could? Because he wanted answers? What a strange way to get her to talk.

She wasn't complaining because the kiss from yesterday, no matter how short and brief it had been, had played through her mind all day. This kiss ranked just as sweet.

Moaning from the delicious tingles enveloping her body, she started to wrap her arms around his neck when he suddenly pulled away.

"Who do you think sent those flowers?"

Why did he stop kissing her? She hadn't wanted him to stop.

"Derek." Wow. That popped out without thinking.

He frowned as he dropped his hands and backed away. "Deputy Graham? Is that who you're talking about?"

"Yes."

She stared at him, unable to keep a frown from appearing. Why did he back away from her? Did he truly kiss her to mess with her? She didn't like being played with.

"Why would he send you flowers? Are you two... together?"

"I don't want to talk about this." Kat walked around him and headed for the kitchen. "And quit kissing me. I don't like games."

She pulled open the fridge door and grabbed a bottle of water. Closing the door, she dropped the bottle and jumped back, surprised to find Danny standing right there. She hadn't heard one footstep follow her.

He advanced on her, her retreating until his body was pressed up intimately against hers, blocking her against the counter. "I don't play games."

"Then why'd you kiss me again?"

"Because I couldn't help myself. I like kissing you. And I shouldn't damn it." His hands slid to her waist. "Why would Deputy Graham send you flowers as an apology?"

"Why do you always insist on calling people by their titles? Can't you ever use their first names?"

His brow lifted. "Now who's avoiding the question?"

"We were dating these past few weeks, and recently, I... broke it off."

"What did he do for that to happen?"

"Nothing."

"I have a hard time believing that."

Kat put her hands on his chest intending to push him away, instead, she found herself resting her hands there and looking away from his questioning gaze. "He's a good guy. Derek deserves better."

Danny lifted her chin. "I don't know you that well, Kat, but what I do know is you don't seem like the kind of woman who would put herself down. I'm surprised you would. You deserve a good man. Apparently, he wasn't good enough."

"That's not true. He was perfect. He treated me exactly the way a woman should be treated. I didn't treat him well enough. We were planning to go to my family's cabin and I... I never showed up. I didn't even call. He didn't deserve that."

Danny looked confused. "So why would he be sending you flowers?"

God, he glossed over what she did to Derek. She knew Danny wouldn't be kissing her anymore after hearing how coldhearted she could be. Even though he hadn't moved away from her yet, she knew he wouldn't kiss her.

No more kissing. She shouldn't want any more kisses from him.

"He showed up at my house wanting answers, which he deserved to have, and words were exchanged. We both said things that hurt, but Derek's the kind of guy that would feel bad, so I'm pretty sure it was him who sent them."

Danny finally took a step back and glanced at the flowers. "Pretty sure and knowing for sure are two separate things. Deputy Graham would probably also write his name on the card, wouldn't he?" He looked back at her.

"What are you saying, Danny?"

"Any other problems you're having? Anyone suspicious you noticed hanging around you?"

Shivers ran down her body as she thought of Erik and his creepy friend. That had been an innocent encounter. Hadn't it?

"Don't be silly. It had to be Derek."

His brow rose. "Like you first thought it had to be me? You hesitated. What aren't you telling me?"

"Nothing. Geez, get a grip, Danny." She walked past him and snatched her bottle of water that rolled halfway out of the kitchen.

"Get a grip? Sure, I'll do that when you start telling me what you're hiding. My sister chose not to tell me about her concerns. I didn't notice she was holding something back until it was too late. She was kidnapped and missing for three damn months. I'll get a grip as soon as you start talking."

The anger in his tone should've had her backing up, but the pain mingled in each word had her stepping toward him.

"I'm sorry, Danny. You know what happened to Aubrey isn't your fault, right?"

His face turned hard. "Wrong. It was my fault. She's my sister, and I was supposed to take care of her. I didn't. I won't let what happened to her happen to you."

"They're flowers. Nothing's going—"

He gripped her hard by the shoulders, not enough to cause pain, but enough for her to feel the anguish swarming his body. "Don't you dare say nothing's going to happen. Aubrey said that one time and look what happened. Something did. Now she has nightmares and memories I don't even want to know about. I keep telling myself I don't like you, or anyone in your family...but that's not true."

He relaxed his grip, running his hands down her arms softly before letting go of her completely. She shivered from the loss of his touch.

"Your brother called me today."

"Why?"

"He's worried about you. He didn't give me a reason, but I figured it had to be something pretty big for him to call me. We don't exactly like each other to be making friendly phone calls."

Kat shoved her hands to her hips. "My brother actually called you and what...asked you to check on me?"

"Yeah, and now I'm glad he did. Talk."

"Derek's his best friend. I have no idea if he said

anything to Logan, but I never did. That's why he's worried. No other reason for him to be worried."

"I don't like to repeat myself, Kat." Danny's eyes veered to the flowers.

Kat sighed. Danny could be the most obstinate man, and yet, it oddly made her feel special that he cared so much.

"I met a guy yesterday walking into the building. He was nice, nothing weird or strange about him. His friend on the other hand, gave me the creeps a little. I never spoke to the guy. I'm sure Derek sent the flowers."

"Do the nice guy and creepy guy have names?"

Danny still looked angry, maybe even a little angrier than before. The way he said the word nice hadn't sounded nice at all. Was that a bit of jealousy?

"The nice guy's first name is Erik. No idea about the other guy. I'm sure—"

"Yeah, I know. You're sure it's nothing. Let me be the judge of that."

"What are you going to do, Danny?"

"Well, first I'm going to call your brother and determine whether Deputy Graham sent the flowers. Then, I'm going to call for a pizza. After that, I figured we could tackle the pile of books all over the floor."

Kat whipped her head to the mess she had created in the living room. She had no idea Aubrey loved to read so much. She didn't add any books to the list to bring home to Minnesota, but some books had been so worn as if Aubrey loved re-reading them, that she started to make two piles.

Books to keep. Books to give away.

"You want to help me?"

"If you're going to make messes like that, then yes." He shoved a hand toward the piles and piles of books. Yet, she had seen the sparkle in his eyes. Almost like he wanted to laugh.

He had the best laugh. So deep and energetic. When he actually chose to let loose which didn't happen often.

She'd like to hear him laugh again.

"I can call my brother. You call for pizza. Things will go much quicker that way."

The corner of his lips slowly rose. "Want to get rid of me fast, uh, Kat?"

5

DEREK PULLED his phone out of his pocket and glanced at the screen.

Logan again. For the third time.

Why couldn't he leave him alone? He didn't want to talk about what happened. He didn't want to admit the woman he loved saw him as nothing more than a friend, that she stood him up.

That's what Derek couldn't understand. Kat ignoring him seemed so out of character for her. She never ignored things. She was always in-your-face about everything. It was one of the many reasons he loved her so much. He knew he'd always have honesty with her.

Yet, he didn't. She turned away from him instead of meeting him at the cabin and saying, "This isn't going to work."

He would've respected that. The way she ditched him made him want to lose some respect for her. Yet, he didn't. He still loved her.

"We're better as friends. It was never pity, so don't make me look like some no-good bitch."

"Well, gee, Kat, I think you earned that title when you stood me up."

Then he had to call her a bitch. The minute he said it, he regretted it. Hurting her was the last thing he wanted to do. His words had hurt her.

And there it was. The hurt. He knew deep down, she hadn't wanted to hurt him either. That's why she stood him up, because, while Kat excelled at getting everyone to talk about their feelings, to look at their feelings, to look at their actions, she always hid behind her own.

He could still remember when her father died. Logan had been shaken to the core. He had been close to his father. The Caldwell family was a tight-knit group. It had shaken the entire family. After the funeral, Kat had been buzzing around the house, letting Logan lean on her, her mother, her other brother. She offered a shoulder to everyone to cry on and share their anguish over the loss of such a great man. She made sure the food didn't run out, the drinks stayed plentiful. She had run herself dry until Derek noticed she wasn't in the house anymore.

After a quick search, he found her behind the shed in the backyard, staring out into the woods. No tears marked her face. She sat there with her knees bent, arms resting on her legs and a blank expression that told him nothing about how she was feeling. Even alone, she kept her emotions inside.

Derek had sat down next to her without a word, put his arm around her, and listened to the quiet nature around them. They sat for more than an hour—in silence—not one tear left her body in all that time.

Kat didn't like to show her emotions to anyone.

Maybe he did understand why she didn't show up at the cabin. He should've expected it. The few short weeks they dated, he gave more of himself than she had. Obviously, because he loved her, and she still only saw him as a friend.

He had to help her see him as more than that. They could be so good together. He knew it.

He didn't hate her for reacting the way she had. He wasn't mad anymore. He was hurt, but not mad.

All he needed was a little time. Thankfully, Logan decided to give him some. Not that he gave Logan a chance to disagree.

His phone vibrated in his hand.

Logan—again.

He couldn't keep ignoring him. He couldn't risk it.

"Hi, Logan."

A heavy, relieved sigh sounded in his ear. "You had me worried, Derek. Don't ignore my calls."

"I wasn't."

"Something's obviously going on between you and Kat. I don't want to pry, but one of you has to confess. She's not, so tell me. What's going on?"

Derek ran a hand through his hair, then down his face. The stubble that rubbed against his hand made him shiver. He hated that feeling. The first thing he was going to do when he got off the phone was shave. He should've done that this morning. No more feeling sorry for himself.

"It didn't work out, Logan. We're better as friends, I guess."

"Says you or her?"

"What do you think?"

"Shit, Derek, I'm sorry, man. I know how much you care about her. Just give her some time." A slight pause. "Did you send her flowers?"

Flowers. Would flowers put a smile on her face? Would

flowers show her a different side of him? Would flowers show her how much he truly cared?

"No."

"Do you want to get a beer? We can talk some more."

He didn't want to talk about it. He only wanted to fix the problem. Apparently, to Kat, he was the problem. How could he show her how perfect he was for her?

"Not right now." Derek glanced at the clock. "It'll be getting dark soon. You know Aubrey doesn't like to be alone at night."

"Seth can hang out with her. She likes hanging out with him."

Seth had his own issues. Logan and Kat's younger brother still hadn't gotten over the thought that his best friend Evan had something to do with Aubrey's disappearance. Evan was adamant he had no clue his brother Wayne was involved. Aubrey was positive Wayne was the only one she remembered. Yet, Seth was sure that Evan was lying.

Seth hadn't been around them much lately. Would Logan be able to find him to hang out with Aubrey?

Well, it didn't matter. He wasn't going out with Logan. He couldn't.

"Thanks, Logan, but not this time. I'm fine. I'll see you in two weeks." That was his nice way of saying, "Quit calling."

Derek tossed the phone on the bed after Logan said goodbye and walked over to the sliding glass door. Stepping outside onto the balcony, Derek let the rush of heat sink into his bones.

Florida was hot. He had never been to Florida. The heat in December surprised him. Nothing like the cold winters in Minnesota.

Florida was beautiful.

Kat was beautiful.

Maybe coming here wasn't the greatest idea.

He walked back inside his hotel room and debated what his next move should be.

———

DANNY TOSSED the pizza crust onto his plate and grabbed a book that he knew Aubrey loved. She read it so many times, half the corners of the pages were dented. She hated book-marks. She always folded over the corner of a page to mark her spot. Something he loved to give her crap for, abusing a book in such a manner. Not that he could talk much because he rarely read anything, unless it was to skim a news article in the papers.

"Keeping?"

He looked at Kat and nodded. She grabbed the book and placed it in the box that was going to Minnesota.

"I had no idea she loved to read. That book you handed me was a fantasy one. I don't know why, but I never pictured her as a fantasy fan."

"Oh, Aubrey always loved fantasy things. Even as a little girl, she loved creating forts with pillows and blankets and pretending she lived in a big castle with gnomes and trolls and giants and anything else you could think of. When..." Danny paused as he ran his hands down another great fantasy book she loved. "When our parents died, she turned from books to getting into trouble—going to parties and drinking. Dating losers that never treated her right. Started smoking."

"Aubrey smoked?"

He glanced at Kat and gave her a crooked grin. "Yeah, she did, for about a month. She was only seventeen. Deke and I had her boyfriend, who was twenty-one, arrested for providing alcohol and tobacco to a minor."

Kat laughed. Her face lit up with such delight, he gripped the book harder to prevent himself from leaning closer to kiss her. "You sure know how to play hardball, Danny. You had her boyfriend arrested, and just like that, she quit smoking?"

"Well, I grounded her for a month as well and told her I'd follow her like a hawk if she didn't quit drinking and smoking."

"Did she listen?"

Danny tossed another book in the to-go box to Minnesota. "About the smoking, yeah. She said she didn't like it anyway. The drinking...I still had a hard time getting her to stop going to those damn parties."

A soft chuckle made his heart skip a beat. Kat stared at him with the sweetest smile yet of the night. "You never went to parties and drank?"

He shrugged. "That's different. That was me." He laughed with her. "Eventually, she settled down. She started to read more and do less partying. College had me worried, but she focused on her studies and partied only occasionally."

"How old was Aubrey when your parents died?"

"Fifteen. I had just started with the FBI. Deke and I became close right away. I was very thankful when he stepped in and helped me with Aubrey. It wasn't easy raising a teenager, especially when we were used to being brother and sister. Suddenly I had to almost act like her dad. I didn't like doing that. Now...now I can't help it sometimes."

"It's weird to hear these stories about her, or to see the clothes in her closet. It doesn't fit the Aubrey I know."

"She has changed...once again. I like her new wardrobe.

I hated most of the clothes she wore before she... disappeared."

"I bet. She has some short, tight dresses in the closet. But the clothes were on her list for me to take home, so I imagine Logan will enjoy seeing her in some of those outfits."

Danny raised a brow as his lips thinned into a straight line. "Did you really just say that to me?"

"He will enjoy it." Kat bit her lip as a sly grin appeared.

The damn woman was trying to irk him. Did she realize that making him mad almost made him hot for her? Her smirk grew with his silence.

Maybe she did know what it did to him.

"If Logan is like me, he'll appreciate those clothes if he's the only one seeing it. I'm not too fond when other men eye my woman."

Her smile fell. "I had no idea you were dating someone."

"I'm not. I meant when I am dating someone, I don't like it when other men stare. The clothes Aubrey has, men stare quite easily."

"Yeah, I can imagine. The red dress I—" Kat stood up. "Do you need another drink? I need more water."

Danny eyed the empty water bottle in her hand. Running from the conversation, or actually thirsty? "Did you try on Aubrey's clothes?"

"We *are* the same size. You do realize the clothes she wears now are mine."

"You love avoiding some questions, do you know that?"

"So do you." Kat walked away to the kitchen.

Danny figured she tried on at least one piece of Aubrey's clothing—a red dress.

He had no idea the clothes Aubrey wore were Kat's. Although, when he looked at Aubrey in the simple, plain clothes he only sighed in relief that she was covered up properly.

When he looked at Kat in her comfortable yoga pants and T-shirt, he only pictured what lay underneath. It left his imagination to run wild.

Now he wanted to see her in the red dress she started to talk about. How could he get her to try it on?

He stood up abruptly and grabbed his jacket on the couch. "I have a busy day tomorrow. I should get going."

Kat looked confused, then smiled. "Thanks for the help."

"You mean that?" He chuckled, finding it hard to believe.

"I do. I never say something I don't mean."

His eyes glossed to the flowers, then back to her. "You told me Logan said Derek didn't send the flowers. I'm going to look into this Erik guy you met. Let me know if you see him again. Keep your distance. I'll stop by tomorrow."

"All you have is the first name. How in the world are you going to find him? I'm a big girl, Danny. I don't need a babysitter."

He kept his feet firmly planted in his spot when all he wanted to do was walk up to her and kiss her. To shut her up. He hated when she talked like that. If he wanted to check on her, then he damn well would.

"I have my ways. I'll find him. I'll be here tomorrow whether you like it or not. There's a lot to pack. It isn't going to kill you to have help."

"Fine. You're not going to listen to what I say anyway, are you?"

He smiled. "Nope." Walking to the door, he opened it and turned around, surprised to find her right there.

"Let me guess. You were going to say lock the door on my way out." She smirked at him with one hand planted on her hip.

He was starting to find that gesture sexy as hell. "I *was* going to say that. You might be good at taking care of yourself, but has it ever occurred to you, sometimes people like taking care of you?"

"Are you saying you're one of those people? You want to take care of me?"

He stared into her eyes, wondering how to answer that loaded question. "Aubrey wouldn't like it if something happened to you."

Her eyes dimmed with the happiness, the anticipation, as he answered her question. Did she want him to take care of her? Did she want more from him? Like another kiss. He wasn't about to stick around to find out.

He took a step into the hallway and nearly ran into Aubrey's neighbor from across the hallway.

"Hey, Jared. How's it going?"

Jared smiled and clapped him on the back. "Not bad, Danny. How are you? How's Aubrey?"

"She's good. I'm helping Kat, a friend of ours, pack up Aubrey's stuff. She's moving to Minnesota." Danny gestured to Kat. "This is Kat." Then he looked at Kat, surprised to see an angry expression on her face. "Kat, this is Jared. He lives right across the hall."

Jared turned his smile up a notch as he held out his hand toward Kat. "Nice to meet you."

She eyed his hand, her anger still plain as could be. Did these two meet already? Did Jared send the flowers for some reason? The questions swirled around Danny's mind, suddenly afraid to leave her alone for the night.

She thrust her hand into Jared's and shook it briefly. "You're the jerk who wouldn't hold the door open for me. I know you heard me. We made eye contact. Your smile isn't going to sway me."

Shit. Danny turned his attention back to Jared. Maybe he did send the flowers.

"I apologize. That was extremely rude of me. I had to run an errand, and while I was out, I realized I left a pot on the stove. I forget stuff like that all the time. I didn't want the building to burn down."

A brow slowly rose as both hands went to her hips. "You seriously expect me to believe that story?"

"It's true. I get distracted easily. Don't I, Danny?"

Danny glanced between the two. Jared looked eager for him to agree. Kat looked annoyed and so damn beautiful he wanted to shove Jared into his apartment so he could have Kat alone.

"He does get distracted easily. He's a musician. Works on his music all the time and forgets to eat. Aubrey used to bring him meals because he forgot he was cooking something one time and the smoke detector went off." Danny offered her a smile, then turned to Jared. "It was rude not to hold the door. Is this your first apology to Kat?"

"Yeah, I didn't even know she was staying in Aubrey's apartment. I truly am sorry. Perhaps I can buy you dinner to say it again." Jared's smile turned into the most devastating smile he'd ever seen. He didn't even use that smile with Aubrey.

Thankfully, Kat seemed immune to his charm. "Thanks, but no. I accept your apology. It was a long flight. I was tired, so maybe I overreacted." Or maybe she wasn't that immune. A small smile formed on her lips as she stared at Jared.

This was all wrong. Danny didn't want her to look at another man that way. He wanted her to look at him that way.

Whoa! Did he want that? Shit. He needed to leave.

"I'll wait for you to lock your door, Kat. Nice seeing you, Jared."

"You, too, Danny. Maybe I'll see you around, Kat." Jared smiled once more, gave a brief wave, and headed into his apartment.

Jared's door closed with a soft thud.

"You thought he might've sent the flowers."

Danny turned toward Kat. "It crossed my mind. He's a decent guy, although sort of absent-minded. He's always so absorbed in his music." His lips curled into a devious grin. "You know, you haven't been here long and already managed to have quite a few suspects who could've sent those flowers."

"Makes life interesting." She chuckled, then slowly stopped when his expression turned into a frown. "I'll be okay, Danny. Flowers shouldn't be a bad sign. Flowers are normally a sign of happiness."

"Yeah, except this time, the person who sent them doesn't want you to know who they are. What's that a sign of?" He gently pushed her into the apartment. "Lock the door."

She listened, not even offering a word of goodbye. As soon as he heard the lock click, he walked away.

Standing there any longer would've tested his patience. He wasn't sure how much longer he could continue to resist her. Sure, he kissed her twice now. The problem was he wanted to do so much more than kiss her.

Maybe they were starting to get along, but going further than a kiss would be a terrible idea.

Now he couldn't keep his distance. He had to figure out who sent her flowers and keep her safe. He would never let what happened to his sister happen again, to anyone.

He might not know Kat well enough, but he'd never let anyone hurt her.

6

_____

THE CONSTANT MUNCHING in his ear was sending him insane. "Seriously, Deke, do you have to stand that close while you're eating that damn doughnut?"

Deke's hand paused midair, the half-eaten doughnut a few inches from his mouth. "Oh, is it annoying you?" He laughed, then took another bite, overemphasizing his chewing to the extreme.

Danny shook his head and turned back to the computer screen, squinting his eyes in concentration. He had a ton of shit to do today and not enough time. Only nine o'clock in the morning and he already wanted to see Kat. Too damn early to see her.

He could call.

No. She'd find that odd. He even thought the urge to call her was odd. Sure, he wanted to make sure she was okay, but a part of him simply wanted to hear her voice. He knew that Kat could take care of herself. He knew she was a smart woman who could fight well.

He still wanted to hear her voice.

"Do you know how many people live in Aubrey's apartment building? What happens if this Erik guy doesn't even live in the building? What are you going to do, then?"

Danny barely spared Deke a glance. "I'll find him."

"Are we sure Derek didn't lie about sending the flowers? That would be the best answer." Deke chuckled as he went from perched on the side of the desk to the chair in front of it and wiped his hands after finishing his doughnut.

"What's with the damn chuckle?"

"I'm surprised Kat thought you sent them."

"Yeah, that surprised me, too."

"You're not that type of guy."

His fingers stopped typing as those words rushed through him. "What the hell does that mean?"

Deke spread his fingers wide and interlocked them behind his head. "We both know you're not the romantic type. You date now and then, but you've never had a serious relationship. And the ones that could almost be classified as one, you didn't do romantic things, like give them flowers."

"Shut up, Deke."

"Ah, my cue that you don't like what I have to say. Also translates into, 'please change the subject'. Will do, buddy. Not sure you'll like the subject change." Deke dropped his hands down to his lap. "Our serial killer's first two victims were killed on the east coast. Less than an hour drive between locations. He suddenly changes course and heads to the west coast, almost a four-hour drive. Why the big jump?"

"We could answer that if we found a link between our victims. So far, nothing. Victim number one: Tonya Clark, a thirty-year-old Asian female who worked as a teacher at a local high school. Victim number two: Debra Cooper, a twenty-two-year-old white female who worked at a gas station. Victim number three: Sheila Crowler, a forty-two-year-old white female who worked as a secretary at a law firm. Their age, race, hell, even their occupations are all over the map."

Deke leaned forward. "You didn't hear a small connection as you said all of that."

He repeated everything in his head. "All their last names start with a C. Slim connection and impossible as hell to predict the next victim."

Deke's face went dark. His lips fell into a frown. His forehead wrinkled with worry lines. His tone of voice even became soft, almost like a whisper. "Maybe you forgot because I know you're worried about a lot of things right now, but the first victim received something three days before she was murdered."

"Yeah, I guess I did forget. Enlighten me." Danny wasn't sure he wanted Deke to say anything. He didn't like the look on his face.

"She received a box of chocolates."

He did forget that. "Her mother said her boyfriend sent those to her. He's been out of the country on business. We haven't had a chance to question him yet."

"Her boyfriend Tate called me earlier this morning as soon as he heard the news. He recently got back from Italy. He never sent those chocolates. I called her mother again. She said there wasn't a name on the card, but that Tonya assumed they were from Tate. He sent her flowers, gifts, little trinkets all the time because he traveled so much. Having no name on the card never registered with her."

"Shit." Danny grabbed Tonya's case file and flipped through the reports they had already gathered, which wasn't much. This killer didn't leave evidence behind. Ever. Except for the last crime scene. They made sure Detective Larson knew how important it was they processed the evidence as fast as possible.

"What are you looking for?"

"I don't know." Danny dropped the papers in his hands as panic rose, expanding to the point of pain. Every muscle, every joint in his body ached from the pain. He couldn't understand why he suddenly felt this kind of panic. "What did the card say again?" He started to organize the photos from the latest crime scene on his desk.

"It's time." Deke shrugged. "Her mother said Tonya assumed Tate meant he was coming home early. She never thought any of it was odd."

His movements stalled.

The bouquet of roses sitting on the shabby wooden table in Aubrey's apartment hit him right in the gut. The card lying next to it, the words seared into his brain. *Please forgive me.*

Were they innocent words from someone looking for forgiveness from Kat? Or dooming words from a serial killer?

He knew the reason for his panic. Because there might be a correlation between his serial killer and the flowers Kat received.

Impossible.

The first victim received a box of chocolates.

Sinister words from a killer.

Kat received a bouquet of roses.

Nothing sinister in the words on the card.

"Goddamnit!" Danny slammed his hands on the desk. "Kat's last name…"

Deke nodded with a wary look. "It's Caldwell. Do you think the killer followed us to Tampa? Followed you?"

KAT HESITATED.

She rarely did that. A simple knock on the door shouldn't frighten her. Not much scared her. Losing someone she loved, now that scared her. Seeing someone she cared about in pain, unable to help them, that scared her.

Walking to answer the door. That shouldn't scare her.

Her day had been productive so far. She woke up, worked out, had a cup of coffee that didn't taste nearly as good as yesterday's batch, and tackled more of the living room. She even managed not to think about Danny the entire morning. That was a feat in itself.

Those kisses.

No. Not thinking about him. That was dangerous territory.

The day had been going well. Nobody had bothered to call her. Not her brother Logan. Not Aubrey. Not Danny. Nobody. Not even Seth, her other brother.

That one concerned her. She knew Seth was struggling since him and his best friend Evan got into a serious fist fight. Seth firmly believed Evan was lying, that he knew something about Aubrey's disappearance.

Since that fight, Seth was very touchy. She almost had to be careful what she said around him, afraid he would get upset and leave, refusing to talk to her for several days.

Kat had been so engrossed in her own issues that she never saw or talked to Seth before leaving. So unlike her. And he hadn't called her once. So unlike him.

She would answer the knock at the door and then call her brother. She suddenly needed to hear his voice, make sure he was okay.

Or she could call him right now.

Another knock sounded.

Stalling. She never dragged things out like this.

It's just a knock. Nothing sinister about that.

Times like this, she wished she had her small ankle holster gun.

Glancing through the peephole, the blood all rushed to her head. Dizziness threatened to consume her.

For the first time in her life, she passed out.

DANNY STEPPED off the elevator and checked his watch. Two-thirty. Not too early and not too late.

His first reaction when Deke told him about the chocolates had been to rush to Kat's side. As a friend? As a concerned brother to one of his sister's friends? As an FBI agent? As something more?

He couldn't answer any of those questions.

The longer he sat, thinking, he had started to calm down. Only a fraction. Enough not to rush to the apartment.

He worked hard all morning going through the entire case, photo by photo, paper by paper, looking, searching for that one anomaly that would rip the case wide open.

But nothing.

Not a damn thing popped up.

It could all be a coincidence. Chocolates weren't the same as flowers. But the similarities had him panicking. He couldn't let it go. As far as they knew, nothing was sent to victims number two and three, but Deke said he would start looking into it. He needed to check on Kat.

A serial killer could've followed them to Tampa and

latched onto Kat immediately. That was only one of the theories they talked about.

But she wasn't. She couldn't be. He wouldn't let her get hurt.

Stopping in front of Aubrey's door, his hands glided to his pockets until he realized he didn't have a key anymore.

"Damn it."

He knocked. A mellow sound drifted through the door.

Kat liked classical music. Interesting. He pictured her more of the hard rock kind of girl. The way she always let loose with her words, her eyes dancing with fire, hard rock would fit her much better.

Classical music? It didn't fit her, which made her even more intriguing—a woman with so many layers.

What was taking her so long?

He knocked again.

The music wasn't on that loud. She should be able to hear him. Maybe she was simply ignoring him. That sounded plausible. He refused to be ignored.

"Screw this."

Danny walked two doors down to Mrs. Bederman's apartment, a sweet, eighty-year-old woman who took care of Aubrey's apartment when he couldn't find the time.

Her door swung open. Soft wrinkles covered her face, almost hiding her beauty. She might be eighty, but he still thought she was a beautiful woman.

"Ah, the handsomest man finally graces me with a visit, besides my Harold. No one can surpass my Harold's looks. May he rest in peace."

Or maybe he thought she was beautiful because her personality was so refreshing. She always said he was the handsomest man she ever met, besides her Harold. She always added that.

He had passed away two years ago. Any time she mentioned his name, she always ended it with, 'May he rest in peace.' Such love. Danny envied her in that respect. He wasn't sure he wanted love, but if he did, he'd want exactly what Mrs. Bederman had with her Harold.

"The most beautiful woman still manages to make me blush," he replied, eliciting a hearty laugh from her. She was a small, frail-looking woman, but she had a deep, heavy laugh that always put a smile on a person's face.

"What can I do for you? How's Aubrey? Come on in." Her tiny hand waved him in.

"Aubrey's fine. Thanks for asking. I don't have my key to her apartment. Can I get yours?"

"Problems?" She walked over to a beautiful cabinet that Harold had handcrafted himself. Her husband had been a carpenter, creating the most beautiful furniture Danny had ever seen.

"Of course not. Aubrey's friend is packing up her apartment. She's moving to Minnesota. I want to check on the progress."

Mrs. Bederman opened the top drawer, shuffling her tiny fingers around. "I'm sorry to hear Aubrey didn't come as well." She looked at him. "Are you okay?"

"I'm fine."

She made a clucking noise as if she didn't believe that statement. Walking back over to him, her tiny steps slow and steady, she grabbed his hand and placed the key in his palm.

"You don't sound fine, so don't try to lie to this old woman." She squeezed his hand before letting it go. "Aubrey's friend is a very beautiful woman."

"You've met her?"

"No, but I saw her walking down the hallway. Very beautiful."

Danny chuckled and winked as he turned to leave. "Don't try to play matchmaker, Mrs. Bederman. That beautiful woman is the sister of the man Aubrey's with. Talk about weird."

"Oh, so you agree she's beautiful." She winked back and closed the door.

Danny couldn't help but laugh some more as he walked to Aubrey's door and unlocked it. Swinging open the door, his laughter died like a knife slicing his chest open as the door hit a bit of resistance.

"Kat!"

Sliding into the apartment without pushing the door into Kat too much, Danny then knelt down to Kat's crumpled body and lifted her head gently. A sticky substance coated his hand.

"Shit. Kat, sweetheart, wake up." He couldn't tell how badly her head wound appeared. The floor wasn't coated in a pool of blood, but the side of her head was bright red. She had to be okay.

A small moan escaped from her sweet lips.

"Wake up, Kat. Let me see those beautiful eyes. That fire in them." He pressed a kiss to her forehead when she moaned again.

Scooping her up, he carefully walked her to the couch and laid her down.

"Kat..." He swiped a tender hand across the top of her head and then grabbed for his phone. Something he should've done immediately. She needed medical attention. How stupid could he be?

He started to dial for an ambulance when a soft hand

covered his. He glanced up. Her beautiful eyes shimmered with relief.

"Who did this to you?" It came out a little harsher than he intended, but seeing her lying unconscious on the floor still wouldn't evaporate from his mind.

Her eyes fluttered closed.

"Kat, don't—"

"Danny, stop yelling at me. I have a headache," she whispered, then slowly opened her eyes again.

He grabbed her hand that still covered his that was holding the phone, and squeezed. "Then don't scare the shit out of me. You probably need stitches. What..." He took a deep breath so it wouldn't come out harsh again. "What happened?"

Her free hand ventured to her head. She winced when it touched the wound covered in blood. "I fainted."

"What?"

A small smile appeared. "I fainted. I've never done that before in my life. I don't know what came over me. I... fainted."

"Did you eat lunch? You can't overwork yourself packing shit up here. You have to take care of yourself. I thought someone did this to you. Shit, Kat." He turned his head away, trying to reel in his emotions. He couldn't even stop the pounding of his heart.

"I did skip lunch today, but only because I was making such good progress. I...it shouldn't have..."

Meeting her gaze again, he saw it. Something he never thought he'd see in her eyes.

Fear.

Even two months ago when they pulled her and Aubrey out of the dark chamber, smoke swirling around them as a fire nearly took their lives, he never once saw fear from her.

Only persistence and determination. That's all he ever saw in her eyes. Always so strong and tough.

"What happened, Kat? Just tell me." He pulled her hand to his lips and lightly kissed it. Her body trembled, the fear slowly melted away as desire started to lace the depths of her eyes.

That look he could handle. He'd rather handle that look, even as wrong as it was to want, than the terror he saw moments before.

"Someone knocked on the door. I don't know what came over me. When I looked through the peephole, I got dizzy, and everything went...black."

"Who was on the other side?"

Her body trembled again, this time with fear.

"A delivery guy. He was holding another bouquet of flowers."

7

KAT FELT STUPID. Utterly dumb at her reaction to a guy delivering flowers. Fainting. She couldn't believe she fainted at something like that.

She should've eaten lunch. She needed to take better care of herself. That's why she fainted—lack of food.

Definitely not because the sight of the flowers scared her. She refused to admit it. To anyone. Especially Danny. He was already going overboard about these stupid flowers.

The minute she told him about the flowers, his face had paled, which was a difficult thing for him to do. His body held such a gorgeous tan, bronze-toned skin that made her wonder when he ever spent time outdoors. He didn't give the impression he did anything but like to argue with her and work too much.

He appeared very fit, though. Much more fit than the last time she saw him. Two months ago, he was almost homely, his clothes had hung off him like an old raggedy doll. Now, his clothes showed every little definition, every sexy thing that made her body yearn for more.

Last night, when he had taken off his jacket, it wasn't hard to notice his muscles wanted to bust free. When he rolled his sleeves up, the definition, the golden skin, it all went straight through her. The urge to run her fingers up and down his arms and make their way to his buttons on the front of his shirt had been strong. She wanted to take everything off.

Feeling him up in any way would never happen. She wouldn't allow it. She wouldn't allow him to freak out over some silly flowers either. She fainted from a lack of eating, not because she had been scared.

"Did you really need to call Deke?" Kat rolled her eyes as she adjusted the IV line poking in her arm.

Thank goodness, she had talked Danny out of calling an ambulance, but she hadn't convinced him she was okay not to go to the hospital. After receiving four stitches in her head, she figured he had been right to insist she come here. Now she might be stuck overnight for observation. Falling to the ground, no one around to catch her and nothing soft to break her fall, she had suffered a minor concussion in addition to the gash on her head.

At least her hair covered the stitches so she wouldn't have to explain anything to Logan when she returned home. Not unless she wanted to confess what happened, which she didn't. She didn't want to talk about anything. Not the problems in Florida. Not the issues with Derek. She couldn't even believe she managed to ask him to ask Derek if he sent her flowers without going into too much detail about why she wanted to know. The less Logan knew, the better. He had enough to worry about with Aubrey.

So dumb fainting. So dumb not taking better care of herself. She had one slice of pizza last night, not even able to finish the whole piece. No breakfast but a cup of coffee.

Then she skipped lunch. Her body needed food. She'd never be that dumb again. As a nurse, she knew better.

"Hey, aren't you happy to see me even a little bit?" Deke asked with a devilish grin.

Kat smiled despite the crabbiness that wanted to stay on the surface. "I am, actually. You're so much nicer than Danny."

Danny, who sat next to her bed poking at his phone, scoffed at her but didn't glance up.

"A lot sexier, too." Deke winked. "You shouldn't scare us like this."

"I didn't eat much since last night. That's all this was."

"Sure it is," Danny mumbled but still didn't look at her.

"I'm sure the flowers are nothing. I think you might be overreacting a bit, especially with all the questions you asked me."

On the drive to the hospital, Danny had spit out question after question. Did she remember what the delivery guy looked like? Did he have on a uniform? Did she know what flower company it was? Did he say anything? Did he try to get into the apartment? Did she notice anything else strange? Had she seen Erik again or his creepy friend?

The excruciating pain echoing in her head couldn't handle his barrage of questions. Everything he said only intensified the pain. Since being stitched up and given some painkillers, his questions had ceased, and silence had descended. Now he sat next to her barely giving her the time of day as he played on his phone.

"You didn't tell her?" Deke asked, his voice so quiet, it unnerved her.

She shivered from the dangerous look in Danny's eyes when he finally looked up from his phone to Deke.

"I've been busy." He still refused to look her in the eye.

She could easily solve that problem. "Typical Danny, being a jerk by not telling me anything. What should you be telling me? Don't play with me."

His gaze snapped to her, unnerving her even more than Deke's soft tone, the pain and anxiety in his eyes. Why did he look at her like that? Why was he scared?

"I already told you I don't play games, Kat. You could've gotten more seriously hurt. You annoy me a helluva lot, but I don't like seeing you in the hospital." He looked back at his phone. His eyes narrowed into tiny slits.

She annoyed him? Well, he annoyed the hell out of her. What were these two keeping from her?

"This is ridiculous. Tell me whatever it is. I have more packing to do. I don't have time for this. And if I annoy you so much, forget about helping me anymore."

Surprising her, he abruptly stood up and came within inches of her face. His hot breath, minty smelling, was like a kiss upon her lips. She wanted him to close the distance so she could determine exactly what kind of mint flavor.

"Let's get a few things straight. You're going to start taking it easy. I'll tell you things when I'm damn well ready. You annoy the shit out of me way too much. I sure hope we don't kill each other in that apartment."

"What are you talking about?" Just one more inch. That's all he needed to close the distance. Would he kiss her in front of Deke?

"Until I figure out who's sending you flowers, I'll be staying in Aubrey's apartment with you."

"Like hell."

He backed away. "Not up for discussion."

"I don't want you there."

He sat down and went back to fiddling with his phone.

"Are you seriously ignoring me?" She heard the squeak in her voice. He must've as well because he glanced at her, gave her a funny look she wasn't sure she wanted to decipher, and then went back to his phone.

"Danny, stop messing with your damn phone and tell me what's going on. You're not staying in Aubrey's apartment with me. I don't need a babysitter."

"What you need is a good smack on the ass." His head jerked to her, desire touching the tips of his irises.

Her cheeks flamed with heat. She honestly didn't have a good comeback. That kind of sex didn't turn her on. But when Danny said it, it didn't sound so bad.

She looked away from him when she heard a soft chuckle. Deke thought it was funny. Nothing about this was funny. Not fainting. Not having a concussion. Not getting flowers. Not her attraction to Danny. None of it.

She pinned her eyes to Deke. "Tell me."

He ignored her. "Who are you texting on your phone, Danny?"

She couldn't believe they were both ignoring her. She wanted to jump out of bed, get in Danny's face, and shout her anger at him.

"Rogers. I want him to go over the security tapes at the apartment."

"Oh my God, you're having someone look at the apartment's security cameras. It was just flowers." Kat shook her head, then froze when Danny was suddenly in her face again.

Why did he think getting in her face was a good idea? She could shout at him from a distance. That would be so much better than him so close to her. All she could think about was kissing him.

"Get it into that thick, pretty little head of yours. It's not *just* flowers. You have no idea."

She released a slow breath. "You're right. I don't, because you won't tell me anything."

"I'm going to go get a soda. I'll be right back," Deke said.

She didn't glance in his direction, and neither did Danny. They stared at each other, the silence in the room almost deafening.

"Danny?"

"What?"

"Why did Deke leave the room like that? What won't you tell me?"

He finally turned his head, like he was unaware that Deke left. Then he looked at her, his mouth still precariously close to hers. "Who knows why he left."

"Are you going to kiss me again or continue to stay in my face like this?"

The question had him jerking away. "There will be no more kissing between us. Absolutely nothing between us. I'm staying at the apartment only to –"

"You're not staying with me."

He pinned a hard stare at her. "This is one fight you won't win." He sighed. "Do you want me to tell Logan about this?"

She blanched. "Of course not. He'll worry for no reason. He won't leave me alone if he knows."

"Then stop arguing with me because I'll tell him."

"You're threatening to tell my brother if I don't peacefully agree. God, you're such a jerk."

"Don't ever forget it." He walked around the bed and out of the room.

DEKE FOUND Danny outside Kat's room looking at his phone, but not really seeing anything on the screen.

"You okay, man?"

"Just peachy."

He didn't know what Deke expected him to say. Of course, he wasn't okay. Kat got hurt on his watch. Technically, it was an accident and her own fault, but still. He felt responsible for her, especially after Logan asked him to watch out for her.

He threatened to call her brother, which he knew she didn't want, but he was tempted to call regardless, and not simply because of the threat. Because, as a brother, he knew how much it would bother him if he didn't know his sister had been hurt. He felt like Logan deserved that level of respect and concern.

But so did Kat. If she didn't put up a fight about him staying in the apartment, he'd respect her wishes more.

"What are you going to do?"

Danny glanced away from his phone to look at Deke. "I'm going to wait right here until Rogers gets back to me about the surveillance video in the apartment building."

"Not what I was talking about." Deke sighed and waved a hand to the room Kat was in. "Her. Admit it. You like her."

"She annoys the hell out of me."

He snickered. "Yeah, I know. You could cut the sexual tension in that room with a butter knife."

Danny stood up tall. Not that he towered over Deke. They were about the same height. But he needed to show some sort of dominance over him.

"I'm not sleeping with her. I barely like her."

Deke took a step closer, almost getting nose to nose with him. "I think you like her so much it scares the hell out of you. You hide your emotions inside so damn much, one of these days you're going to explode. I'm waiting for the moment it happens. I figured you would've already after finding Aubrey. What the hell are you so afraid of?"

He poked him hard in the chest. "You might be my best friend, but don't tell me how I feel. I know how I feel. If you say something stupid again in front of Kat, we'll be having more than just words with each other."

Deke's eyes narrowed, then dropped into sorrow. "You can hit me if it makes you feel better. Maybe that'll help unleash the tension that's been taking over your body since Aubrey disappeared. What I said to Kat about the case was a mistake. It won't happen again."

Danny's anger depleted. Hit his best friend? He'd never do that, even as tempted as he was sometimes. He stepped back and fell against the wall. Yeah, he had a ton of tension eating at him, and he wasn't sure how to fix any of it. How to fix any of the problems in his life.

The minute Aubrey went missing, he forgot to do the simplest of things, like eat and sleep. Nothing mattered other than finding his sister.

When he finally found her, to see her alive and well and fallen in love with a man he wanted to hate, the tension still didn't disappear. It just morphed into a new kind of tension. One he didn't want to acknowledge or admit. His sister was a grown woman. She could choose whom she wanted to love. He had no say in the matter, even if he wanted to.

What was his problem with Logan? He was patient, kind, and loving to her. Those weren't horrible qualities in a man. In fact, those were the exact things his sister needed. Now, more than ever.

Perhaps his problem was he wanted her to need *him*. For him to help her through her turmoil. He wasn't able to protect her, but he wanted to help her. Like he promised his parents he'd do if anything ever happened to them.

And he failed. Miserably at it.

When he left his sister behind in Minnesota, he took the tension racing through his veins and tried to stomp it out by working the hell out of his body. Lifting weights and running every morning helped the anguish somewhat. It also helped him look more like a human being instead of a gangly alien from another planet.

Even still, the tension wouldn't go away. Flaring to new life the minute he saw Kat.

Sexual tension.

Damn, if Deke wasn't correct on that account.

But he couldn't do anything about it. Touching her would be a mistake. A deadly one. If he screwed up, which he'd probably do, Logan would hate him, possibly even hurt him. And Aubrey. She adored Kat like a sister. It'd tear her up inside if he hurt Kat in any way. He'd never hurt his sister like that.

Nope. It was best if he kept his hands to himself where Kat was concerned. No more kissing.

"Danny?"

"Just...stop. I'm not going to hit you. I don't want to talk about Kat again."

Deke pressed his lips together like he wanted to argue, but instead nodded.

His phone pinged. He looked at the text he received from Rogers and grinned. "Looks like Erik does live in the building. You up for giving him a little visit?"

"Who's going to stay with Kat? You don't really want to leave her alone, do you?"

"Shit." No. Of course he didn't want to leave her alone. Never again.

"I'll stay with her."

They both turned to the right at the sound of the voice.

Looking grim and sad and like a pathetic little puppy stood Deputy Graham.

What the hell was he doing here?

8

KAT HAD a hard time looking at Derek. Although ever the gentleman, he was giving her space, even though she could see it in his eyes he didn't want to.

He would definitely think she was a colossal bitch if he knew what she was thinking right now.

As crazy as it seemed, she wanted Danny next to her bed. Not Derek.

Danny might aggravate her, upset her, and make her want to strangle him, but he also made her feel safe. He made her feel special.

Because the minute he told her, in his abrupt manner, he was leaving to go talk to Erik, she realized she never doubted him. She knew he'd find Erik. He had an intense look in his eyes that said she shouldn't doubt him—at all.

Then he stepped to the side and there stood Derek. Danny said he would stay with her until he returned. He left without another word.

Derek didn't say much other than to ask her how she was feeling. The silence in the room grated on her nerves.

"Why are you here? Does Logan know?"

Derek lifted his eyes, his hands resting gently in his lap, yet she saw the tension in every facet of his body. He looked like hell. His face, always clean-shaven and smooth, was sprinkled with a light beard. It looked so foreign on him.

"Does Logan know you got hurt?"

She narrowed her eyes. "How did you know I was here? Danny would've never called you."

He sighed as he leaned back in his chair and lifted his gaze to the ceiling. "You always avoid what you don't want to talk about. I hate it."

"So you're going to avoid my questions in return?"

He looked back at her. "Seems fair, no?" His face crumbled. "I don't want to hurt you like that. And I know you don't want to purposely hurt me when you avoid things you don't like talking about but damn it, Kat, I care about you. I want to help you. Talk to me."

She dropped her eyes to the bed, wringing her hands together. "Please don't call Logan. He'll worry, and he has enough to worry about. This was an accident. I didn't eat enough, got lightheaded, and fell. That's it. Nothing more."

"Agent O'Rourke said someone delivered flowers to you yesterday. That's why you fainted today." A low sigh left his mouth. "I guess I know why Logan asked if I sent you flowers. He didn't elaborate and I..." A strangled sound erupted. "I'm sorry, Kat."

She glanced up at the pain in his voice. "For what? Derek, I'm the one who's sorry. I hurt you and I never meant to. Never. You have to believe me. I'm sorry it didn't work out between us, but that doesn't mean I want to lose you as my friend. I know that'll be difficult, and you probably—"

"Stop." He abruptly stood up and rushed to the side of her bed. "Just stop." He bent his head. "The delivery guy today with the flowers...I came to the apartment because the flower company called saying they were unable to deliver them and asked what I wanted to do." He looked at her. "I sent the flowers today. I thought Logan was…I had no idea. I decided to deliver them myself and then found out what happened. Dumb flowers. I threw them away."

She closed her eyes as the ache swept through her. Derek tried to win her heart and be the sweet, gentle guy he was, and she overreacted at seeing a simple delivery guy.

Did Danny know he sent the second bouquet of flowers?

"You're hurt because of me, and that's the last thing I ever wanted. I should tell Logan what happened. I—"

She grabbed his hand, threading her fingers with his. "Please…don't tell him, Derek. Aubrey's struggling right now. He has enough to worry about with her. Even Seth. I haven't talked to him in days, and I'm worried about him." She squeezed his hand. "It isn't your fault I fainted. Flowers were a lovely gesture. I wish you hadn't thrown them away. Please say we can still be friends."

"I'd like that." He snatched the chair with his foot and dragged it closer to the bed to sit down, not releasing her hand once. "I could even help pack up Aubrey's apartment."

She smiled. A sort of fake smile that she hoped he wouldn't see through. He should hate her right now, not accepting only friends. She knew how much that probably hurt him to agree.

But she didn't want him here.

If she was really honest with herself.

She wanted Danny to stay with her.

She wanted Danny. That's it. Plain and simple.

Just Danny.

That was probably the worst thing she could ever want.

DANNY KNOCKED LOUDLY on the door. A few seconds later, it swung open to a guy in his mid-twenties with black hair covered by a black knit hat and dressed from head to toe in black clothes. Even his hands were covered with black gloves. It was unnerving and creepy. In his line of work, not much made him pause.

"Yeah?"

"Special Agent O'Rourke." Danny produced his badge, then his hand swung to Deke, who stood next to him. "This is Special Agent Sumnter. We have a few questions for you and your roommate Erik Townsend. You're Michael Johnson, correct?"

Danny already knew he was by his driver's license photo he saw before arriving. When he wanted information, Rogers always came through. Michael also matched Kat's description of the man who wore all black.

"He's not home." His eyes narrowed and shifted between them slowly, warily.

"When will he be back?" Deke asked as if they had all the time in the world to wait for an answer.

Which they didn't.

Danny was already itching to get back to Kat. The feeling was strange and unnerving, especially concerning a woman, this urge to be by her side. It bugged the hell out of him. He didn't want to want her.

The guy shrugged. "He didn't say."

Danny shoved his badge in his back pocket and grinned. "Have you seen anything strange lately? Any problems in the building?"

"No. I don't leave much."

Danny's brow rose. "But you left a few days ago and met a woman. Exchanged a few words with her."

Not much expression lit up his features, only mere boredom. That's what he looked like—bored with the conversation.

"I didn't talk to any woman. Is that why you want to talk to Erik? Because he talked to some chick the other day. Helped her carry in some boxes. I have no idea what they talked about."

"And were you leaving the apartment or heading home?" Deke asked.

They knew the guys left. At least, that's what Kat assumed.

"We left."

Danny looked at him intensely, as if to make him elaborate more, but he didn't do anything but stare at them. He wasn't about to offer any more information. It was like pulling teeth with this guy—a man of few words.

"Have you seen her since that day?"

His hand gripped the door harder. "Like I said, I don't leave much. So, no."

"Where did you go the day you saw her?"

"I don't think that's any of your business."

Like that, his demeanor went from bored to defensive. Danny wanted to know what the hell he was hiding. But he knew resistance when he saw it. He wouldn't be eliciting any information out of this guy today.

Danny pulled his wallet out and handed Michael his card. "Tell your roommate to call me as soon as he gets back."

Michael took the card.

"Are you cold?"

Michael's head jerked to Deke at his question, obviously curious about the gloves on his hands.

"Sorry I couldn't help you more, Agents. I'd like you to leave now."

Danny nodded and didn't argue when the door swung closed in their faces. He didn't know what he expected when they drove here. He didn't think, if Erik or Michael were responsible for sending Kat flowers, or even murdering three women, they would confess if asked. But he wanted to get a feel for them.

He was definitely getting the creepy kind of vibe with Michael.

They headed out of the apartment building. No words were spoken until they were driving toward the hospital.

"What was with the gloves?"

Danny glanced at Deke. "Totally weird. He ignored your question about it. What do you think?"

"Well, he had the creepy vibe going on, that's for sure. You think those two are partners?"

"I didn't get the feeling from the three crime scenes there could be two perpetrators, but I guess it could be possible." His hands gripped the steering wheel tighter. "We could be completely wrong about all of this. Maybe none of it's related."

"Do you really want to take the chance?"

"No. We'll keep investigating like it's related. Kat's not leaving my sight."

"What about Deputy Graham?"

Danny had no answer to that. He didn't know what to think about Deputy Graham's arrival in Florida other than the obvious. He was trying to get Kat back.

As soon as he got the text from Rogers, he asked Deputy Graham how he knew about Kat being in the hospital. He said he knocked on the apartment door for a few minutes before a sweet older lady, most likely Mrs. Bederman, came out of her apartment and informed him of what happened. He booked it to the hospital immediately.

He didn't stick around to ask any more questions because he didn't want to know why he was in Florida. It couldn't be anything good for him.

No. Kat could do whatever the hell she wanted. With whomever she wanted. He had no claim over her, nor did he want to.

They parked the car and walked to her room quickly. At least, his feet moved faster than he normally walked. Something Deke annoyingly pointed out.

When he opened the door and saw Deputy Graham sitting close to her bed, holding her hand as if he'd crumble to the floor if he let go, he knew.

He knew he kept lying to himself over and over.

He wanted Kat.

He wanted her so badly he wanted to dive over the bed and shove Deputy Graham away from her.

But apparently, she made her decision. She forgave him. They were a couple again.

Damn, if that didn't pierce his heart with an aching feeling he wasn't familiar with.

Well, this sucked.

KAT TURNED toward the doorway as Danny and Deke walked in. The dark, brooding expression on Danny had her worried until she realized that was a normal look he wore. Did they find something, or was he acting like his typical self?

Derek's hand suddenly felt clammy and uncomfortable. She didn't want to be holding hands with him while Danny was in the room.

Well, why not?

It's not as if she and Danny had a thing going on. Not even close.

Still, it felt awkward to be holding his hand when she knew she only wanted friendship. Nothing more. Derek took everything she said in stride and accepted it without issue. Since their big fight, things were starting to feel more normal between them. It made her so happy. She didn't want tension between her and Derek, especially since he was her brother's best friend.

"Well?"

Danny cocked a brow as he stopped at the foot of her bed. "Well, what?"

She narrowed her eyes. "What did you find out?"

"Nothing for you to worry about."

Her cheeks instantly burned as the anger rushed through her. Why did he have to leave her in the dark about everything? So aggravating and unnecessary.

A calm hand touched her shoulder. She turned her head to look into Deke's kind face. "We were only able to talk to the creepy guy all in black. We didn't find out much."

Her anger slowly depleted, thankful that at least Deke trusted her enough to tell her something. She glanced again at Danny. His expression turned hard as his eyes shifted from her confused face to her hand wrapped inside Derek's.

"How are you feeling?"

She gingerly smiled at Deke, trying to ignore the weird signals she was getting from Danny.

"Better. The doctor was in here a little bit ago and said as long as someone is with me the first twenty-four hours, I can probably go home tonight."

"I already said I'd stay with you."

Kat smiled lightly at Derek and squeezed his hand. Even though she didn't want anything more than friends, she was grateful for his kindness. She'd let him stay tonight and find a polite way to tell him to go back home tomorrow. She still wanted to be left alone.

"How long are you planning to stay, Deputy Graham?"

Her head whipped to Danny at his clipped tone of voice, the movement made her cringe in pain.

"Hey, are you okay?" Deke asked quietly.

"Yes," she whispered, feeling a bit nauseous after jerking so strongly. She was feeling better, but not *that* much better, apparently.

Her hand slid out of Derek's grip as she fiddled with her blankets and tried not to press a hand to her head that suddenly hurt worse than before Danny and Deke walked in.

Derek stood up. "I'll be staying for as long as Kat needs me." He cleared his throat. "You guys left so quickly before I could tell you…"

Danny's brows dipped lower. His frown looked menacing. "Tell us what?"

"The delivery today…was from me. I had no idea she received an anonymous bouquet of flowers before and that this would happen." His eyes turned to her. "I'm sorry, Kat. I never wanted you to get hurt because of me."

"It wasn't your fault, Derek. Don't make me keep repeating myself. Please." She knew she sounded exasperated, but she couldn't take it anymore. The tension in the room. The awkwardness. It was too much.

"Why were you sending her flowers? Why are you here in Florida?"

Kat couldn't keep the surprise out of her expression. Why did Danny sound so harsh? Did he honestly think Derek was out to hurt her? He wouldn't hurt a fly.

"I don't think that's any of your business, Agent O'Rourke," Derek replied in a firm tone.

"Actually—"

"I think we all need to talk a little quieter and remember that Kat has a concussion. Arguing is not helping her," Deke said gently as he cut off whatever Danny was about to say.

"You're right." Danny looked at her. "I apologize if I caused you any more pain. I'll take you home soon."

"I already said I'd stay with her tonight," Derek shot out.

"Arguing again..." Deke piped in. "How about you two leave that decision to Kat. Maybe she wants me to stay with her."

Kat couldn't stop the chuckle at Deke's words that were probably meant to lighten the mood and make her laugh. Deke was so good at breaking the tension. He excelled at it when they had been cooped up in Logan's small house, searching for the man who hurt Aubrey.

"See, that sounds like you want me." Deke winked at her.

"You are a charming devil." Kat smiled at him, then closed her eyes because her head still pounded like crazy.

She heard footsteps drift away, curious to see who left the room, but unable to open her eyes. The doctor said she could go home, but maybe it'd be better if she stayed.

"Hey, Kat..." She opened her eyes to Deke's soft voice, noting he was the only one left in the room. "I motioned for them both to leave. Surprisingly, they listened."

"Thank you. My head hurts again. Maybe I should stay."

"Is that what you want?"

What a loaded question. As much as she didn't want to admit it to herself, she wanted Danny. She shouldn't. Not only was it strange, but it was completely wrong. Half the time they didn't even get along. She wanted everything to go back to normal. When she and Derek were comfortable and friendly with each other, and there wasn't anything weird between them. She wanted her brother Logan not to be so stressed and worried about Aubrey. She wanted Aubrey to feel better and safe and have no nightmares anymore. And she wanted her brother Seth to be best friends with Evan again.

That's what she wanted.

"I want to feel better."

Deke smiled tenderly. "Me, too. I don't like seeing you like this. I know neither does Danny or Deputy Graham." He looked away, almost as if he was unsure of what to say. "I don't know what happened between you and Deputy Graham or why he's here, but I get the sense you don't want him here."

Deke might be a jokester, but he was very insightful and watchful of everything around him. She imagined it made him one of the best FBI agents out there.

"We dated a bit." She fiddled with the blanket. "I want some time to myself. I want..."

Well, she wasn't going to admit to Danny's best friend she wanted him. That would only increase the awkwardness.

"Done." She looked up at Deke. "I'll tell Deputy Graham as nicely as possible he can go home."

"I should tell him myself."

"Your head hurts. Do you think he'll understand and go peacefully without arguing with you?"

Kat pondered for a moment. Derek was always a gentleman, besides the big fight they had. He'd respect her wishes. But she also hurt him. Would he take her words easily without argument? Regardless, she had to. It wouldn't be fair to have Deke talk to him.

"I appreciate your thoughtfulness, but I'll talk to him."

"And Danny? What about him?" Deke scrubbed a hand across his jaw. "I know you two don't always get along, but he means the best. He just has a funny way of showing it sometimes."

"I don't make things easy on him either. What about him?"

"Are you going to let him stay with you?" He gave her a wily smirk. "Or do you want me to stay with you?"

Oh, no. She wanted Danny to stay with her. Even as wrong as it was.

She chuckled, though, because if Deke stayed with her, she knew she'd be safe from the tension, the awkwardness. From it all.

Maybe it would be best if Deke stayed with her.

9

KAT WALKED into the apartment slowly, resisting the urge to hold her head. It's not like the gesture would take away the pain, but she didn't want Danny to see how terrible she felt. She wished the medication she had taken before leaving the hospital would kick in.

Maybe she should've spent the night there.

"Are you hungry?"

At the sound of Danny's voice behind her, she upped the maybe to definitely should've stayed in the hospital. The tension before they left the hospital followed them into the car and all the way to the apartment. What she couldn't determine was whether it was sexual in nature or plain old tension because he annoyed the hell out of her.

He was being thoughtful right now. She hadn't eaten much at the hospital. Hunger wasn't on her mind. She wanted to lie down and make the ache in her head go away.

"I think I'll just lie down." Without turning around to look at him, she walked toward her room.

Grateful, as she sat down on the edge of the bed, she realized he didn't follow her. Grateful didn't even begin to describe how she felt. She knew she needed time to herself and no more tension. It wasn't helping her head.

Derek hadn't been happy when she thanked him for his thoughtfulness and coming to see her, but she wanted him to go home. His eyes had been clear, he wanted to argue. Perhaps he didn't because of the slight concussion she had. Or maybe he knew he wouldn't have won the argument. Regardless of the reason, he didn't argue. He gave her a hug and a kiss on the cheek in front of Danny, making him scowl like a mad hornet, and then said goodbye.

Danny didn't say he was taking her home, even though Deke joked about it some more until the doctor officially discharged her, insisting that someone keep a watchful eye throughout the night. As soon as she was dressed properly, he led her outside and to his car. Not much was said between them. What was there to say? She wanted him to take her home, even as wrong as it was.

Thinking was hurting her brain. Right now, she needed rest. Changing into her pajamas as quickly as she could, she then slid under the soft covers and promptly fell asleep.

An insistent shaking jarred her out of a deep sleep, one that made her head ring with a slight ache. She batted at the hand that touched her shoulder and tried to go back to the peaceful sleep she had been enjoying.

"No, you don't, Kat. Open those eyes. Look at me."

She batted away the hand once more.

"Stop fighting me. I need to see you're lucid and okay, or I'm taking your ass back to the hospital."

Soft, yet a firm tug to her chin had her opening her eyes to see Danny hovering close to her face. The concern shining within the depths of his eyes sent a tiny shock through her. Was he that concerned about her? He barely tolerated her at times. What did he really think of her?

The firm gesture on her chin turned tender as he swept his fingers up her cheek, brushing gently. "Don't scare me, Kat. I had a hard time waking you up. You should see the doctor again."

"No," she murmured so quietly, she wasn't sure he heard her because a dangerous glint entered his eyes. One that said she wouldn't be able to fight him if he wanted her to go back.

"How are you feeling? I have another pill if you need it with a glass of water."

She wanted to shake her head no, instead whispered it.

"That doesn't help me think you're okay. All I hear from you is mumbling."

He started to back away, probably to yank the covers off her and rush her to the hospital. That was the last thing she wanted. Exhaustion consumed her. She needed to close her eyes. She reached out and touched a hand to his cheek that was full of a day's growth. She had to admit, she liked the feeling and how handsome he looked with so much scruff.

"It's too soon for another pill."

He lowered himself back to the bed, her hand still touching his face. "It's not. I tried to wake you a few hours ago, and you mumbled in your sleep but barely stirred. It's almost two in the morning. I'm worried about you."

Her eyes closed.

"Open your eyes, Kat."

She promptly listened, her hand still attached to him, almost as if she were afraid to lose the connection. Something swirled around them. Desire? Sexual tension? Tenderness? She couldn't quite define it, her addled brain too groggy to focus, but she knew she didn't want to let her hand fall away.

He moved away. Her hand fell before she could stop him

this time. She almost cried out in anguish from the loss of his touch. He was back by her side before she could utter one protest. Slipping a hand underneath her head, he gently raised it as he put a pill near her mouth.

"Come on. Your head hurts. I can tell. Take this."

She didn't have the energy to fight him. She let him put the pill in her mouth and took a sip of water from the cup he held. A few drops of water slid down her chin.

His eyes flared in heat. She thought for a moment he was going to kiss her, instead, he moved away to set the glass of water down on the nightstand.

"I'll be back to wake you up again in a few hours. You better wake up more lucid next time or we're going back to the hospital whether you like it or not."

She turned to her side. Her eyes drifted closed as she smiled at the fierce glare on his face. She never realized how adorable she found that look. Maybe that's why she enjoyed his kisses as much as she did. Maybe that's why she wanted him to take her home and not Derek. She liked his assertiveness and honesty. He never pulled any punches with her. She liked that.

"Did you hear me, Kat? Answer me."

Without opening her eyes, she reached out and hit his arm. "Stay...so you won't worry so much. You worry too much, Danny. I'm fine."

Sleepiness wanted to take over. Very strongly. She had no idea if he would stay or not, but she suddenly wanted him to. Badly. She wanted his strong arms around her. To comfort her. To take the ache in her head away. Although, as a nurse, she knew he wasn't capable of that.

Her hand fell as he jerked away from her. Too tired and a little hurt by what she considered rejection, she kept her eyes closed. She didn't want to see him walk out. She was too tired to care, anyway.

The bed shifted. A warm, soothing heat surrounded her as Danny laid next to her. She didn't hesitate as she threw an arm across his stomach. A slight disappointment slid through her that she couldn't feel his bare skin. Of course, why would he get completely naked? This wasn't about sex. This was to make sure she was okay.

"Thank you, Danny."

A hand wrapped around hers that rested on him. "Shh, Kat. Go to sleep. And wake up more lucid when I wake you next time."

A smile graced her face before she let the slumber take her once again.

DANNY STIRRED the eggs as he glanced at the timer. About two more minutes and the bacon would be done. Then he could wake up Kat.

Not a task he relished doing. Waking her up every two hours last night had been complete torture. He hated the times she almost refused to wake up, the terror running through his veins that he should take her back to the hospital. His heart raced every time, the indecision intense.

But every time, he managed to wake her and get a semi-satisfactory response.

Until that last time.

Stay.

As soon as he heard that word, he wanted to flee from the room and never return. He almost did. Then he found himself crawling into bed and letting her shift closer. He barely got a wink of sleep with her warm, soft body cradled next to his.

Of course, she was injured so it wasn't as if he could've acted on his raging emotions, but he sure wanted to.

He wanted Kat.

Badly.

More and more it was becoming hard to resist her. He wasn't sure how much longer he could hold out.

First things first, she needed food. A good breakfast that would give her some energy. He needed the old Kat back that gave as good as she got. Not the one that looked hurt, small, and so very fragile.

He shoved two pieces of bread into the toaster, then glanced at the timer again. One more minute. Then he'd have to wake her up and resist the temptation in front of him. He barely resisted the temptation lying next to her.

When he woke up this morning, he hopped out of bed so fast he was afraid he woke her up and jolted the pain in her head because she moaned, but then rolled to her side and continued to sleep—something she desperately needed, obviously.

Boxes were scattered around the house, some filled to the brim, some half empty. She was working herself too hard. And chaotically. He couldn't understand why she didn't start in one room and move to the next when it was finished, instead of jumping from spot to spot. Not that he wanted her to finish at all. As soon as everything was packed and ready to be donated, or making its way to Minnesota, it meant Aubrey was officially never coming back. He absolutely hated thinking about it.

Yes, he wanted his sister to be happy. Yes, he wanted her to move on and heal from the horror of what happened.

But no, he didn't want her to do it without him. It hurt like hell.

"That smells delicious."

He whipped around so fast he almost flung eggs everywhere. Kat stood looking rumpled with sleep, her hair messy, her eyes filled with fatigue, but none of it mattered. She looked gorgeous. He wanted to drop the spatula to the floor, wrap her in his arms, and hold her. A kiss would be nice, too. But he just wanted to hold her and reaffirm she was okay and safe.

"I love bacon."

The timer buzzed, knocking him out of his stupor. "Good. It's done." He turned away from her, set the spatula down, and turned off the stove and oven.

Grabbing a potholder, he pulled the bacon out of the oven and gestured his head toward the dining room table. "Have a seat. I'll bring you a plate."

"I can get it myself."

His jaw clenched, then he relaxed his features. He didn't want to argue with her anymore. They needed to find common ground and get along. He turned toward her.

"Let me do this for you, Kat. Please, relax today and let me take care of you."

She stood silent, staring at him. The way she pierced her golden eyes his way unnerved him. He couldn't say why, but she never looked at him that way. A way he couldn't even describe. He wanted to know what she was thinking. Not that he'd ever ask such a thing.

To his relief and a giant surprise, she gently smiled and nodded. "Okay."

He let out a breath he didn't realize he had been holding and made a plate for her. The plate, filled with a decent amount of eggs, bacon, and one slice of toast, thumped quietly as he set it in front of her.

"Would you like coffee, milk, or orange juice?"

She looked warily at him as if wondering why he was being so nice. He knew how to act like a gentleman, he simply didn't do it most of the time. Clearly, it was time for him to change his ways, especially when it came to her.

Not just because he was attracted to her.

He might want to sleep with her, but he'd never act on it. He wouldn't hurt his sister like that, and no doubt, it would happen when he and Kat didn't work out. It was only sexual tension between them, nothing else. There couldn't be anything else.

"Kat? What would you like to drink?"

Her eyes veered away from him and to her plate. "I'd love some tea, but since there isn't any, I'll suffer with some coffee. Please."

He chuckled at the poutiness in her tone, then poured her a large cup of black coffee. He added a small container of sugar next to her cup on the table, and then grabbed his own plate of breakfast. As he sat down, he noticed Kat didn't reach for the sugar, taking a large sip of the black coffee. Not one wince touched her face. He made his coffee strong. A little part of him was impressed. Not many people enjoyed his coffee or went without commenting on how strong he made it. If Kat didn't like it, she definitely would've voiced it.

Or maybe not. She still wasn't acting like her usual Kat-like self yet.

They ate in silence. A comfortable silence that felt normal, like something they had done many times before. Sure, he ate with her a few times in Minnesota when they found Aubrey, but Logan, Aubrey, and Deke were always in the room as well. This was the first time he ate with her like this, with a meal he made. He wasn't trying to impress her with his cooking skills, but he felt lighter inside every time a small smile graced her face as she took a bite.

His nerves started to jangle, which was crazy. Women didn't make him nervous, especially a woman like Kat. He knew where he stood with her. That was one thing he really enjoyed about her. He always received honesty, and he never wanted anything less.

"Thank you, Danny."

He lifted his gaze slowly to hers. Her eyes glowed with kindness, appreciation, and if he really wanted to dig deeper, a hint of desire. He wanted to act on that like a kid on Christmas morning dying to open their presents. He wanted to stand up, wrap her in his arms and carry her to the bedroom. He wanted to kiss her until he branded her as his, and then plunge deep inside until she knew she'd never be with anyone else.

"You're welcome." He stood up so abruptly, his chair wobbled but didn't fall backward. His plate clattered in the sink as he tossed it without thinking whether it would break or not, then he hightailed it to the bathroom. For safe measure, he even locked the door behind him. Not that he thought Kat would follow him. But to stop him from going out there and doing exactly what he wanted to do.

He wanted to claim Kat.

He wanted her as his.

He just wanted her.

How in the hell was he going to survive being in the same apartment without touching her? Because, until they found who was bothering her, he wasn't leaving her side. Not for even a second.

He hoped he didn't lose his sanity before then because keeping his hands to himself would definitely test his resolve.

10

LOGAN SAID hello to Charlotte without getting caught in a conversation and headed for his office for a moment to himself. Sometimes he needed that. He loved Aubrey with all of his heart. He'd do anything for her. But sometimes he felt so lost and confused.

She had another bad night, and she didn't want to talk about it. Hell, he hated hearing about it, but if she refused to go to therapy, she had to talk to someone. He knew bottling what happened inside wasn't good. She was bound to explode eventually if she didn't let it out.

He could see the terror in her eyes this morning about him leaving for work. She had to work, too. But he could see the ache to ask him to call in sick, and the two of them stay home.

Except Derek was on vacation and Bolt just came back to work. He was needed here.

He was also needed at home.

Thank God he wasn't needed in Florida. Danny was there to watch over Kat for him. One less thing for him to worry about.

He swung open his office door and skidded to a stop, surprised to see Seth waiting in his office. "Hey, Seth." He let out a breath and continued inside, shutting the door, and then hung up his jacket.

Seth didn't say a word as he got situated behind his desk and sat down. For a few seconds they stared at each other.

"You okay?"

Seth shrugged, slumped in the chair. "I saw Evan. We had some words again."

Logan didn't see any bruises on his face so he figured it had literally just been words. Because the last time they spoke, they used a different form of communication, their fists.

"Where's Kat? I've been looking for her and can't find her. I even tried calling her, and she didn't answer."

The last part surprised him. Kat normally answered her phone. Yeah, he knew he'd been annoying her lately with questions and figured she might ignore his call, but he didn't think she'd ignore Seth.

"She's in Florida packing up Aubrey's apartment. Aubrey wasn't ready for that. Where have you been?"

Seth averted his eyes. "Working. Does Kat need help?"

Logan almost groaned. Both of his siblings obviously hated dealing with their issues and thought running away sounded like a better plan. He knew Kat would be okay, eventually making things right with Derek. But Seth. He'd been trying tirelessly to get through to him since the incident with Evan. And nothing. He didn't want to talk about it. He didn't want to hang out as much. He wanted to be left alone. Logan hated it all.

He wanted to help his little brother.

"She has Danny to help her."

Seth glanced at him and chuckled. The sound made

Logan happy for the second it lasted. Because he chuckled once and then went right back to frowning. "They can't stand each other."

"They'll be fine. Aubrey misses you. Why don't you come over for supper tonight?"

Seth ran a hand through his hair, then sighed. "Yeah, I'd like that. I'm sorry, Logan. I know I've been a mess, but I... he's hiding something."

Logan leaned forward. "Aubrey's been having some bad nights lately. Most of the time we talk about it. She doesn't remember Evan being involved. It was only Wayne. Whatever you think he's hiding, I don't think it's about that."

Seth leaned forward as well, his expression harsh and foreboding. "You're wrong. It involves Aubrey. I know it. I will get to the bottom of it."

That's what Logan was afraid of. Seth would keep digging and digging and digging until he couldn't dig anymore.

What would be left of him?

He already felt like he lost a part of his brother. He didn't want to lose the other half.

And Kat. Why didn't she answer Seth's phone call?

Maybe he should've called in sick. He didn't want to deal with anything anymore. He wanted to take Aubrey, head to the cabin, and lock themselves inside for days, enjoying each other.

That would be considered running away. Something he did not do. Ever.

"I hope I'm not wrong, Seth. But whatever you do, don't bring it up around Aubrey, please. She's been having a rough few days."

"I would never do that." Seth stood up, his expression still fierce. "I'll see you tonight."

His office door closed. He was finally left alone like he originally wanted. The silence was deafening. A huge roaring sound, like a heavy waterfall beating against the ground.

A weird prickling sensation hit him. Almost from the moment Seth said Kat didn't answer his call.

He grabbed his phone.

If she didn't pick up, he'd be forced to call Danny again.

Because he needed to know his sister was okay.

But he trusted Danny when he said he'd keep an eye on her.

Nothing was wrong.

Maybe if he kept repeating that, he might actually believe it.

———

KAT TRIED NOT to groan as she disconnected the call and tossed her phone on her lap. First, Seth called her, which she missed because she didn't hear it ring, and then had breakfast before checking her calls. Then Danny acted all weird, being nice and sweet, and then abrupt and distant, his usual behavior with her. The nice and sweet part, not so much. She didn't know what to make of it.

Now Logan was bothering her, wondering if she was okay. He didn't mention the hospital visit, so she assumed he wasn't aware she hurt herself, but she heard the worry in his tone. Something was bothering him, but she didn't think it was only worry for her. Probably a combination of every-thing going on in his life, Aubrey being the biggest worry.

She tried to soothe his worries with words that would have him stop calling, hopefully, and now she wanted to get off this couch and get to packing.

Except Danny wasn't having it. Every time she even thought about it, which she didn't know how he knew when she wanted to get up, he gave her a look that said she better not move an inch.

Part of her was tempted to test his restraint. Because she could see he was holding back. His irritation. His anger. And dare she say, his desire.

That's the one that troubled her. The craving in his eyes every time he glanced her way. It was quick and such a flash of yearning she wasn't sure if she was creating it all in her mind because that's what she wanted. She wanted him.

But another part of her was afraid to tempt that particular beast. What happened if they fell into each other's arms and did more than kiss? What would happen after? Would it be awkward? Would he hate her and her family even more? Would it upset Aubrey? What would Logan think?

All those concerns had her keeping her butt firmly planted on the couch. She didn't want to find out any of those answers, especially when she didn't think they would be in her favor. Danny might be warming up to her somewhat, but she didn't think he'd ever let his guard down enough to go beyond mere friendliness, even if they slept together.

She took sex seriously. It meant something to her. It wasn't a quick thing between the sheets to scratch an itch or relieve an ache. It was so much more. A joining of two people expressing their feelings.

She didn't even sleep with Derek and she could've many times. Each time she saw him, she could see the yearning in his eyes. He wanted her. He probably even loved her, although he never said the actual words. Did she love him? Yes, of course. As a friend. The one reason she always held back when she dated him. That was the biggest reason she never showed up to the cabin as they planned because she knew what would've happened there, what Derek wanted to happen. She wasn't ready to go that distance with him.

She wasn't a novice when it came to sex. Since high school, she'd had two steady boyfriends giving herself to both of them, but sadly, neither could hook her heart into a love she thought would last forever. Both relationships ended amicably. To her relief, although she knew she could've remained friends with them, neither lived in Lucky.

The same could be said about Danny. He didn't live in Lucky. He didn't even live in the state of Minnesota. Therefore, nothing would work between them.

She had to protect her heart. She couldn't sleep with him no matter how much her body was aching to.

Because Danny had the potential to break her heart if she let him, she refused to let him have the chance.

He wanted her to relax while he worked hard packing Aubrey's things. Then so be it. She didn't want to find out what would happen if she tested him by arguing. Their arguments always led to the wrong path. One where he enjoyed teasing her with kisses, which still confused her, even though she enjoyed each kiss.

No more.

"Is everything okay?"

She jerked her attention to Danny, who stood a few feet from the couch. "Yep."

His eyes narrowed as if he didn't believe her. "Are you sure? You looked very deep in thought." He nodded toward her phone lying on her lap. "Was that your brother?"

"Yeah. I guess he's still worried about me."

"You should tell him about the hospital."

"Why?"

He glanced away, a slightly melancholy look she didn't miss before he averted his gaze. When he looked back at her, the expression was gone. "Because I would want Aubrey to tell me if something like that happened."

"I'm okay, Danny. He has a lot on his plate right now. This will only increase his worry. I'll tell him about it when I get back home. Deal?"

Something flashed across his eyes. This time it looked a little like panic. It confused her until she realized he didn't want her to finish packing. Because once she finished everything here, Aubrey was officially never coming back.

"I'm sorr—"

"Sounds like a deal."

He cut off her apology she felt compelled to give and watched in surprise as he bolted out of the room. The longer she was around him, the more he confused her. She didn't understand his up and down behavior. One second nice to her, and the next, running from her as if she would bite his head off.

Resting her head back against the cushion, she closed her eyes. She felt utterly useless. Tomorrow would be a new day. Her head would feel better and she could help pack everything up and go home.

Before she left, she had been excited and eager to get to Florida. Now she was ready to leave.

Being near Danny wasn't good. He was testing her resolve. She just wanted to wrap her arms around him and comfort him. Show him a bit of happiness. Something she didn't think he had felt in a very long time.

"How's it going there?"

"Fine. Give me an update."

He ignored the long sigh from Deke as he waited for him to tell him something good about the case he should be helping with.

"You and Kat..."

"What? Getting along? Sure are. Now, do you have something good about the case or not?"

Another sigh echoed in his ear. "Nothing. I spoke to Detective Larson earlier, and the crime lab is still processing the trace evidence collected at the last crime scene. I spoke to our victim's ex-husband, Tony, and he didn't have much to give me. He has a solid alibi. I still haven't gotten a call from Erik. How about you?"

"No. I don't like it. It's suspicious."

"Or Michael never relayed the message, which is also suspicious. Let's break this down. Do we think these two could be our killers? They happened to be living in the same apartment building your sister lives in?"

Danny clutched the phone harder. "She doesn't live here anymore."

"You know what I meant." Deke's voice softened. "I'm sorry."

He tried to ignore the pain that jabbed him in the heart at Deke's words. "It is kind of farfetched, but they could've sent Kat the flowers."

"We don't know anything at this point. She could've gotten flowers from anyone. Hell, those flowers could've been meant for Aubrey. Kat's name wasn't on the card."

"They were not for Aubrey. Everyone who knows Aubrey knows she's not living here anymore. They were definitely meant for Kat." His patience was starting to run thin. He had to take a deep breath before continuing, "Are you saying I don't have to stay with Kat because she's not in danger?"

"No. That isn't what I'm saying. Until we figure out more about what's going on, you should stay with her. I'm only throwing different scenarios out. We have to keep an open mind about everything."

"Agreed."

Danny pulled his phone away from his ear when he heard an incoming call come through. He didn't recognize the number.

"Hey, someone's calling. I'll check in with you later."

"Okay. But, Danny, stop stalling. Show Kat how you really feel about her."

Before Danny could reply, Deke hung up. He was tempted to call him back and give him a piece of his mind, but resisted the temptation and answered the other call.

"Special Agent O'Rourke."

He tensed after identifying himself and the moment of silence that answered. He could hear light breathing on the other end.

"Hello?"

A soft cough. "Yes, Agent O'Rourke. This is Erik Townsend. My roommate Michael said you wanted me to call you. Is there a problem?"

"There might be. I expected a call yesterday. Are you home right now?"

"Umm...yeah. Look—"

"Don't leave. I'll be there to ask you some questions."

Danny disconnected the call before he could argue with him. He liked to interview people in person. He could always read people better that way. See if they were lying or withholding information. Whether they were scared or even overly confident they were getting away with their crimes.

He didn't want to leave Kat alone, not even for a minute. But he had to interview Erik in person.

Time to get some answers. Hopefully, answers he needed to close the mysterious case about the flowers, and then he could leave Kat alone.

He needed to leave soon.

Because his resistance was slowly melting away. She'd be in his arms sooner or later if he didn't leave.

11

"ARE you sure you'll be okay on your own? I won't be gone too long, and I'm not even leaving the building. Call me if you need me." Danny started to reach for his firearm on his hip. "You know—"

"Stop." Kat's warm hand on his arm sent tingles of delicious intentions straight through him. "I'll be fine. Go. Don't worry about me."

His jaw clenched tightly. Too tightly, where he felt like he would break his teeth. Don't worry? Yeah, right. He hadn't even left and he was worried like crazy.

"Do you want my gun while I'm gone? I know you know how to use it. If it'll make you feel better, I'll leave it with you."

He stood frozen, his hand near his gun, her hand on his arm. At his question, her hand increased the pressure a little bit, enough to make him think she did want his gun.

"I'll be fine. You keep it."

Narrowing his eyes, he tried to read behind the cool gaze she displayed. He couldn't detect any fear or worry on her part, but that slight pressure on his arm still made him think she would feel better with the gun.

Digging deep for strength, for her benefit, he produced a smile as he removed her hand from his arm. Before she could stop him, he unholstered his gun, and handed it to her by the barrel. The gun hung in the air, waiting for her to grab it.

"I'd feel better if you had it."

Kat rolled her eyes but didn't reach for the gun. "You won't be gone that long. You're not even leaving the building. I don't need your gun. Keep it." This time he didn't miss the flash of fear as her eyes connected with his. It was brief, but there.

He couldn't stand it anymore. He couldn't stand keeping his distance when all he wanted to do was wrap her in his embrace and never let go.

Bending down to his knees, he laid the gun in her lap and then grasped her cheeks lightly. "Don't argue with me for once. I need you to keep the gun for my peace of mind."

Her eyes softened. "Did it ever occur to you I'd like you to keep the gun for my peace of mind? What happens if Erik decides to attack you?"

"It'd be the dumbest thing he ever did. He won't."

"You don't know that, Danny."

He moved his lips closer to hers, his hands tightening the grip some. "Just keep the damn thing." His lips connected with hers. He kept it light and gentle, even though he ached to devour her until she moaned in his arms begging for more.

Abruptly, he let go of her and stood up. She looked dazed and so damn beautiful sitting on the couch all wrapped up in a blanket. He knew she didn't like sitting around doing nothing, but it couldn't be helped. She needed at least one full day of rest to recover.

"You need to stop kissing me, Danny."

Her words made him chuckle, especially in that tone of voice, soft and airy, as if she was waiting for more. "You need to make that sound more believable."

"Look, we can't—"

"Don't answer the door to anyone. I'll be back soon." He winked and walked away, closing the door on her angry words she shouted that he was an annoying, arrogant jerk. Locking the door with his key he managed to get back from her after returning the other key to Mrs. Bederman, he couldn't hold back another chuckle.

He could be an annoying, arrogant jerk. With her, it came out more than he liked. But he knew it was a defense mechanism to keep his distance. His distance that was slowly inching to nothing.

He turned around from the door and jumped in surprise. "Uh...hi."

The guy standing in front of Jared's door smiled. "Hey. Sorry if I startled you. Didn't mean to. You headed out?"

Danny didn't know Jared well enough to call him a friend, but he knew enough. He was a musician. He worked from sun up to sun down on his music. He rarely left the apartment unless it was for a gig. He didn't have many friends. Superficial stuff about the guy. But this dude? He didn't recognize him. And why didn't he like his smile?

"Are you?" Danny wasn't about to announce he was leaving. It wasn't this guy's business.

"Yep. Gotta get some groceries. Jared has absolutely nothing in the fridge. I'm surprised he doesn't starve himself with his lack of priorities on eating."

Danny laughed because it sounded like Jared. "And you

are? How do you know, Jared? I'm Special Agent O'Rourke." He held out his hand, making sure to emphasize his title, his gaze stern.

The guy shook his hand. "Jason. Jared's my brother. If I don't visit him, I never get to see him. You must be Aubrey's brother."

"You know my sister?" Danny's eyes narrowed, still unsure what to make of this guy. He wasn't sure if he trusted him or not. He couldn't ever recall Jared talking about a brother.

"Yep. How is she?"

"Fine. I hate to keep you from your shopping. You have a nice day, Jason."

Jason flinched at his sharp words, then nodded. "You, too. Maybe I'll see you around. Say hi to your sister for me." Jason tossed his keys in his pocket and continued down the hallway toward the elevator.

Danny stood in front of the door and waited impatiently until Jason stepped on the elevator and knew it was descending.

He wasn't sure what to make of that guy. But he'd call Aubrey to see what she said. Maybe if she vouched for him, he'd lower his suspicions.

As he took the stairs a few flights above Aubrey's apartment, he knew he shouldn't be wary of every guy he met or saw, but he was.

Until this killer was found, until he knew who was bothering Kat, he didn't trust anybody.

It didn't take long for him to reach Erik's apartment. Not even ten minutes had passed since he hung up the phone with him. If he wasn't still home, he'd know whether this was his guy or not. If he had nothing to hide, he wouldn't be concerned about talking to a federal agent.

He knocked on the door and barely waited a second before it swung open to a clean-cut guy in nice clothes that didn't give off a disturbing feeling, not like his roommate Michael, and a friendly smile that unnerved him.

"You must be Agent O'Rourke. I'm Erik."

Danny nodded and produced his badge. "I am."

"Would you like to come in?"

Danny stepped inside. He wasn't sure what to make of his so-called friendliness. Danny didn't like it. He was being too friendly. Maybe to throw him off his trail, make him think he was a good guy, when really, he loved to terrorize and murder women.

Or maybe he was losing his mind with worry for Kat and creating scenarios that were so farfetched he should get his head examined.

He couldn't decide which one seemed more plausible.

"How can I help you, Agent? Would you like something to drink?"

Danny took his time glancing around the apartment, an exact replica of Aubrey's apartment, although cleaner looking. Packing up Aubrey's apartment made it look like a disaster zone with boxes sitting everywhere, her belongings put in dozens of piles. He had to give Erik and Michael credit for keeping a clean apartment, especially for two bachelors. Not a thing looked out of place. Even the blanket on the couch looked folded with precision, draped across the end as if someone made sure it was lying the way they wanted it.

"I won't be here long. I have a few questions." He took a few steps into the living room, close to the couch. "Is your roommate home?"

Erik's smile widened. "He's not. Did you need to speak to him again? I thought you wanted to speak to me."

"I do want to speak to you. Where were you yesterday?"

"Working."

Danny leaned against the end of the couch, making a point to mess up the blanket. "And what do you do?"

"Nothing too exciting. I'm an accountant. What's this about, Agent O'Rourke? I have to say I was very surprised when Michael told me you stopped by yesterday. Something about a woman I met."

He stood up and walked around the couch, eyeing the kitchen, noting how immaculate that area looked as well. "Yes. You spoke to a woman a few days ago. Helped her bring in some boxes."

"Beautiful woman. Kat with a K. That's all I know. I don't know her or anything. Did something happen? Is she okay?"

"She's fine. So you don't know what apartment she lives in?"

Erik shook his head, confusion crossing his features. "She didn't share that information."

Danny couldn't get an accurate read on him. He was saying all the right things, yet his gut churned like a blender on high. Something about this guy bugged him.

"Have you seen anything lately that looked strange or suspicious?"

"Not that I can recall. If I did, I'd call the police, of course."

Danny chuckled as he walked toward the door. "Of course. Well, if you do see anything strange or suspicious going on here, I'd appreciate a call."

"You got it. I still don't understand what happened." Erik's brows dipped as he walked to the couch and straightened the blanket. He didn't lose eye contact once, as if he knew how he wanted—needed—the blanket situated.

"It's nothing to worry about. We're looking into a small

incident that occurred. I appreciate you taking the time to speak with me."

"Any time."

Danny took one last look around before leaving. He took two steps at a time going back to Aubrey's apartment. He suddenly needed to see Kat. He needed to make sure she was okay.

Why wasn't Michael home? He said he rarely left the apartment. Why did Erik feel the need to fix the blanket as quickly as he did?

Why did every crime scene look clean and precise? As if the killer couldn't leave it looking like a mess?

Did he find his killers he was looking for?

Or was he still creating things in his mind to make it go the way he wanted?

His heart was racing double-time as he unlocked the door. As soon as it swung open and Kat's smiling face connected with him, his crazy nerves that had been jumping like a dog excited to see its owner, calmed down. Not entirely, but enough to produce a smile to show everything was okay.

But was it?

Were they in the same building as not one, but two serial killers?

"I'M SO glad you decided to join us for supper, Seth. I missed you." Aubrey hugged him. "Logan's missed you."

Seth kissed her cheek before backing away. "I've missed you, too, Aubs. Something smells good. What's cooking?"

"Some chicken recipe I found online. I hope it's good. I'm not much of a cook."

Seth rolled his eyes as he laughed. "You're nuts. You're a great cook. You look tired, though." He hesitated. "Have you been sleeping okay? How bad are your nightmares?"

She turned away from him and shrugged as she made her way to the kitchen. "They've been fine."

"That didn't sound fine."

Talking about herself wasn't something she wanted to do with Seth. She didn't even like doing it lately with Logan. The darkness that lived inside was hard to manage. One of these days, she was afraid it would seep out of her and into the people she loved. It seemed better to keep it in.

A soft hand touched her shoulder. "Aubs, talk to me."

She whirled around. Seth's hand fell away immediately. She didn't want his sympathy, his support, or heaven forbid, his pity.

"Then you talk to me first. Why have you been acting the way you have?"

For a brief second his features hardened, then softened as if he never tensed for even a moment. "I don't know what you're talking about. It's been busy at work."

"Don't lie to me."

A muscle in his cheek ticked. "Then don't lie to me either. What's bothering you?"

Whipping her hands out, she shouted, "What always bothers me. My nightmares, Seth. Yeah, they're bad, and I don't want to talk about them." Her hands slammed to her hips. "So, what's bothering you?"

She couldn't stand it. Why did people always think it was okay to insist she talk about her problems, but they didn't have to? She hated it. If she didn't want to talk about it, she didn't have to.

Seth sighed, his gaze drifting to the floor. "I'm sorry, Aubs. I didn't—"

"No. You don't get to do that. You don't get to ignore the problem. You either tell me what's wrong or get the hell out."

His eyes snapped up, shock covering his face. She had to admit, she was a bit surprised herself. She never got upset like this. Yelling, raising her voice as if she had a right to. Pushing an issue when she normally ignored them.

Not anymore. If people wanted to insist she share her feelings constantly, she would insist right back. She hated feeling weak. She hated feeling useless.

It was time to start taking the darkness consuming her inside and manage it. She didn't think she'd ever be rid of it, but she could figure out a way to cope. That started by letting people know she wouldn't be run over any more. They couldn't control her into doing what they wanted all the time. She would start to do what she wanted. Right now, she wanted Seth to talk to her. If he couldn't give in just a little, then she didn't want him here.

They stared quietly at each other.

Finally, Seth nodded. "Have a good night, Aubs. I hope you don't have any nightmares tonight."

He turned around and walked out of the house.

The moment she heard the door shut with a soft click, her bottom lip trembled, her hands shook, her heart hurt as if a deep knife had wedged its way inside.

Her chin was lifted by a soft, warm hand. Logan's sweet smile raised her spirits for a tiny moment before plummeting once again. Why was he smiling at her? She demanded his brother to leave. He should be yelling at her.

A tender kiss landed on her lips before he wrapped his arms around her tightly. "Are you okay?"

Tears fell. "Why don't you hate me right now? I kicked your brother out." The words came out muffled as she buried her face into his chest, the tears raining down heavily.

"Because Seth needs to talk about it, and he won't unless we push him. We need to do it together. You did what Kat probably would've done. I wouldn't yell at her, so why would I yell at you?"

"But I never yell."

"Maybe you need to." His breath hitched. "I know I've been pressing you a lot lately to talk about...you know. I don't mean to be in your face about it, but I don't want you to bottle things inside and then...and then explode."

"I just exploded."

He pulled her back some and cupped her cheeks, wiping the tears away. "No, that wasn't an explosion. But it was real. If you don't want to talk, that's fine, but you need some sort of outlet for the nightmares. For your memories. We can get through this. I know we can."

"I...I just feel so dark inside, Logan. Most days I'm happy. You make me happy. Then, days like today make me feel miserable like it's never going to get better, that the nightmares will never stop. I'm afraid to go to sleep."

"I'll be right there. To hold you, to comfort you. I'll do anything in my power to make the nightmares go away."

She kissed him before pulling him tighter to her. These were things she needed to hear. So often. Too often. At times, it felt like she demanded too much from him, expected too much from him. Yet, he never stopped. He never acted as if he couldn't handle it, or hated it.

How did she get so lucky finding Logan? The entire Caldwell family?

She missed Kat.

"You said I did something Kat would've done." She sniffed, wishing for a tissue but refused to leave his arms.

"What does she do when she needs to let it out? What's her outlet?"

Logan sighed heavily. "I don't know. Kat tends to hold things in, too. She loves to help others, but when it comes to herself, she doesn't always like to talk."

"She seems so put together."

He squeezed her hard. "So are you. You're as strong as her. Every time you doubt yourself, I'll remind you of that. Why don't you call Kat tomorrow and ask her what she does to let off steam?"

"I think I will." She snuggled closer and inhaled his wonderful aroma that usually could calm her down instantly. This time was no different. She was already feeling slightly better. Although, she still didn't want to go to sleep tonight.

The nightmares were getting worse. The memories wouldn't disappear.

12

_____

KAT PRESSED the blankets down around her. Patting here, then there. Almost as if she were tucking herself in.

Of course, it would be highly inappropriate and oh so wrong for Danny to do it.

Danny tuck her in?

What was she? Five years old?

No, she was horny and aching for him since the moment he burst into the apartment a few days ago. Why lie to herself? It was the truth. Part of the truth.

She wanted Danny for the longest time. Probably from the moment she met him, even if she didn't appreciate his cocky and surly attitude.

He had a reason for acting that way. He hurt deep inside because his sister was kidnapped. She understood. Now all she wanted to do was offer him comfort in some sort of way.

Repeating to herself that she only had sex when it meant something—to both parties—wasn't helping her resolve. She still wanted him to walk into her room and take her to the heights of pleasure of which she had never seen. She knew he could. She saw the heat and desire in his eyes sometimes when he looked at her. She knew he was capable of taking that look and touching her in the same way.

And if she did do something as dumb and stupid as that, he'd probably break her heart when he wouldn't reciprocate her feelings.

But she already did something dumb.

She fell in love with the obstinate man.

That feeling cemented deep inside today when he came back from interviewing Erik, although he wouldn't tell her how it went, and had been the most considerate he'd ever been with her.

He made sure she was comfortable, bringing her things to drink or eat, more books, or changing the channel on the TV, even though the controller lay on her lap in her reach. Gone was the brusque attitude from this morning and in popped a sweet and caring man.

She didn't understand it. She didn't understand his up and down behavior.

But for the day, she was happy to see the soft part of him.

Damn him for making her feel this way.

So the least he could do was tuck her in and make her feel good. She'd let him into her bed if he did. She'd give him something she rarely gave to men unless she truly cared for them.

She patted the blankets around her one more time, then gave up hoping he'd come in the bedroom to say goodnight and attempted to close her eyes.

He had no reason to come in here. She already said goodnight in the kitchen when she grabbed a bottle of water to take with her to the bedroom.

He looked tired, too. Not only did he make sure she was comfortable all day, but he also packed Aubrey's things. Slowly, but he made a bit of headway. She couldn't resist watching him as he did. Looking sad and lonely as he placed item after item into the boxes. Her heart hurt for him as she watched the pain in each movement.

Well, tomorrow was a new day. She already felt much better, her head free from any pain. She'd help him pack, and she could probably be home in two or three more days.

Then no more worrying about who sent her flowers. No more keeping her distance from Danny. No more falling completely in love with him.

She turned to her side and tried to shut her mind off. Even though she laid around doing absolutely nothing, she was exhausted.

Squeezing her eyes shut tightly, she prayed she didn't dream about a difficult, handsome man that had crawled under her skin and refused to leave.

Her eyes popped open at the sound behind her. Glancing at the clock on the nightstand, she realized she actually fell asleep faster than she thought. Two hours had passed since she went to bed.

What was the noise?

Her heart pounded at the implications. Either someone broke in and was about to hurt her, or Danny had come into her room.

She hoped it was the latter.

Without turning around, too afraid, hating that emotion, she whispered softly into the dark bedroom, "Danny, is that you?"

Silence answered her.

She knew she heard something. Footsteps near her bed. Now, she heard nothing.

Pushing the panic aside at what she might find, she turned to her other side and looked around.

Danny stood in the doorway, his expression indecipherable. What was he thinking? Why didn't he answer her?

"What are you doing?"

"I was just checking on you to make sure you're okay. I didn't mean to wake you. Go back to sleep."

"I feel much better. You don't have to worry about me anymore."

Even in the darkness, she could see him clench his jaw tightly. "Go back to sleep, Kat. I'm sorry I woke you up." He turned to walk out of her room.

Didn't she fall asleep hoping, wishing, and aching for him to come to her room? He finally came. Perhaps not for the reason she wanted. But he came.

He took two steps out.

"Don't go."

He stopped.

"Stay with me."

SHE HAD no idea the restraint he had shown near the bed when he decided he needed to make sure she was okay before he finally went to sleep. If he took one step back into the room, it would all fall apart, and she'd be naked in his arms.

Was that what she wanted, too? Because if not, he'd embarrass himself if he started to strip her naked.

As much as he ached to do that, he couldn't move. Frozen in his spot, the scenarios of what would happen afterward if they slept together flooded his mind. Too many that didn't look good.

"Please...Danny."

Her soft, whispered words tore through his defenses

without issue. He couldn't stand in the doorway and ignore her quiet plea.

She wanted him as much as he wanted her. That's all he needed to know before he made his move. Some things he didn't have the bravery to enact unless he had some sort of sign.

He turned around and stalked to the bed. He almost flinched at the surprise on her face and realized maybe it was from the way he reacted. Brusque and fierce. It's not that he meant to startle her. His nerves were wired so high with desire, he wanted her now. He didn't want to wait.

Letting out a deep breath, he sat on the edge of the bed, showing more restraint than he knew possible.

His hand ached to reach out and touch her. But he knew if he did, he'd lose it. Lose the ability to speak and function. Only one thing would happen.

Claiming her as his.

Maybe this wasn't such a good idea.

"Are you feeling okay?"

Her brows puckered low. "I'm fine."

"You can't sleep? Is there a reason..." Her hand reached out and touched his arm. His words died on his lips.

"I think we both need to stop dancing around the issue here, Danny. I want you to stay because...I want you." Apprehension coated her eyes. "I'm pretty sure the feeling is mutual. Am I wrong?"

His entire body was coiled tight with tension. If she so much as moved her hand a millimeter, he'd react. He wanted to be buried deep inside her and show her how much he truly ached for her.

"Oh, wow. I am wr—"

"Right." He cleared his throat. "You're right. But is this a good idea, Kat?"

Why was he asking such a dumb question? Of course, it wasn't a good idea. They'd sleep together, and then at family gatherings, when he wanted to see Aubrey, it would be incredibly awkward. Or incredibly difficult to resist taking her in his arms each and every time he saw her.

Her hand tightened on his arm. "At the moment, Danny, I don't care whether it's a good idea or not. It's probably not, but I still want you." Her eyes turned down as her hand slowly slipped away. "Can you at least lay with me for a while?"

"If I get in this bed...I can't—" He jerked to his feet, unable to finish the sentence.

Her eyes closed. She turned her back to him, effectively shutting him out.

Shit. He hurt her feelings. That wasn't his intention. But didn't she understand that if he climbed into bed with her, they wouldn't be sleeping? He'd be loving her body from top to bottom. He wouldn't be able to keep his hands to himself.

He turned to leave. The doorway looked far away. Miles and miles away. The thought of walking out was like a knife to the gut. Brutal and painful.

Why couldn't they indulge for the night? What was so wrong with acting on their feelings? Things didn't have to be awkward if they didn't make it so.

He looked at Kat, her back still turned away. Her entire body looked stiff and tense. He could relax her. Soothe all her aches and pains. Soothe a little of his own.

It might be a terrible idea, but he didn't care anymore.

But first, he needed protection. He left the room quickly, not wanting to leave her alone too long, and tore Aubrey's bathroom cupboard apart before he found a box of condoms hidden behind a box of tampons.

His hand trembled holding the box. One, because he

couldn't believe he was going to do this with Kat as he'd been aching to do for so long. Two, because it was weird to know his sister kept condoms in her apartment. He didn't want to think about his sister having sex.

He ran out of the bathroom and wiped clear all thoughts of Aubrey. Because if he didn't, he'd never go through with this.

Stripping down to nothing in Aubrey's room, the room he was sleeping in, his clothes crumbled to a pile on the floor. Then he grabbed a handful of condoms and walked back to Kat's room. Her back was still to the door. It looked like she hadn't moved a muscle.

The condom packages made loud crinkling sounds as he laid them on the nightstand on his side of the bed. Kat flinched at the sound, but said nothing.

The bed dipped as he crawled under the covers. Without hesitating, he scooted closer to her and wrapped an arm around her waist, pulling her as close as possible.

A contented sigh escaped as he relished in the way her warm body felt snuggled next to his. A strange sensation hit him. Something more than contentment. Something more than desire.

Ignoring the feeling, he dipped his head and kissed her on the neck below her ear. "I want you, Kat. So badly. Screw the consequences. We can be adults about this. It's just sex."

As soon as he said that, his insides twisted with disgust. Just sex? No. Nothing with Kat would ever be *just* sex, but he didn't want to look deeper. He needed to keep it light and carefree. Because he wasn't prepared to share with her how much he cared for her when she probably only thought it was just sex.

How much did he care for her? He honestly couldn't answer that. More than simple sex, that's for sure.

His arm tightened around her, pulling her even closer, her ass cocooned against his hard dick that waited impatiently to plunge deep inside her.

Another kiss hit her neck, then a trail of them down her shoulder. "Say something. Anything. Tell me to get the hell out of your bed...or...I'm going to start doing something I've been dying to do since forever."

She shivered in his arms but still said nothing. She didn't even make a move to touch him back in any way.

He made another trail of kisses back up her shoulder, to her neck, and ended at her ear where his tongue swirled and nibbled before landing one more kiss on her neck that could've turned into a branding mark if he hadn't controlled himself to stop.

Damn, but he wanted to mark her as his.

But she wasn't.

This was just sex.

Maybe if he kept saying it, he might actually start believing it.

"I'm going to make love to you now, Kat. Unless you hate me so much you want me to leave." His breath hitched, afraid she might hate him, because her silence worried him. "Do you hate me?"

13

KAT TREMBLED ONCE AGAIN as his hold on her tightened, his words echoing in her mind.

Do you hate me?

She never hated him. Not even for a second when he acted like an arrogant asshole. Did he upset her? Too many times to count. But hate? No. That feeling never entered once.

She was still trying to wrap her mind around the fact he said he couldn't lie down with her, walking out of the room as if he didn't care, and then sliding under the covers completely naked. Or wrap her mind around the fact his kisses were lighting her body on fire, a deep, brutal inferno that she had never experienced before. They were only kisses. He hadn't even done anything dramatic yet.

How come her two previous boyfriends never ignited this kind of sensation out of her?

Why did it have to be Danny?

If she went through with this, actually let him love her body as she ached to do, she had the terrible fear she'd lose her heart in the process. Was it worth it? Was this one night worth losing her heart to a man who'd probably never offer his in return?

"You do ha—"

"Never." She grabbed one of his hands that was wrapped around her waist and lifted it to her mouth for a kiss. Maybe a dumb gesture, but she couldn't help but to let her lips linger before lowering his hand. He linked fingers with her before she could pull her hand away. "I've never hated you, Danny."

"Do you want me to leave?"

"No."

"Then what's wrong? You feel tense in my arms."

Of course she did. She was on the verge of making a monumental decision. One that would have her mending her heart for far longer than she ever wanted. That's how much she knew taking this plunge with him would do to her.

Once she opened herself to another, she truly did—each and every part of herself. Opened herself to pain and hurt and happiness and...love.

Maybe she should tell him. Get it out in the open.

Yeah, and then he would run so fast out of the room, she'd lose her chance at experiencing at least one night of bliss with him.

Turning around as best as she could with his arms locked tightly around her and her hand still linked with his, she let herself express as best as she could with her eyes instead of with words she knew she could never utter.

"I want this. I want you." She chuckled as she shifted closer. "Even now we can't help but argue. Why is that?"

A silky grin touched his face as he cocked a brow, followed by a tender kiss. "Because it's what we do. And you're adorable as hell, not to mention breathtakingly beautiful when you're angry. I love it."

And I love you.

She tried to keep a smile on her face as the words echoed in her mind. Then Danny removed her nightgown and lace panties before lowering his mouth to hers. She lost all train of thought after that. His tongue swirled and danced and made love to her without moving any other part of his body. If his kisses could make her feel this way, she was afraid to find out what anything else would do to her.

Should she do this? Would she survive after this?

His hands wove up and down her back, igniting tiny shivers of pleasure. His mouth and tongue continued their assault on her lips, sending her desire through the roof.

She might not survive, but it would be worth every second.

He pulled away with a sexy grin. "Have I ever told you how much I enjoy kissing you?"

A giggle let loose as she tested her bravery and ran a hand down his back and cupped his ass. "I can't remember, but I know I like it when you do."

He trembled as she grabbed his ass tightly and pushed into him.

"So you want to skip all the fun stuff and get right to it, huh?"

She bit her lip playfully. "Isn't this fun?"

His lips brushed hers softly. "I could kiss every inch of your body all night and never get enough." A hand trailed from her back to her breast, his fingers tweaking her nipple into pleasure. "I can think of tons of fun stuff I could do to you before taking you completely." His lips met hers once again. Slowly. Softly. So sweetly. "But I need you so badly."

Her eyes closed as he shifted and clamped his mouth

over her hard nipple he had been playing with. "God, yes, Danny. I need you, too."

Although she agreed with him, almost begging him to take her then and now, he took his time savoring her breasts, first one, then the other. Kissing, devouring, and showing a lot more patience than she ever imagined. Each time his lips touched a new part of her body, she soared to heaven. She had no idea it could feel like this. Like she was the most precious jewel in the world. Like he would starve if he didn't feast on every inch of her body.

His kisses trailed a pathway down her body, his tongue circling her belly button, before reaching his ultimate destination. She jerked off the bed the moment his tongue touched the most intimate part of her body. He swirled his tongue in delicious ways she had no idea existed. Were her previous boyfriends really this ignorant when it came to sex? Or did Danny just know how to touch her in the right way?

She couldn't decide. At the moment, it didn't matter as his soft touch made her feel things she never wanted to end.

The instant her orgasm hit, she moaned quietly as she grabbed his hair and pulled. She kept pulling and tugging until he drained every last ounce of pleasure out of her. As he leisurely made his way back up to her lips, pressing a tender kiss to her, she knew one time with Danny would never be enough.

What did she do to herself?

"Damn, Kat, you feel so good, and we haven't even started."

Laughing, she playfully swatted his ass. "Haven't even started? What did you just do to me?"

"I kissed you. That was nothing." His grin said she was in for so much more.

Would she survive it all?

Biting her lip coyly, she then giggled. "I can't wait for you to start then."

Reaching toward the nightstand, he grabbed a condom and tore it open. Sheathing himself quickly, he hovered above her, yet made no other movements. His eyes bore into her, as if trying to see into her soul. The look unnerved her for some reason. Could he see the love she felt? Could he feel it? What was he thinking?

Swiping a hand across his forehead, she brushed a lock of hair back. Temptation almost tickled her to say the words of love, but she held them back. She said nothing. He did nothing but gaze at her warmly.

Then, without any words, he guided himself deep inside her, resting for a moment as she savored how perfectly he fit. She knew then, she would never get over him. She'd never love another man as she loved him.

It royally sucked.

Because would he ever love her back?

Probably not. This was Danny O'Rourke. The man could barely stand her entire family.

He started to move slowly. In and out.

She grabbed hold of him tightly, her hands grazing up and down his back as he moved flawlessly against her. In and out. Softly and slowly, as if she were a princess meant to be treasured with the utmost care.

No words were spoken, not even tiny moans of pleasure.

They stared at each other as they moved as one.

Each time he slid deep inside her, she felt her pleasure step up a notch. She didn't think she had it in her to orgasm again so soon. But the more he kept plunging deep inside her, the more she realized she was achingly close to another one. Probably more powerful than the last.

His head dropped, his lips touching her neck as his movements started to become a little faster. His warm breath against her throat incited her desire even more. His whispered words made her hit her crescendo. "You feel so... right."

Moaning delightfully, she let the pleasure flood her system once again. He tensed, jerking a few more times before going completely still, his lips brushing her neck.

After a few seconds, Danny lifted his head. "I'm glad I grabbed a few condoms."

Kat giggled, especially because she was extremely glad, too. "Are you now?"

A tender smile slowly appeared as his eyes shimmered with satisfaction. "Oh, yeah. Because once is definitely not enough. I hope you're not too tired."

"I had a nap."

Chuckling, his lips met hers. "Good thing. Because you're not about to get any sleep any time soon."

HIS HAND WOVE down her side, barely touching, yet loving the feeling of her soft skin. A tender kiss touched her shoulder.

Now that he had Kat in his arms, he wasn't sure he was prepared to let her go. He thought maybe she was something he needed to get out of his system. A sexual tension that would go away once he slept with her.

Holding her as he was now, he knew that was a lie. He wanted her again. And again.

He wanted her to stay.

Rolling to his back, he blew out a breath. She would never stay. Aubrey didn't even want to come back home.

How did he expect Kat to stay when her life was in Minnesota?

Moving as slowly and silently as possible, he got out of bed and walked out of the room. He took a quick shower and then started to brew some coffee as he looked at his phone. One missed call from Deke thirty minutes ago.

Pressing the phone to his ear, he waited for Deke to pick up.

"Hey, how's it going?"

"Fine." He poured himself a cup of coffee, willing his heart to slow down. Deke could not know he slept with Kat —multiple times last night. If he found out, he'd never get off his case.

"How's Kat doing?"

Danny took a sip of coffee and tried to block out the image of her in bed naked. "She's feeling a lot better. Did you find anything yet?"

"I talked to Fueller in Fort Lauderdale, and so far, none of Debra's friends know if she received anything a few days before her death. We didn't find any evidence in her home to suggest that, so no lead there. I did speak to Detective Larson, who spoke to Sheila's sister. A box of chocolates was left in front of her apartment door two days before she died. No note was found with it. She said Sheila thought it was from her neighbor two doors down. Apparently, he's been asking her out, and he doesn't understand the word no."

"Did Detective Larson speak to this guy?"

"No, not yet. She can't find him." Deke paused, shuffling sounds going on. "His name is Robert Grossman. Thirty-five years old and works at a car wash. No record or any complaints against him. Squeaky clean, other than both-ering his neighbor who happened to be murdered."

"A box of chocolates, like the first victim. What do you think about that? Kat received a bouquet of roses."

"Maybe Kat isn't a part of this investigation. Maybe we have that part wrong."

"I'm not willing to bank her safety on maybes, Deke."

Muttering a vicious curse under his breath, he slammed his hand down on the counter for letting his voice tell Deke exactly what he didn't want to. It wouldn't be hard to deduce by the venom and anxiety in his tone how worried he was about Kat.

"Did something happen last night?"

"Nope. No incidents here."

Deke sighed. "That's not what I was asking, and you know it."

"I don't want to talk about it." Danny took another sip of coffee to refrain from saying something to Deke he'd regret. "What are you doing today? What can I do from here to help you out?"

"Rogers has been digging through Michael and Erik's backgrounds, but so far no red flags are popping up. Neither one has a record. Not even a speeding ticket. Although, strange thing. Michael doesn't have a driver's license. Erik must bring him everywhere."

"He did say he doesn't leave much." Danny leaned against the counter. "Hey, you remember Jared, across the hall from Aubrey's apartment?"

"Yeah. Dude with the music."

"Did you know he had a brother? Jason?"

"No, that doesn't ring a bell. Why?"

"I ran into him last night. I didn't see Jared, but this guy was leaving his apartment."

"What are you thinking?"

Running a hand down his face, he groaned. "I don't

know. I don't know what I'm thinking anymore. Maybe it's nothing. He rubbed me the wrong way. Maybe I'm just suspicious of everyone right now."

"Does Aubrey know him?"

"I haven't asked her yet. I was going to call her next."

"Well, give her a call and give her my love. I'll keep doing the hard work on my end." He paused. "Figure out what you really want."

"What the hell does that mean?"

"You know what that means."

Deke hung up before Danny could argue with him. *Figure out what you really want.* Yeah, maybe he did know what Deke was insinuating, but he preferred not to think about any of that right now.

Hitting a few buttons, he waited for his sister to answer.

"Hi, Danny. How's Kat?"

He hesitated. Why was she asking about Kat? Did she know she hurt herself?

"Danny? Is everything okay? Did something happen to Kat?"

The intense panic in her voice had him feeling like a complete douche, upsetting his sister for no reason. She had only been asking him an innocent question.

"Kat's fine. She's still sleeping. How are you?"

"Sleeping? Did you spend the night?"

Shit.

How did he get himself out of this predicament?

"Danny?"

"Yeah, I did. I figured the more I help her, the faster we can get everything packed up and Kat back home to you."

"I do miss her," Aubrey said softly, almost in a whisper. "I miss you, too."

"Is everything okay, Aubs?"

"Yep." Her voice suddenly sounded cheery. "So you guys are making headway in the packing?"

His eyes moved across the room to the boxes stacked everywhere. They sure were. Soon, Kat would be leaving him. He'd be alone once again.

"It's a lot faster when two people are working. It'll be done in no time." He blew out a tiny breath, wondering if he should even ask her about her neighbor. Aubrey didn't sound like herself. "Are you sure you're okay, Aubs?"

"I'm fine, Danny." Her words were stern.

That, somehow, didn't reassure him at all. He could hear the strain in her tone.

"Was there a reason you called?"

Ouch. He couldn't call his sister for no reason other than to say hi? That hurt more than he cared to admit. But he wouldn't let her know that. He didn't need to add more stress to her life by attacking her. "I met Jared's brother, Jason, last night. I didn't know he had a brother. Did you?"

Aubrey hummed a little, a tiny gesture she sometimes did when she was thinking about something. God, he missed that sound. He missed his sister. An ache punctured his heart, deep and brutal as if someone was taking their time to carve it out.

"It sounds familiar. I might've met him once, but I can't recall when. My memory isn't...it's not what it used to be."

The sadness that coated her words hurt him deep inside. He was millions of miles away from his sister, and he couldn't stop her hurting. Couldn't help take the pain away.

"Your memories are fine. If you only met him once, it makes sense you wouldn't recall much. Nobody has a perfect memory."

"Why are you asking about him?"

"No reason. I never knew he had a brother." He pushed

away from the counter and grabbed his coffee. "I'll let you go. I know you have to start getting ready for work." A slight pause. "I miss you, Aubs. I love you."

"I miss you and love you, too, Danny. Take care of Kat for me."

Yeah, he was taking care of her just fine.

As he set his phone down, his gaze drifted toward the hallway. He could go take care of her again. Remove the pain centered deep in his heart. Ease the ache settling in the pit of his stomach. Let his worries drift away by burying himself deep inside her.

Maybe taking care of her wasn't such a good idea.

Because the more he let her in, the harder it would be to let her go.

14

———

KAT JERKED IN HER SLEEP, the loud jangling of music jarring to her senses. Sitting up, she rubbed her eyes, then focused on the spot where Danny should've been lying. Where was he?

Her eyes blurred. Did she dream about last night? Did she really sleep with Danny?

Music was still playing loudly. Turning her head to the nightstand, she realized it was her phone. Reaching over to grab it, her body protested and tingled in all the right places.

Oh, she *so* did not dream about last night. The delicious aches coating her body was evidence enough to confirm she slept with Danny. Multiple times. He loved her body three separate times. Each time better than the last.

Groaning at the screen, she almost didn't answer.

"Hey, Aubs. Good morning."

"You sound...funny. Are you okay?"

Rubbing her eyes again, she chuckled. Was she okay? Probably not. "You woke me up. I'm still trying to get the sleep out of my eyes. Is everything okay?"

"Danny slept over."

Heart pounding, she froze. How did Aubrey know that? Why did she sound so angry?

"He's been helping me pack. I didn't think it'd be a big deal if he helped."

"He sounded stressed when I talked to him. What's going on there?"

Too much. Everything. *I slept with your brother.* Ha! She couldn't say that.

"What do you mean? We're packing. Do you want to come down and help?"

"I yelled at Seth."

"What?" Kat couldn't hold in a laugh. Aubrey sounded funny. Like something was bothering her. "He probably deserved it. What's the matter, Aubs?"

Aubrey started breathing heavily as if she were trying to hold back tears. "I...it's...Kat...are you coming home yet?"

Home? Why did that word not sound appealing at the moment?

Her eyes glanced at the doorway, and to the soft sounds she could hear going on in the kitchen.

That's why it didn't sound enticing.

She didn't want to leave Danny yet.

"Soon, Aubs. We're almost done. Did you," she paused, hating to ask, "did you have another bad night?"

"They won't stop. I can't handle the nightmares. I didn't mean to yell at Seth." Her words sounded choppy, the tears definitely coming out strong. "It's okay if you sleep with Danny."

"Aubs! What?" Kat started to laugh. Loud and boisterous. Of all the things, she never expected Aubrey to say that out loud.

To her relief, Aubrey started laughing as well. The tears started to subside, her laughter stronger.

"This is why I need you home. You always make me feel better. Forget my apartment. Come home."

"I can't."

Silence.

"Aubrey, it's not because I don't want to."

"Because you do want to sleep with my brother."

She chuckled. "Enough about Danny. That's not why." Liar. "I don't want to be your crutch. You can do this."

"I don't think I can. I don't know how to cope with it. I feel so weak and useless."

Kat sighed, thinking maybe she should go home. Nothing would ever work between her and Danny. Why stay and let him in even more? Cut it off quick and clean.

"You're not weak. You're the strongest woman I know."

"How do you cope with...everything?"

"I run." A strangled laugh came out. "I hate running. But I run when I'm stressed. A lot. In fact, I run every morning to clear my head and focus myself for a new day."

"Yeah, running doesn't sound..."

"Maybe you should take those karate classes Mr. Strommer is offering. Release some of that anger, some of that fear. Learn how to protect yourself. If you feel weak, which you're not, build yourself up."

"Karate classes? Isn't his place next to Mrs. Dunburry's boutique, the biggest gossiper in town?"

Kat rolled her eyes. "Yes, but she can take her nosiness and stick it up the butt. Who cares what anyone says? Do what you want. Unless you don't want to do it."

"I actually like the sound of that. It sounds... empowering."

Happiness started to melt the worry away as she heard the eagerness in Aubrey's tone. "Hey, when I get back, I'll join, too. We can do it together. But don't wait for me. Sign up today. You're right. You need another outlet. Not just Logan, or me, or Seth. You need something for yourself."

Kat didn't even suggest talking to a professional, something she did every so often. Every time she did, Aubrey went into a tailspin, vehemently refusing to do anything that involved speaking to strangers.

"Thank you, Kat. I'm starting to feel better already. When do you think you'll be home?"

"I need a few more days."

"Well, don't be afraid to jump my brother's bones while you're there."

An outrageous giggle escaped. "Aubs! Stop saying things like that."

"Why? I know you two like each other. I'd like to see my brother happy again. He's always so sad."

She knew all too well what Aubrey was talking about. The sadness was easy to detect in Danny. "Even if I wanted to jump your brother," she laughed, knowing how much she enjoyed jumping him last night, "it would never work out between us."

"I knew it. You just admitted you like him."

"Yeah, I do. You got me. But it wouldn't work."

"Said a person who doesn't want it to work. And you, Kat, always find a way to work things out."

Kat said goodbye to Aubrey, her words ringing over and over in her head.

And you, Kat, always find a way to work things out.

Maybe she could. But did she want to set herself up for potential heartbreak? A heartbreak so strong, she might never recover from it?

Pushing those thoughts away, she got out of bed and grabbed some clothes before heading to the bathroom. She brushed her teeth, dressed, and pulled her hair back into a ponytail, then bounded to the kitchen as if nothing were wrong. As if no awkwardness existed. And there wouldn't be any if neither of them made it awkward.

Danny turned around from the coffee pot and smiled at her as soon as he heard her step into the area.

"Morning. Cup of coffee?"

She declined with a quick shake of her head. She was getting sick and tired of coffee. She wanted her tea.

Then she wanted something else.

Her body tingled with anticipation as his eyes looked her up and down. Slowly and deliciously. The intent clear on what he wanted to do.

"Why do you look dressed as if you're going for a run?"

A wide smile. "Because I am."

Danny nearly choked on the coffee as he started to take a sip. "Like hell."

With a hand to her hip, she arched a brow. "I feel better. A lot better. I'm going nuts. Aubrey called me and—"

"Is she okay? She sounded weird on the phone, like something's bothering her."

Her expression softened. "She had a bad night. Her nightmares are...tough. She wanted to know how I cope with stress. I run."

Danny nodded, the pain clear in his entire posture how much it hurt that Aubrey didn't share any of that with him. "Aubrey was never much of a runner."

"Yeah, she didn't like that idea. So I suggested Karate classes. That lifted her spirits." Kat stepped closer, close enough for Danny to grab her, which he thankfully did to her trembling nerves. She almost sighed in contentment. "I know it's hard. I'm sorry."

"I just want to be there for her."

"You are. Trust me. She wants you to be happy as much as you want her to be happy."

"How do you know that?"

The conversation with Aubrey jumped to the front of her mind. She chuckled as a light blush coated her cheeks. "I just know."

Danny's arms tightened around her as he pressed a tender kiss to her lips. "Are you feeling okay this morning?"

"I said I was."

"I mean...about last night."

Her hand reached up and caressed his cheek, his rough stubble filling her heart with giddiness. She loved the feel of his skin everywhere. Smooth in some places, rough in others. Like the man himself. Inside and out.

"I'm hoping we have a repeat later."

A smile brightened his features as he stole another kiss. "Why not right now?"

"Because I'm going for a run."

"You're not."

She patted his cheek. "I am, Mr. Macho Man. So you can either change and come with me, or stay here and worry like crazy?"

"Can we have shower sex when we get back?"

A laugh, so carefree and wonderful, let loose. How would she survive leaving this man?

"I thought you'd never ask."

As LOGAN REACHED for his coffee mug, a knock sounded on the door.

"It's open."

Taking a drink, he scalded the roof of his mouth when

too much hot liquid slid down his throat as the door opened and the last person he expected to see walked in.

"Derek. Hey."

Derek offered a weak smile as he closed the office door and took a seat in front of his desk. "Are you busy?"

"Not really. I'm catching up on some paperwork." Logan couldn't help wonder why Derek was here and dressed as if he was ready for work. It didn't make sense. He asked for time off. Insisted on it. What was he doing here? "Is everything okay?"

Derek nodded. "I should've known she'd never love me. I was an idiot."

Kat.

He finally wanted to talk about her. Not a subject he wanted to touch, but he knew he couldn't leave his best friend hanging.

"It didn't hurt to try. I'm sorry how it turned out. Maybe when she gets back from Flori—"

"I went to Florida. It's over between us."

Speechless.

He honestly had no clue what to say. Derek followed Kat to Florida?

"I thought maybe if I wooed her somehow or did something romantic," Derek gave a half-hearted laugh, "maybe even groveled on my knees, she would give me another chance. I was wrong."

He opened his mouth to say something, anything, but he still didn't know what to say.

"I think her and Agent O'Rourke like each other."

Logan leaned forward. "Are you sure? They normally don't get along. Danny doesn't get along with any of us. He practically hates us because Aubrey stayed here."

"That's not what I saw."

Derek had to be wrong. He had to have misread the situation. Danny and Kat? No. He didn't like that scenario.

"I can see by the expression on your face you're not happy about that. I'm glad I'm not alone in that feeling."

He cracked a smile for Derek's benefit. "Yeah, I can't say the idea makes me happy. Danny is...difficult." Logan sighed as he ran a hand down his face. "He's also Aubrey's brother. I can't hate the man."

"Even if he wants to date Kat?"

Logan's brow lifted. "Come on, Derek. Maybe you saw attraction, but can you honestly see him moving to Minnesota? He left as fast as he could."

"Maybe. But what about Kat moving to Florida?"

Kat leave?

No.

No, his sister couldn't leave.

His heart started to pound, loud and heavy, like a drummer banging hard and fierce. Was this how Danny felt when Aubrey wouldn't come home with him? Like his heart had been ripped out of his chest. Like the world tilted on its axis.

His sister couldn't move away. He'd miss her too much.

The door to his office swung open. Charlotte held a look of panic in her eyes. He stood up slowly.

"Charlotte?"

"You need to get down to Barry's Garage. Evan and Seth are going at it."

"Shit." Logan rounded his desk, grabbed his jacket from the coat rack near the door, and followed Charlotte down the hallway.

Loud, echoing footsteps followed him.

"Is your vacation over, Derek?"

"Yep."

He held open the door and let Derek step outside first, then followed him, the cold bite of the wind sinking into his cheeks. "Let's have a beer tonight. We can talk about everything."

Derek followed step for step as they made their way to his truck. "Nothing to talk about. Shit happened, and she moved on." Derek hopped into the passenger seat. "But I will have a beer."

He grinned as he started the engine. "Good. Let's go see what Seth got himself into."

"I can't believe he's still holding the fact that Evan is lying."

"Aubrey can't remember Evan involved, but Seth swears he's lying about something. They both need to let it go."

"Well, if it's at the shop, then it sounds like Seth approached him."

Another hand ran down his face before he took a hard left. "Aubrey's been tense and on edge. Her nightmares have been bad lately. She kicked Seth out of the house last night because he wouldn't talk about what's going on."

Derek chuckled. It was good to hear his friend sounding a little like himself again. "No shit. Good for her."

He chuckled, too. "That's what I told her, but she felt horrible about it. I said it was something Kat would've done." Tension immediately swarmed the truck. "This is going to be awkward for a while, isn't it?"

Derek sighed. "I don't want it to be. But yeah, hearing her name...it'll get better. I'm sorry, man."

"No, I'm sorry it didn't work out. I would've loved if you two would've made it work."

"Now her and Agent O'Rourke..."

Logan groaned. "Please don't say that."

A laugh filled the space. Logan couldn't stop the laugh

that bubbled to the surface, joining Derek as they laughed at something that wasn't that funny. He honestly didn't know what to think if his sister and Danny started to date.

Was Danny even capable of treating his sister the way she deserved?

Less than five minutes later, he pulled in front of Barry's Garage and jerked to a stop. Seth and Evan were rolling around the ground, fists flying, snow churning in the air. They had a light dusting last night, but not enough to cushion the ground with a blanket of snow. Some parts were icy.

They stormed out of the truck and attempted to break up the fight, getting right down to the ground and into the fray. Derek grabbed Evan as he made a move for Seth.

Seth was strong. Even as kids when they used to horse around, him being nearly ten years older than Seth, Seth held his own. He never let his age hold him back in a fight. He didn't hold back now.

"Calm down, Seth. Stop it."

Logan tried to hold Seth tightly by the arms, Seth's back to his chest, but Seth refused to cooperate.

"That son of a bitch deserves his ass beaten! Let me go."

"Don't make me arrest you."

Logan's grip tightened as Seth struggled to break free. Without warning, a hard kick hit his ankle. His hands loosened, and Seth stumbled away.

"Goddamnit, Seth. That hurt."

Seth's eyes darted between him and Evan, who stood behind Derek looking calmer than Seth.

"Don't do it. Don't try to hit him again. I will arrest you if I have to." Logan had no idea if threatening his brother would work because the murder in his eyes right now said nothing would work to calm him down.

"Move out of my way, Logan. I want him to feel the pain. I'm doing this for Aubrey."

Logan stepped closer, attempting to block Seth's view. "What for? Why? Aubrey doesn't remember—"

"I just know. I don't need her to remember anything. Now get out of—"

"No," Logan said with a growl as he grabbed his brother by the jacket and made him back up a step, "I won't let you do this. I won't let you ruin your life over some supposed theory. Knock it off, and grow up!"

Seth pushed at Logan, disengaging his hand. Before Logan could react, a fist went flying in his face.

He went down hard, his head smacking the snowy ground so roughly, the ringing in his ears sounded like a teakettle about to explode.

His brother hit him.

Kat liked Danny.

Danny liked Kat.

Aubrey's nightmares were getting worse.

The ringing intensified.

Then nothing penetrated his mind as everything went black.

15

THE SOFT FABRIC tickled her skin as she pulled it over her head and down. Getting dressed sucked. She'd rather have Danny's hands sliding down her skin than a shirt, even if it felt soft and warm.

Like he made her feel in the shower.

Their run had been exhausting. Taking a few days off threw her rhythm out of whack. But not wanting to look weak or pathetic in front of Danny, she pushed through the tiredness and kept up to pace with him. By the time they came back an hour later, they were both dripping with sweat and drinking what felt like gallons of water.

Then they showered just as Danny had promised. Together.

When Danny wasn't worried and agonizing over things he had no control over, he was fun and playful.

Happy.

But how could it last? A relationship between them would never work. He lived in one state, and she lived in another. As much as she enjoyed Florida, she could never move away from Minnesota. Although she knew Danny would love to be closer to Aubrey, she couldn't see him leaving his job and moving to Minnesota, he loved his job too much.

So she had to put a smile on her face and pretend everything was okay when inside she felt her world crumbling down around her.

Bracing herself, putting on a happy face, she left the bedroom and found Danny in the living room closing a box.

"You got a lot finished yesterday. What's on our agenda today?"

Danny glanced up from the floor and smiled. Every time he smiled, her heart did a little pitter-patter. A little jolt of desire straight to her core. "I did get a lot done. I think we could probably make a few trips to the donation center. Then come back and assess what's left. I think we're almost done."

Her heart rate sped up, speeding dangerously, afraid she would crash and burn soon. Almost done? That meant she would leave. Say goodbye to the first man to make her think she could find happiness like her brother found.

Life was so unfair sometimes.

She smiled wide to hide the pain at the thought of leaving and clapped her hands. "Great. We could stop for lunch afterward. You could bring me to your favorite spot. Show me a little of Tampa."

He stood with a sexy grin, his eyes heated with desire as he snagged a hand around her waist and pulled her against him. "I know just the place. The ribs there are to-die-for. Do you like barbeque?"

"Yes. Nice and messy."

"I'll clean you up afterward." He chuckled and then bent

his head toward her neck, peppering tiny kisses in playful delight.

Stern, arrogant Danny, finally lighthearted and wonderful. Making sure she was happy and comfortable. Teasing her. Joking with her. Loving her body as if she were a treasure, a piece of glass that could break if he didn't touch her slowly and tenderly.

How would she ever give this up? Why didn't they have more time together? How slow could she pack everything and not give it away she was stalling?

A sharp ring broke the peace.

"I should get that."

His tongue licked up her neck, and his teeth nibbled her ear. His silky voice whispered, "We might not make that donation run today after all." He let her go, stepping away with a dirty wink filled with promises for later.

She couldn't stop the giddy smile that touched her lips. Perhaps she wasn't alone in her feelings. He didn't want her to leave either. Not yet, anyway.

Heading for the kitchen where she left her phone on the counter, her spirits dipped when she saw it was Aubrey calling. She should be at work already. Her nightmares must've been worse than she realized, otherwise why would she be calling?

"Hey, Aubs."

"You need to come home. Right now. I need you. You need to come home."

"Okay, calm down. Did something happen? What's going on?" Her eyes darted to Danny, who looked worried, the happiness from moments before completely gone. He stalked her way.

"You need to come home, Kat. Please." Aubrey's voice cracked as tears mingled with her words.

"You need to tell me what's going on. Right now, Aubrey."

"Seth..." She sniffled, then her tears increased in strength.

"What about Seth? Is he okay? You're scaring the shit out of me, Aubrey. Stop crying and tell me what happened."

A warm hand touched her shoulder. She looked at Danny, his eyes sparkling with concern, his hand a comfort.

Aubrey slowed her crying, a few hiccups echoing in her ear before she heard Aubrey slow her breathing down, just as she practiced with her. When Aubrey got upset, sometimes she didn't know how to calm down, spiraling into chaos until Kat taught her breathing exercises. They normally helped. Like, now.

"Seth got into a fight with Evan. Logan showed up with Derek, and they broke the fight up. Seth wouldn't calm down. He hit Logan." Her breathing started to pick up speed, tears making an appearance again. "Logan arrested him. He...he blacked out. Seth hit him, and he blacked out."

"Shit. Is he okay? Is he in the hospital?"

"The big dummy won't go. I'm worried about him. He locked up Seth, and he's acting like it's no big deal. Seth won't talk to anybody. I'm..." Aubrey screamed. Kat had to pull the phone away from her ear. Danny's hand tightened on her shoulder. The look on his face said he was about to grab the phone from her when Aubrey stopped screaming. Kat held a hand for him to stop.

"Aubrey?"

"I'm okay. I feel better."

Kat giggled. "Well, that's good. Maybe you should scream more often."

Her giggles became louder until she was laughing like someone told her the joke of the century. To her relief,

Aubrey was laughing with her. Danny's hand still held her shoulder tightly, his expression read he wasn't amused. By any of it.

"Thank you, Kat. I needed that. I wish I could give Seth the answer he wants."

"Seth needs to grow up and let this Evan business go. You don't remember him, so it didn't happen."

"I don't care about my apartment or my stuff. Come home, please. We all need you."

"I'm on the next flight home. I'll be there soon."

Kat hung up with Aubrey and set her phone down on the counter.

"I heard Aubrey scream, but that's about it. What the hell is going on?"

She turned toward him and reached up to smooth his cheek, hoping to erase the frown and replace it with the smile she adored.

His hand left her shoulder and grabbed her hand, stopping her from touching him. He squeezed her hand tightly. "I'm two seconds away from getting pissed."

"It figures this happiness between us wouldn't last. We're already gearing to yell at each other." Her gaze turned down.

A hand wrapped around her waist, pulling her snug against his body. His mouth dipped, his lips brushing her neck. "I don't want to argue, but you need to tell me what's going on. Why did my sister scream like someone was hurting her?"

She grabbed hold of his waist and dug her fingers in, hating every word she was about to say. What was wrong with Seth? Why would he hit Logan? Was Logan okay? Blacked out? Shivers wracked her body.

Danny dropped her hand and pulled her tightly against him, hugging her fiercely. "Whatever it is, I can help."

Maybe he could. Maybe he could help Seth see reason.

"Seth got into a fight with Evan, again, for the millionth time. He won't let it go that Evan isn't lying. Logan tried to break up the fight and...and...Seth hit him. He hit Logan." Suddenly, she wanted to cry, just like Aubrey. Let loose a torrential downpour of tears. She inhaled sharply, hoping to keep her control. "Aubrey said he hit him hard, that Logan blacked out for a moment. She said he's okay, but he did arrest Seth. I have to go home."

A soft kiss touched her neck. "I'll go with you."

For once, she didn't argue with him. She didn't want to. The thought of Danny coming with her, of helping, filled her heart with joy.

She wasn't ready to lose him. She would latch on to any small way to keep him for as long as she could.

"I'd like that."

A LARGE BREATH escaped before he stepped inside the house he didn't expect to enter again for a while. But he was glad to be here. To see his sister. To have Kat a little longer before it would all fall apart.

He wasn't too thrilled about the weather. It was cold as shit in Minnesota. He didn't have a winter jacket, but Kat told him on the plane he could borrow one of Logan's. He would be the happiest man alive when he finally got that.

A smile touched his face as Aubrey flung her arms around Kat, holding her tightly. His eyes connected with Logan's, who stood near the kitchen sporting a nice shiner on his right eye. Seth hit him in the right spot.

"Danny? You came, too." Aubrey squealed excitedly, her

arms wrapping around him. He hugged her, lifting her off the ground.

"I missed you, Aubs. I hope you've been okay."

"I'm much better now that Kat's home, and you're here, too." Her breath hitched as wetness hit his neck as if she were crying. "I want you to stay. Don't go back to Florida."

What could he say? He had a job in Florida. A life. What would he even do if he moved to this small town that offered almost nothing for him, other than his sister, of course?

And Kat.

If he moved here, he could have Kat. Couldn't he?

"Silly me. I know that won't happen." She sniffed and backed away, wiping at her eyes.

"I'm here now." That's about all he could say at the moment.

Aubrey grinned but said nothing else.

"Hey, girl. I have some goodies for you. Come on. Help me unpack this stuff." Kat grabbed Aubrey's hand, met his gaze briefly, and then started walking toward the hallway that would lead to the bedrooms with a suitcase wheeling behind her.

Logan watched them leave the room, as did he. Then Logan turned toward the fridge and pulled two beers out.

"Want one?"

"I do." He snatched one of the beers and took a long sip. "So, Seth hit you. Nice shiner there."

A lame chuckle let loose as Logan placed the cold bottle over his eye for a moment. "Never thought he'd do that or that I'd have to arrest my own brother. He's still sitting in lockup, and it's killing me not to pay his bail even though I put him there."

"Kat said it was about Evan again."

Logan took a seat at the table. "Yeah, it's always about Evan lately. Seth won't let it go."

Danny joined him at the table. "How's Aubrey been doing?"

Logan fiddled with the bottom of the bottle before meeting his gaze. "I don't want to lie to you. It's been a shitty few days. Her nightmares have been bad. She's been stressed." He sighed, muttering a curse under his breath. "It just occurred to me they started when Kat left for Florida. It's usually not this bad."

"Her and Kat are close. Maybe she was stressing because she wasn't near her. Hopefully, she sleeps better tonight."

"God, I hope so. It's..." Logan looked down. "It's hard sometimes, but I love her so much. I'd do anything for her." Logan suddenly jerked his head up and pinned him with a fierce stare. "Derek told me something."

Danny cocked a brow. What did the deputy say? He promised Kat he wouldn't tell Logan about the hospital. "Yeah?"

"Do you have something going on with my sister?"

All of Danny's friendliness washed away. His grip tightened on the beer bottle as he clenched his jaw. Who did the sheriff think he was, questioning him about Kat, when he was sleeping with *his* sister?

"And if I do, Sheriff?"

Logan's expression hardened at the way he said his title so condescendingly. Well, tough. He wasn't about to take any of this shit.

"I know you don't like the idea of me and Aubrey, but whatever you're doing with Kat better not be—"

Danny stood up and reached across the table, grabbing Logan by the front of his shirt. "Don't finish that sentence. Don't disrespect Kat that way. I would never toy with her.

And if you ever hurt my sister or mess with her, you'll see how dangerous I can truly be."

Logan didn't back down as they stared at each other. "Why? Why Kat?"

Danny's grip loosened a notch. "Because sometimes you can't help who you like. You should know that feeling well, Sheriff, don't you think?"

Understanding reflected clearly in Logan's eyes as he nodded. "If you hurt her..."

"Oh, I think we both understand each other clearly. You hurt my sister, I hurt you. Vice versa." Danny let him go and sat down as he laughed. "I think we're more alike than I care to admit."

A grin touched Logan's lips. "Maybe when it comes to our sisters." Then his smile fell. "Aubrey doesn't know."

"Don't be so sure. My sister is smart as a whip." Danny took a long, hard swallow of his beer, then almost slammed the bottle to the table. "I'll be staying at Kat's house while I'm here. You got a problem with that, Sheriff?"

Logan squinted his eyes in irritation. "I don't have a choice, do I?"

Danny smirked to aggravate him. "Nope."

"How long are you staying?"

The case waiting for him in Florida, the one that worried him centered around Kat, shifted through his mind. Should he tell Logan? Should he tell him how he didn't want to leave Kat's side until the killer was caught?

"I don't know yet."

Confusion sparkled in Logan's eyes. "What's going on, Danny?"

"Can't take you for a dummy, that's for sure."

"Gee, thanks." Logan took a swallow of beer.

"I'd like to talk to Seth."

"That's why you're not sure how long you're staying?"

Kat would be pissed at him if he confessed everything to Logan. Beyond pissed. But, from one brother to another, he felt like it was his duty to tell Logan.

"No. But I told Kat I'd help in any way I could. Clearly, you're not making any progress with him. So let me talk to him." Danny leaned forward. "Maybe a fresh set of eyes on this case I'm working on would help me. I help you, and you help me."

"What case?"

He took a deep breath, refusing to avert his eyes and act like a coward. If Logan didn't already hate him, he'd despise him after he confessed.

"There's this serial killer running around Florida killing women." His jaw clenched. "The case that I think...might have targeted Kat as the next victim."

HER BLOOD BOILED as Danny's words rang in her ears like someone stood near her blowing hard on a whistle.

"What the hell are you talking about, Danny? A serial killer after my sister? What happened in Florida?" Logan demanded as his hand slammed down hard on the table.

"Nothing happened," Kat said with a laugh as she stepped into the kitchen with a smile on her face, even though the anger was spreading fast and thick like a wildfire.

Her gaze met Danny's. He looked sympathetic, but not apologetic. Damn him. What was he thinking?

"Somehow, I don't believe you, Kat." Logan stood up. "I know about you and Danny. Are you planning on telling

Aubrey? Or am I keeping that a secret? It seems we like to keep secrets now."

Kat flinched as Logan's tone of voice told her exactly how much she hurt him. That wasn't her intention. She simply didn't want to add more worry onto his plate.

Danny stood up slowly, stepping closer to her side, the expression on his face stern. "Watch what you say to her."

"Don't." Logan jerked a finger at him. "Don't act like you give a shit. What's really going on here, Danny? Why are you really sleeping with my sister?"

Danny's hand clenched. Kat grabbed his arm before he could take one step toward her idiotic brother. She felt the rage flowing, inching to let loose. If she let go, he'd take a swing at Logan, and he'd probably be sporting two black eyes before they left.

How did Logan even know they slept together? How did this night turn sour so fast?

"Please, Danny. Back off. Please," she whispered.

He turned his head in her direction. The fire blazed in his eyes how much he wanted to hurt Logan. For her. She found it endearing that he cared that much.

She waited, holding her breath until he finally relaxed a little and took a step back. A breath escaped, air filling her lungs instantly, and some relief. Her hand fell away from his arm that she had been holding in a death-like grip. She could feel his anger emanating behind her as she took a few steps toward Logan.

"I don't want Aubrey to hear any of this. She's already stressed out. I'll come by the station tomorrow, and we'll tell you everything. But not tonight. Don't do this in front of Aubrey." Taking another step, she laid a hand on his shoulder. He was coiled tight with tension. "This isn't you. Talking to me like this. I'm sorry about Seth, but I don't deserve to be attacked, too."

Logan's anger instantly vanished, anguish taking its place. He grabbed her by the shoulders and hugged her. "I'm sorry, Kat. Shit, I'm sorry. I'm worried about Aubrey. About Seth. Now, I'm more worried about you. I...I..."

She squeezed him, trying to offer the comfort she knew her big brother needed. "I know. Which is why I told Danny...and Derek," she hugged him tighter as he stiffened, "not to say a word to you. I didn't want to add more worry to your plate. I'm fine. Everything will be fine."

"A serial killer? That doesn't sound fine."

"That could just be Danny being overprotective. We'll talk about it tomorrow. Please, Logan. For Aubrey's sake."

He nodded, hugged her tightly one more time before letting her go. "What is Aubrey doing?"

"Hanging her new clothes up. I came in here to get us some drinks." She turned toward Danny, who stood near the counter, his expression blank and his arms crossed together. "Do you want to help Logan cook supper?"

She could see he didn't like that idea at all, especially when he glowered in Logan's direction.

"Sure."

A smile touched her lips. He might not be happy about it, but she couldn't stop the little jolt to her heart that he was willing to overlook his anger for her.

"Thank you, Danny."

She grabbed two cans of pop from the fridge, then started to walk out. A hand grabbed her arm, twirling her into a warm embrace.

"He gets a hug and I don't? Doesn't seem right," Danny whispered in her ear. A kiss followed. Light and airy. A promise for later.

"Please don't argue with him anymore tonight."

"Yeah, I know. For Aubrey's sake." Another kiss hit her neck. "For your sake." One more kiss. "I'm staying at your house. No arguments."

She smiled, her grip tightening around his waist as best as she could holding the pop cans. "None."

Now, how did she explain to Aubrey why her brother was going to be staying at her house and not Logan's?

16

THE FRONT DOOR slammed harder than she intended, the wind helping the task. Listening to the news at Logan's last night, she knew there was snow in the forecast the next few days. Maybe they'd get a blizzard so she could hide away in her home from everything.

Her morning run had been exhausting and difficult. When she first stepped outside, the freezing morning air lifted her mood and invigorated her for a nice, long run. As soon as the wind started to impede her strides, her mood dipped until she realized it made her work harder at putting one foot in front of the other—something she desperately needed.

Last night had been stressful, to say the least. The tension between Logan and Danny had been off the charts. After the small argument, they did make nice. Or at least when her and Aubrey happened to be in the room.

Kat hadn't wanted to spring the news about Danny staying with her, so she told Aubrey while they unpacked in the bedroom. Surprisingly, Aubrey loved the idea. She had been giddy at the news. Her spirits definitely lifted.

Which made Kat's mood dip down drastically.

How would Aubrey take it when Danny left? How would she react when this thing between them turned out to be nothing?

Aubrey would be heartbroken. Devastated.

Kat knew that was the only likely outcome. She couldn't see any other way they would work out. She had been worried Aubrey wouldn't like the idea. Now, she worried Aubrey liked it a little too much.

Sure, they were dynamite in bed, something they proved once again last night, but that didn't mean they would last forever. They got along just fine between the sheets. But the ride home had been tense.

Grabbing the pitcher of water from the fridge, she set it on the counter, then opened the cupboard in front of her to grab a glass.

"Where did—"

Startled, she jumped, twirled, and dropped the glass in one smooth move. Pieces of glass shattered between her and Danny, who stood a few feet away.

A brow rose, the worry evident in his steely gaze. "I didn't mean to scare you. I woke up, and you were gone. Don't do that to me, Kat. Where were you?"

Brushing a shaky hand across her upper lip, she didn't like the concern in his gaze. She wasn't a child. She could take care of herself.

"I went for a run."

"By yourself? Kat, you can't—"

"Don't tell me what to do, Danny." Turning, she grabbed another glass, setting it gently on the counter. She didn't trust herself to hold it while pouring the water.

"It's for your own safety."

Her own safety? Was he serious? They weren't in Florida anymore.

After pouring a full glass, she chugged the entire thing, then refilled it.

"Don't ignore this, or me. This is serious."

She twisted her gaze toward him. "We left Florida. I'm fine now."

His expression said he didn't like how nonchalant she appeared. Well, she honestly believed she was fine. She didn't think the issue was that serious in Florida like he did, especially when she didn't know what was fully going on since he wouldn't share it with her. It's his own fault if she didn't appear more concerned.

"You don't know that. This guy could...he could've followed you."

"Are you trying to scare me, Danny?" She set her glass down slowly, willing herself not to slam it on the counter. "Because it won't work. I don't scare easily."

"Maybe you should. You're not taking any of this seriously right now. Gallivanting off on your own. Not even telling me you're leaving."

"You're not telling me anything about what's going on. What should I feel scared about? Okay, some jackass sent me flowers and didn't leave a name. Whoa, so scary."

Glass crunched as Danny stomped to her, the anger imploded on his face, the fear blazing in the deep depths of his eyes. He grabbed her shoulders, his fingers dug in fiercely. "I can't—I won't let what happened to Aubrey happen to you. I can prevent it this time. I will. You have..." His breathing turned rough. "You have no idea how I felt when I woke up and couldn't find you. You didn't even leave a note."

His fingers were strong, his nails digging into her skin.

She wouldn't be surprised if he left bruises, he was holding her so tightly. But she didn't care about that. She only cared about how much she could feel the trembles in those tough fingers. His fear traveled from the tips of his fingers and straight to her gut, making her shiver with unease.

What was she supposed to be so scared about? She didn't like the feeling, especially the unknown.

"I'm sorry, Danny. Nothing is going to happ—"

"Don't," he whispered, as his fingers loosened their hold, "don't say that. I didn't think anything would've happened to Aubrey, but it did. I had no control over it. I can now."

Reaching up, she grabbed his hands and linked fingers with him. "You can't control me, Danny. I went for a run."

He squeezed. "Then I go running with you." He shivered. "Even if it is cold as shit here. I have no idea how you can run outside in this weather."

She smiled, knowing how unbearable it would be for him to run here. She was used to the cold weather. She didn't even wear a jacket, just a long sleeve shirt when she ran. The cold air always pushed her to go faster.

"If you want me to even entertain the idea of letting you act like a macho guy, then you have to tell me what's going on."

His jaw clenched, his fingers tightened their hold once again. His fear was inching its way back in. Why couldn't he tell her?

"I can take care of myself. I don't need a keeper."

"Even if I want to be one?"

She almost smiled but stopped herself before one little corner of her mouth could move. He didn't mean that the way she wanted.

"When you leave, I'll be my own keeper. So why bother now?"

Sorrow coated his eyes immediately. He pulled her closer, bending his mouth near hers. "Indulge me for now. I don't like feeling this way. This panic. Don't leave me like that again. That's all I'm asking, Kat."

She ached to close the distance. To feel his soft lips upon hers. But not yet. "Then tell me why? Tell me what you wouldn't in Florida."

A tender kiss touched her. Soft and sweet, and over entirely too fast. "Let's get ready and meet your brother at the station. I'll tell you everything at the same time I tell him."

Her blood boiled that he wanted to tell Logan everything. Then she'd have not one but two overbearing men trying to control her life. Ridiculous.

Maybe Danny sensed the change in her demeanor because he grinned and let go of her hands. He stepped back, the glass crunching under his shoes.

"You're so beautiful when you're angry." His eyes softened, yet his stance was determined. "But I don't care if you get angry with me. I'll do anything to protect you. Anything."

"You can't control me, or tell me what to do."

He glanced around the room, then stalked to a door down the hallway and came back with a broom and a dustpan.

He started to sweep up the mess. "Go get ready. I'll clean this up."

"Go ahead and ignore me, but I'm not a woman who'll just obey. Don't mistake me for someone weak."

His gaze connected with hers. "I never would. And don't mistake me for a man easily swayed. I will do anything in my power to keep you safe, even if it makes you hate me. I can live with that."

She broke eye contact and fled the kitchen.

Hate him?

No. She loved the big dummy.

But she was afraid it could turn to hate if he didn't give her breathing room. If he didn't put some trust into her ability to take care of herself.

She showered and got dressed quickly, ready to leave and find out the truth about what was going on.

Danny would soon learn what type of woman he was dealing with.

───────

HE TRIED to shake loose the nerves slithering everywhere like a bunch of leeches coating his body, wanting to wreak havoc and suck every drop of blood out. It barely worked because he was about to tell Kat and Logan what was going on.

Telling Kat seemed like the worst idea. She wasn't a woman to sit idly by and let things play out. He could see her taking matters into her own hands to solve the problem. How? He didn't know. That's what scared the shit out of him.

But if she insisted on pretending nothing was wrong, if she would leave the house to go for a run without telling him, then he had to give in. He had to tell her what kind of madman they were dealing with.

Pressing a light hand to her back, he guided her inside the station and nodded at Charlotte, who sat behind the counter. He inhaled deeply and let the warmth from the building heat him up from the cold outside. Even with Logan's thick winter coat, he was cold whenever he stepped outside.

"What? No hello? No, great to see you?" Charlotte

cocked an eyebrow that he figured most men would cower at.

"Hello. It's nice to see you again." He even threw in a smile when he was far from feeling any kind of happiness.

Rolling her eyes, she waved a hand toward her right. "I guess that'll do. Logan's in his office. Where's the cute one? Why didn't you bring him with? He's a lot friendlier."

Danny chuckled. "I'll let Deke know you said hi."

A tint of red coated her cheeks. "Please do."

Kat laughed, too, then grabbed his hand as she started toward Logan's office.

He leaned closer to her ear, pressing a light kiss to her neck. "I love hearing your laugh."

Her steps almost slowed, but they kept walking as she smiled gently. "I love hearing yours more."

Moments like this he cherished complimenting a beautiful woman and garnering a delicate smile that hit him straight in the heart. Hearing a compliment back surprised him. Kat liked his laugh? Laughing felt foreign to him, he hadn't done much of it lately. Now, because he knew she liked it, he wanted to laugh, just for her.

He wanted to pull her in the opposite direction and leave, take her home, and love her body from head to toe. Forget about all of their worries, all the tension, all of the arguments.

Arguing with her this morning wasn't fun. When he heard the door slam and found her in the kitchen, unharmed, looking sexy and sweaty from a run, he couldn't stop the intense rage that hit him. She left him to worry without a word goodbye.

The moment he woke up and found her gone, his mind ran to what happened to Aubrey, and scenario after scenario flashed before him.

He'd lose his mind if anything happened to Kat. She didn't fully understand that. He didn't even know if he could properly explain how he felt.

Kat knocked once on the door, dropped his hand, and opened the door. He missed her touch immediately, but as soon as he walked into Logan's office, he put his game face on.

Logan stood in front of his desk, a cup of coffee in his hand. Derek stood close to him, also with a cup of coffee. He tensed, jealousy instantly swarming his veins as his eyes connected with Derek. What was he doing here? Why did he feel jealous? They broke up. Kat was his now.

His?

Was she truly his? Maybe for the moment. The future remained to be seen.

"Good morning. There's some coffee in the break room," Logan offered with a smile that looked forced.

"I'm fine." Kat glanced at him. Her look said he was welcome to grab a cup, but she was itching to move this along. She wanted to know everything.

"I'm good." He couldn't resist. "What's he doing here?"

Derek stood taller. "Is there a problem, Agent O'Rourke?"

Kat stepped closer, brushing shoulders with him. "No, there isn't."

The jealousy from moments before, which he didn't think he needed to feel, ramped up even more. Did she just take Derek's side? He didn't need to be here. His question was fair.

"Why don't you tell me what you refused to last night?"

Kat whipped her head in Logan's direction. "That's not fair, Logan. He didn't refuse. We decided it would be better if Aubrey wasn't around."

A muscle in Logan's cheek started to tick. "You're right. I'm..." He blew a breath out. "Can you start talking, Danny?"

Yeah, he might as well. The tension floating around the room was going to give him hives soon.

"Kat received a bouquet of roses. She received these before the ones from Deputy Graham. A card was attached with no name, but it said, "Please forgive me." I didn't like it."

Logan's eyes narrowed as he shifted his gaze away from him and to Kat. "Why didn't you tell me there was more to this flower business, Kat?"

"I didn't think it was a big deal." She shrugged.

"Don't get like that with her, Logan. Just...don't." Danny's entire posture said he was ready to defend Kat in any way, including with his fists.

Logan's expression immediately softened toward Kat, then he nodded, indicating Danny should continue.

"She thought maybe Deputy Graham sent them, but then we figured out he didn't. Why else would someone send her flowers like that?" Danny decided not to tell them Kat thought he sent them. Because then he'd have to explain how they argued when she first showed up.

"It's probably nothing," Kat insisted.

"You don't know that," he replied.

Kat huffed. "And you're not saying anything that I don't know. Like, why you think someone wants to hurt me."

"Tell us about the case," Logan said, appearing nonchalant as if they were talking about a normal case when it was anything but. Danny didn't miss the way his cup trembled as he took a sip of coffee.

"Okay. I'll tell you everything I know." He ran a hand through his hair as he stepped away from Kat. "The first case popped up in Miami. A 30-year-old woman, Tonya

Clark, was raped and murdered, quite brutally. A box of chocolates with a note 'It's time' was left at her door a few days before she was killed. She thought her boyfriend sent it. The killer did, though. Next victim, a 22-year-old woman, Debra Cooper, died in Fort Lauderdale in the same manner. As far as we know, nothing was left on her doorstep. But we're positive something was, and she just didn't tell anyone. Maybe she threw it away. The latest victim, a 42-year-old woman, Sheila Crowler, died in Tampa in the same exact manner. She was also left a box of chocolates, although no note was found. I'm not saying the flowers sent to Kat are related, but I'm also not taking the chance." He looked at Kat. The intensity of how much he refused to take a chance on her safety was fierce. "No chances."

"A box of chocolates isn't the same as flowers. I don't see the connection," Derek muttered.

"Then you're an idiot," Danny retorted.

Logan stood up and set his coffee down. "Let's not argue."

"Well, I admit, the cases sound brutal, but two victims received chocolates, not flowers. It's a loose connection, if anything," Derek said, rolling his eyes.

"And this is my sister we're talking about, Derek. I don't care how loose the connection is." Logan looked at him. "I heard the other thing."

Danny nodded. He knew Logan wasn't an idiot.

"Heard what?" Derek asked.

"Their last names. They all start with C," Logan said quietly, "which is what really connected the dots with you, isn't it, Danny?"

"It was enough to make me worry. Maybe this has nothing to do with Kat. Maybe it does. Maybe this killer is following me now. He was killing on the East coast and then changed tactics to the West. I don't know. What I do know is I'm not letting Kat out of my sight."

"Grown woman. I can totally take care of myself."

Danny stalked to her, grabbing her by the shoulders, his fear instantly surfaced by her nonchalance at the entire thing. "Get it through your thick, pretty little head. You will stay by my side, your brother's side, hell, Deputy Graham's side, but you are not to be alone until I solve this. I can't lose you. I won't..." his voice broke, "I won't lose you like I lost Aubrey."

"But you didn't lose her, Danny."

His hands fell away. "Are you sure about that?"

Air. He needed air.

Without glancing at anyone, he walked out.

17

KAT STARED at the empty doorway, willing Danny to walk back in. She hated the anguish she heard in his tone. The pain that always echoed in each word when he talked about Aubrey.

She heard Logan and Derek whispering but ignored them.

Ignoring everything that happened would be nice, too, but she knew she had to face reality. If a serial killer did have his sights set on her, she wasn't stupid. She wouldn't purposely put herself in harm's way. If it made Danny feel better, lessen his stress levels, she'd stay by his side. It certainly wouldn't be a hardship. She enjoyed spending time with him. The last few days, him taking care of her, had been nice. Too nice. Something she could honestly get used to.

"Are you okay, Kitty Kat?" Derek asked.

She turned away from the doorway, surprised to see him standing next to her and that he called her by a nickname he loved to use with her. One she didn't particularly care for, but she knew it was a sign they were heading back to the friendship they once had. "I'm fine, Grahamikins."

A bright smile lit up his face. "Good." He left the office.

She found it odd he didn't elaborate but figured it would take time for their friendship to go back to normal. And it slowly was, especially when they felt comfortable enough to use nicknames again.

Her gaze connected with Logan's, but she didn't know what to say.

"It's a lot easier to understand how Danny feels about what happened to Aubrey when I think about the same thing happening to you. I thought I understood what he was going through, but I was fooling myself. I had no clue." Logan walked over to her. "The thought of someone hurting you...I get what he said, about feeling like he lost Aubrey. She turns to me more than anyone. Now I feel like a complete jackass."

Kat touched his shoulder and squeezed. "Don't do that to yourself. You're helping Aubrey. He knows that. Maybe if he..."

"If he moved here." Logan smiled as he shook his head. "That's not fair. That's not right. I would hate it if you moved away. So I understand why he hates me now. I guess I chose to ignore it before."

"He doesn't—"

Logan squeezed her hand and then removed it from his shoulder. "He does, Kat. I don't blame him either. When Derek mentioned there might be something going on between you two, I hated the idea. Last night, when I confronted him about it, I wanted to pound his face in for even entertaining the notion. I can't explain why I felt that way because I don't necessarily hate the guy. Now...I'm confused. Everything is crazy right now."

"I won't do anything stupid." She ignored the bit about him hating the idea of her and Danny together. Maybe the situation was a little odd, but she didn't care. Logan would have to get used to the idea and accept it.

Not that they had a future or anything.

"Of course not. You won't be alone to do anything stupid." Logan grinned. "I'll see if I can get all the case files to each murder. Danny said he'd like a fresh eye on it. We'll solve this, and we can all move on. You guys can move on."

She decided she needed some distance and stepped away. Why did he keep bringing up her and Danny? "What do you think is going to happen, Logan? You know I won't move away. I could never be away from my family. And I can't ever see Danny moving here either. Aubrey's so excited, and...I'm afraid we're setting her up for some serious heartbreak."

"Don't treat her like a fragile doll. She's not. She's tough. If—" he laughed boisterously, "wow, I can't believe I'm saying this. If it doesn't work out, she'll get over it. But I hope, if he makes you happy, it works out."

"Do you really mean that?"

"If he makes you happy, then yes. I only want you to be happy and to be with a man who'll treat you right. I won't stand in the way of that. Maybe he'll eventually start to like me. I don't like arguing with him or him hating me. I want everyone to get along."

"Well, I'm still technically on vacation. What am I supposed to do if you and Danny are going to comb through a bunch of cases? I might've wanted to know what is going on, but I'm not excited about helping."

Logan stepped closer and threw an arm around her shoulder. "I wouldn't let you anyway. Why don't you hang with Charlotte up front? I have to talk to Danny. I said I'd help him with his case, and now he has to help me with mine."

"What case is that?"

"Seth."

DANNY DIDN'T TURN toward the person who stepped outside as he leaned against the side of the building, fiddling with his phone as if it was the most important thing he should be doing right now. He hated the cold here, but he needed air so badly he walked outside without hesitating. His throat didn't start to unclog from the feeling of suffocation until he stepped outside and breathed in a deep breath of the brutally cold air.

"You okay?"

He nodded with a tight jerk of his head, then glanced at Logan. "Of course."

"I'm sorry."

"What for?"

Logan's gaze trailed to the ground. "For assuming I knew what the hell you were going through when you finally found Aubrey. I thought I understood what that would feel like, but I had no clue until..." his eyes met his gaze, "until the thought of Kat getting hurt or going missing hit me. I've stood in your way since the moment we met concerning Aubrey, and I feel like total shit about that. If I could—"

"Stop." A grin, surprisingly, hit his lips. "You've helped Aubrey more than I probably ever could. I don't hate you, Logan. I'm still pissed at myself for letting her get hurt in the first place. It was my job to protect her, and I failed." He stood to his full height. "I won't fail Kat. She can hate me all she wants, but I won't let anyone hurt her."

"She might not make that easy on you." Logan chuckled as he shuffled his feet.

"I never expected it to be easy. She never makes anything easy on me." Danny honestly wouldn't have it any other way. Kat was special. He loved her just—

Well, hell.

What a moment to realize he loved Kat, while standing right in front of her brother.

"You have a panicked look on your face. Is there something I need to know? Did something else pop up in the case you didn't want to say in front of Kat?" Logan's tone held the bit of terror he always felt when working on Aubrey's case. He could so easily relate.

Shaking his head, unwilling to share what made him pause, he smiled. "I told you everything I know. I spoke to Deke, and there's nothing new to report."

"Would he be willing to fax over everything so I can take a look? I don't mind."

The eagerness in Logan's expression helped some of the dread slip away. It never hurt to have a fresh set of eyes, especially if the case involved Kat. He'd do anything, including working with Logan, to make sure she stayed safe.

"Definitely. Not sure how much we can do from here, but it wouldn't hurt." He gestured toward the door. "Would you like me to help you now?"

Logan groaned as he ran a hand down his face. "Good luck talking to him. He's not the friendliest lately."

"Have you talked to him since you arrested him yesterday?"

"Nope." A finger grazed over his bruise. "I don't know what to say to him."

"Sometimes tough love is the only route. Aubrey didn't

make her teenage years easy on me." Danny laughed as memories coated his mind.

A tiny grin lit up Logan's face. "I can't picture Aubrey being a hell-raiser."

Danny's eyes bulged. "Oh, I can tell you some stories, and you'd never believe me."

Logan chuckled as he dug in his pocket and then produced a key. "I'd like that, actually. Here's the key to the lockup. I'll let you go talk to Seth before I see him."

He grabbed the key. "If you're sure."

"Evan's back there, too. Feel free to talk to him as well. Get them to let this shit go. I don't want to arrest my brother again, but I will."

"I'll try my best."

Danny started for the door to the station.

A chuckle echoed behind him. "Wow. Did we just have a friendly conversation without getting irritated with each other? Like we're almost friends or something?"

Danny's hand tightened on the door handle as he turned in Logan's direction. "I think so. Hell, if we're dating each other's sister, we might as well."

Alarm touched Logan's features. "That sounded really weird." His expression softened. "But I can live with it. Don't hurt her, Danny. Kat seems strong and tough, but deep inside...she holds everything in. I don't know what's going on between you two, but I'm okay with it. Just please, don't hurt her."

He swallowed hard, his grip tensing even more. "I would never hurt her...intentionally. I don't know what's between us either. It's all confusing right now."

That was the honest truth.

He loved Kat.

But did they have a future together?

He honestly didn't know.

Logan gave a quick nod but didn't say anything else. He remembered how to find the lock-up area from the last time he was here when he finally found his sister again, and they arrested the bastard who hurt her.

He hung up his jacket in Logan's office and then made his way to the lockup area. He passed one cell, glancing at Evan, whose eyes widened at the sight of him, then he stopped in front of the cell where Seth sat on a cot, his arms folded over his knees, his eyes downcast.

Unlocking the cell door, Seth didn't look up until the loud creaking hinges signaled someone opened the door. He looked shocked but didn't say a word. If anything, his expression turned fierce and unfriendly instead of the lost and innocent look from moments before.

"Let's go."

Seth didn't move. "Where are we going?"

Danny jerked his head toward the end of the hallway where the interrogation room was. "We're going to have a chat." His eyes glided to the cell next to Seth's. "You're next."

He watched as Seth and Evan shared a look before Seth stood up and walked out of the cell, leading the way down the hallway. Seth opened the door and took a seat at the table centered in the room. Danny followed suit after he closed the door.

"What are you doing here?"

Danny couldn't hold back a smirk. "That's not how interrogation works, Seth. I ask the questions."

"But why am I being interro—"

"So let's start with why you'd hit Logan?" Danny leaned back in his chair, unaffected at the way panic coated Seth's eyes.

"Is this like an official FBI thing? I don't—"

"Why did you hit Logan?" Danny crossed his arms, prepared to interrupt him at every opportunity. He could do this all day.

Seth's eyes turned down. "I didn't mean to. I was so... pissed. It just happened."

"Pissed about what?"

A roll of his eyes, something that always bothered him when Aubrey did it as a teenager, made him jittery in his seat. He didn't feel like an FBI agent right now. He felt like an older brother reprimanding a younger brother. Hell, if he married Kat, then they'd be—

Married?

Wow. Talk about his mind wandering to the craziest things. Marriage? With Kat?

He slammed his hand down on the table pissed for letting his mind drift the way it had, and it upset him that Seth wasn't answering his questions immediately. "I asked you a question, Seth. We can do this the easy way, or the hard way. You pick."

"Nobody believes me. Not even you." Seth leaned forward. "And that pisses me off because Aubrey deserves the truth."

A vein throbbed in his neck. "The truth about what? I'd do anything for my sister."

"Except find out why Evan's lying. He's lying. He's my best friend, but he's hiding something. It's eating me alive. I can't stand it."

Danny leaned forward as well, close enough where he could reach out and grab Seth by the shirt if he wanted to. "Don't tempt me to hit you. Don't ever insinuate I wouldn't do anything for my sister."

Slowly, Seth retreated, slouching in his chair. "Logan must hate me. He locked me up, and...I haven't seen him once. I never thought my brother would hate me." His eyes looked glossy, as if on the verge of tears. "Aubrey's never hated you."

"And Logan doesn't hate you. But you hit him. He doesn't know how to respond to that. He only wants you to let this Evan shit go."

"Well, then, I guess I can sit here until my trial because I won't."

"What is it you think he's hiding? Aubrey doesn't remember, and from what I gather, she remembers quite a lot." Too much. Danny hated to picture exactly what his sister remembered.

Seth spread his arms wide as he pressed his hands to the table. "I have no clue, but he's hiding something. You have to believe me. Beat it out of him if you have to, but he's hiding something. I would never jeopardize my friendship with him, a man I've been friends with since I was five years old, if I didn't think he was hiding something."

Danny had to admit, he believed that. Why would Seth risk his friendship if he didn't believe with his entire heart he was lying?

"Okay."

Seth tensed. "Okay? What?"

"He'll tell me what he knows."

"How?"

A silky smile that spoke of dangerous intentions touched his lips. "Don't worry about it. He will."

Seth sat back and put his hands in his lap. "Okay, then."

"You can be released," he held up a finger, "if you apologize to your brother," he held up another finger, "and if you leave Evan alone. If I find out he's not lying about anything, then he's not. If you can't abide by those terms, the charges will stick, and you will stay here until your trial. I will make sure of it myself."

Twitching in his seat, Seth's eyes glittered with a touch of fear. "Logan will drop the charges for hitting him if I stay away from Evan?"

Not that Danny talked logistics with Logan, but he knew for a fact Logan never filed charges for the assault against him. Last night, he went into detail about what happened and how he locked them up for assaulting each other, not for Seth hitting him. In true Caldwell fashion, Logan was prepared to let assault charges against both of them slide if Seth let it all go. He wanted his brother to move on.

"Do you honestly think your brother wanted to lock you up? I've never seen a family so protective of each other as I have with you guys. He's hurting as much as you are right now."

Seth nodded. "You have a deal. Can you tell me now why you're here?"

Danny stood up and gestured for him to leave. "Because my sister called Kat, upset because of what happened. She demanded Kat come home. I said I would come home with her."

Seth jerked in surprise. "Home?"

An eyebrow rose as he tried to hide the surprise himself. Since when did he think of Minnesota as home? Seth was right to question him.

He yanked open the door. "Your brother should be in his office." Maybe Seth had a right to question him, but it didn't mean he'd answer it.

Seth paused in the doorway. "How long are you staying?"

"I haven't decided yet."

"Thanks, Danny. I know Aubrey's happy you're here."

Seth started to walk away.

"I'm not just here for her." And he realized how true that was. He wasn't ready to lose Kat so soon. When she said she was going home to Minnesota, he knew he had to go with her, if only to have a little more time with her.

Seth's footsteps slowed as he turned toward him. "Oh?"

"I'm here for Kat, too."

18

KAT ROSE from her chair and rounded the counter, stopping short of pulling Seth into her arms. The sisterly part of her wanted to hug him and wipe the sadness from his eyes. The angry part of her wanted to slap him on the back of the head for his actions.

"I'm sorry."

She hated how his head dipped down, his entire posture slouched inward. "What for? I'm getting kind of sick of hearing your apologies all the time. Are you really sorry?"

His eyes slowly met hers. "Yes."

"I'm not the one who deserves an apology."

Seth looked down the hallway that would lead him to Logan's office. "I'm not ready to talk to him." He sighed heavily. "Pretty sure he doesn't want to talk to me. He hasn't since yesterday."

She couldn't stand it. Couldn't stand the heartbreak in his voice. Grabbing his arm, she jerked him into her arms and hugged him. Seth didn't hesitate to wrap his arms around her, a slight shiver coating his body. Gradually, the tension she had seen left his body.

"You're an idiot."

He nodded.

"I'll take you home."

Backing away, he smiled. "Thanks."

Kat turned toward Charlotte, who didn't look happy. "What?"

Charlotte leaned over the counter. "You're supposed to be hanging out with me, not leaving."

She knew she couldn't go running around by herself, but she wouldn't be by herself. She'd be with Seth. If she wasn't safe with Seth, then she'd have some nasty words for Danny.

"I'll be fine. I'll stick with Seth the entire time."

"I don't like this. We should talk to Logan." Charlotte's lips thinned into a tight line. "Or Agent O'Rourke."

"I'll be fine. Don't bother either one of them. They're both busy." Kat threw out her most charming smile, not that she thought it would work on Charlotte. Not much did. If Charlotte thought something, it was almost impossible to change her mind.

"What's going on?" Seth asked as he stepped near the counter. "Why can't Kat come with me? Does Logan think I'm a danger? That I'd hurt my own sister?"

Kat whipped toward him, placing a reassuring hand on his shoulder to calm the anger and hurt she heard in his tone. "No. Absolutely not. I'll tell you on the way."

"Kat..." Charlotte slapped her hand on the counter. "Why do you always have to be difficult?"

"I promised to stay with someone. Seth is someone." Kat planted a hand on her hip. "Look who's talking about being difficult?"

A slow grin emerged on Charlotte as she leaned away. "I don't like this. Can't you at least say goodbye to Logan?"

Kat looked at Seth, then back to Charlotte. Did she need to explain why she couldn't say goodbye? Seth needed some time to himself before he talked to Logan. Even though she wasn't happy about him hitting Logan, she wanted him to be ready to talk on his terms.

"We'll be fine. Can you hand me my purse and jacket?"

Charlotte gazed at her for the longest time before reaching for her purse and jacket sitting on the side of the desk. Her purse hit the top of the counter with a loud thunk. "I'm not happy about this."

"Duly noted." Kat laughed to help erase the tension, but it did nothing but further upset Charlotte.

Nodding toward Seth to follow her as she put on her coat, she led the way out of the station and to her car. Before starting the car, she looked at Seth.

"Are you sure you don't want to speak to Logan before we leave?"

"Not yet, Kat. Please."

An understanding smile touched her lips as she turned the key. "Why don't I take you to my house, and I'll make you something to eat. You can shower while I cook. Then we can talk about what's going on."

"Yeah, I think we should talk." A slow grin, one that always reminded her he was about to do something mischievous, punctured his otherwise melancholy face. "I'd like to know what's going on between you and Danny."

DANNY PULLED out the chair across from Evan and took his time sitting down. He could see how nervous and anxious Evan looked since he pulled him out of the cell and into the interrogation room. That could mean one of two things.

One, he was hiding something, and Seth had been right all along. Two, he didn't like sitting in an interrogation room with a federal agent.

Since speaking with Seth, Danny was inclined to believe the former. He was hiding something. Nobody would be leaving this room until he found out what.

"Why are you here?"

"Wow. Maybe it's a small town thing." Danny leaned back as he folded his arms casually. "Or maybe it's a best friend thing."

"What?" The confusion on Evan's face almost made Danny want to chuckle. He loved this part of interrogations, throwing people off balance, making them think and question every single thing.

"Seth did the same thing. Asking me questions, when that's not how this works." He leaned forward so quickly, his hands landed hard on the table. Another chuckle wanted to let loose when Evan flinched. "I ask the questions. Not you."

Evan's eyes rounded with alarm, yet he said nothing.

"So, why don't we start with what you're hiding?"

"I'm not hiding anything. I don't know how many times I can say it."

Danny decided to lean back in his chair, relishing in the way Evan squirmed in his seat. "Well, you can keep saying it, but I don't believe you."

"You obviously believed me a few months ago because you left."

A brow rose slowly at the tone in Evan's voice. The audacity of him to sit there with a smug tone as if he knew everything, as if he knew what he thought and felt.

"You don't know what I believed. I can tell you right now, I believe you're hiding something, and neither one of us will be leaving this room until you tell me exactly what it is."

"You can't do that. You can't keep me here."

"I can and I will."

"On what charges?" The nervousness started to slowly wither away, and annoyance took its place. Danny wanted to laugh even more. Evan was letting his hand show by not hiding his emotions.

"Well, we could start with obstruction and then work our way up to kidnapping and whatnot. How does that sound?"

"Kidnapping?" Evan's eyes bulged in shock. "Who? When? I didn't—"

Danny slammed his hands down hard on the desk as he stood up and leaned across the table. "My sister. You're hiding something, and it concerns my sister. So I will throw every little charge I can think of at you...unless you start talking."

"Look, I don't know what Seth said, but I don't know anything about what happened to your sister. I swear."

"Your words mean nothing. You could swear on your mother's grave and I wouldn't give a shit. You have five minutes to tell me what you know, and maybe I'll consider not charging you with everything under the sun."

"This is crazy. I don't know anything. Seth is nuts."

Danny backed away, but he didn't sit down. Evan squirmed even more as Danny pushed his chair in, then started walking around. Nowhere in particular. Just back and forth in front of the table.

"Is he nuts? He's your best friend. He knows you better than anyone else. He's held the belief you've been lying from the beginning. Your best friend thinks you're lying."

Evan's eyes shifted down to the table, his irritation from moments before dwindling away.

"Your best friend believes it so much, he hit his own

brother. You and I both know how much that family loves and protects each other. So, for Seth to knock his own brother out, he's never going to stop believing that you're holding something back. Am I wrong?" Danny stalked to the table and slammed his hands down. "Am I, Evan?"

"I swear I know nothing about what happened to Aubrey." Evan lifted his gaze.

Danny stared hard at him, willing the truth to come out. The longer he stared, the more he believed Evan. "Okay. I believe you."

"Really?"

He shrugged. "Yeah, you know nothing about what happened to Aubrey, but you're hiding something. I think it's time you came clean. It's gotta be eating you alive. I mean, you lost your best friend over it."

Evan's shoulders sagged as sadness ripped throughout his features. "I miss my best friend."

"I'm sure you do. And hey, maybe you and Seth can get past all of this...if you start talking."

"I'm pretty sure he'll never get over this."

"You won't know if you don't start the steps in that direction."

Danny watched in fascination as acceptance fluttered across his face. Evan was on the verge of spilling his guts. He knew it. He sensed it. He could see it. It was moments like this when he was interrogating a suspect that he loved the most. The moment right before triumph struck.

"I saw..." Evan swallowed hard. "I saw Wayne once. About a month before Aubrey escaped."

His heart started to pound like mad. He told this asshole he believed him. He said it had nothing to do with Aubrey, and he had the audacity to lie to his face.

"You said this had nothing to do with my sister."

"I swear, it doesn't. He didn't say much to me. He didn't even mention her."

Danny took a deep breath to control the rage suddenly flowing through him, to stop the temptation of throttling the man before him. "So, what did he want?"

"He stopped at the garage while I was working. I was by myself. He..." Evan's voice quivered as his hands shook in his lap.

"He...what? Don't mess around with me, Evan."

"He wanted to know if I wanted to work with him."

Arching a brow, Danny couldn't stop the intrigue from entering. "With what?"

Evan met his gaze. "Drugs. I told him a flat-out no and to leave me alone." Evan shivered. "Wayne is just like my dad. They both love to torture me and treat me like I'm a piece of shit. He wasn't asking, he was more like telling me."

"So you've been running drugs for your brother?"

Evan shook his head. "Hell, no. I wouldn't let him scare me. I would've let him kick my ass every which way, except..."

"What?"

"His friend stepped out of the car. I didn't realize he wasn't alone. He told Wayne to forget it and to leave me alone. The look in his eyes when he said it..." Evan shivered.

"Does this friend have a name?"

"Joshua." Evan took a deep breath. "Joshua Barten."

Danny almost staggered at that revelation. "Barten? You have another brother?"

"I guess so. Apparently, my father had an affair, like the bastard he is, and I have a half-brother. I don't know how Wayne found him, and I don't really care. He might've told Wayne to leave me alone, but he scared me as much as Wayne did. Maybe even more."

"Wayne wanted you to get into the drug business, I'm assuming, running it through Lucky here. He was partners with Joshua. When you said no, Wayne was going to force you to, but Joshua stepped in and said forget it. Am I understanding you correctly?"

Evan nodded.

"Why the secrecy? Why couldn't you tell Seth this?" Danny pressed his hands down to the table. "Why wouldn't you tell me this when we originally questioned you? My sister might not remember anyone but Wayne, but that doesn't mean he was the only one involved."

Evan's eyes turned away, his shoulders dipping in defeat. "I didn't think about that, Agent O'Rourke. I was ashamed. I find out I have a half-brother and he's just as terrible as my other brother, if not worse." His voice dropped to a whisper. "I had a friend who was like my real brother, and now I don't even have that. I didn't want Seth to hate me."

"As far as you know, they only approached you about drugs?"

"Yes. That's it. I would've told you everything if I knew it involved Aubrey." His eyes glanced up. "Now what?"

"Now, I find out what Joshua Barten's been up to."

———

Kat flipped the sandwich in the pan, then grabbed a plate from the cupboard. She wasn't hungry, but she figured Seth had to be starving. He looked terrible. Tired, strung out, and like he hadn't eaten in days. She knew they didn't let him starve overnight, but he didn't look like he'd been taking care of himself.

Grabbing the pan from the stove, she slid the sandwich onto the plate, cut it in half, then set the plate on the table. She then grabbed the bottle of ketchup, a cup of milk, a napkin, and set everything next to the plate. The only thing missing was her brother. She took her time making him something to eat, but she wasn't about to let him hide from her forever. He'd been showering long enough, or more like, distancing himself from her. No more.

Stalking to her bathroom, she banged on the door.

"Time's up. Your food is ready. Let's go."

She took a step back, crossed her arms, and waited. If she had to wait and bang on the door again and again until he came out, she would.

Only a few seconds went by before the door swung open. A drift of steam followed as Seth walked out.

"Did you waste all of my hot water?"

A tiny smile touched his lips. "Not all of it. Most, but not all."

A happy sigh released. "You look better."

"Yeah, that shower did wonders. I feel better."

"Come on. I made your favorite." She walked away. When she got close to the table, she stepped back and made a big sweep of her arms toward the plate on the table. "This delicious meal also happens to be someone else's favorite, too."

Seth rolled his eyes. "Subtle much?"

"When are you going to talk to him?"

Seth took a seat at the table. Kat relished in the way his eyes lit up at the grilled cheese sandwich sitting before him. Grabbing the ketchup, Seth squeezed until he had a healthy amount on his plate.

"Seth?"

"Can I at least enjoy this meal before you get on my case? I'm starving."

"Fine." Kat decided to give him this small reprieve and went to the kitchen to clean up her mess.

He would talk to her. Seth wouldn't be leaving her house until he did. Did she think making his favorite meal, the same meal that happened to be Logan's favorite, would get him to talk? Maybe. But she also made it because she knew it'd make him feel better. Those two were easy to please, especially when they were feeling down. One simple grilled cheese sandwich always managed to lift their spirits.

Ten minutes later, after picking up and washing all the dishes and wiping down the counters about three separate times, Kat marched back over to the table and sat down. Seth had finished eating. His plate was cleared of every crumb, and his glass of milk was half consumed.

"I don't know what to say."

"Start with an apology. That can usually get a conversation going."

Seth turned his gaze toward her. "Do you think he'll forgive me? I hit him. I didn't just hit him. I knocked him out. You have no idea—" Seth sucked in a harsh breath. "I can't believe I did that. I didn't even mean to hit him."

Kat reached for his hand and squeezed. "I know. Logan knows, too. It's not like you guys haven't gotten into it before."

"I've never hit him like that before."

"What do you want me to say, Seth? Logan isn't going to hold a grudge. Why are you acting like a baby?"

Chuckling, Seth slid his hand out from under hers. "I don't know. Because I am the baby of the family."

"Yeah, and we never let you get away with it, so don't think we're going to start now."

Seth stood up and grabbed his plate. "Are you going to tell me what the deal was with you and Charlotte?"

Kat followed him to the sink with his glass and pushed him aside to wash his dishes. She started vigorously washing the plate and glass in the water she hadn't drained from the other dishes.

A hand to her shoulder stopped her rigorous movements.

"What's going on, Kat? You want me to talk, but you won't. You know that's not fair."

With her hands still in the water, she turned his way. She couldn't explain it, but she always had an easier time spilling her guts with Seth than she ever did with Logan. Maybe because he was the baby of the family. Logan was more of the leader, the big brother always in her business. Seth was the younger one, usually trying to get her to do things she shouldn't.

It all poured out, from fleeing Minnesota to get away from Derek, to running into Danny, to the delivery of the flowers, to her crazy relationship with Danny. Every single thing came out until she felt herself building to tears.

Sucking in a deep breath, she blinked a few times to hold the tears back. She wouldn't cry. She refused to cry.

Seth didn't say a word as she told him everything, right down to the last conversation between her, Danny, Logan, and Derek, where she couldn't even be alone until they solved the case. His only response was to pull her into a hug. She accepted his embrace and hugged him back. A hint of a smile touched her lips as her wet hands soaked into his shirt.

"This thing sounds serious."

"I'll be fine. I can take care of myself."

A low chuckle escaped. "Oh, I know you can defend yourself. I wasn't talking about some killer. I was talking about this thing with Danny."

Kat stiffened. Seth squeezed her tightly, then let her go, a goofy grin on his face.

"Does he know?"

Laughing, Kat rolled her eyes. "Know what?"

Seth relaxed against the counter and smiled. "Come on. Don't pretend with me. You tell me the truth, and as soon as we're done, I'll go back to the station and talk to Logan."

Her gaze drifted to the ground. "It'd be kind of dumb if I let him know...that...I love him."

Just saying it out loud, even to her brother, felt like an enormous weight lifted off her shoulders. Strangely, she felt better. She didn't even realize how scared she had felt until Seth made her confess.

"Why?"

Jerking her eyes to his, she let out a crazy laugh. "Was that a serious question?"

He stuck his tongue out. "Yeah."

"He doesn't even live here. He doesn't get along with Logan. He barely tolerates us Caldwells."

"I'd say he tolerates you fine. Everything is semantics. Are you really going to let him leave without telling him how you feel?"

"It might be better if I did."

Because she wasn't sure she'd survive his rejection.

Swinging an arm around her shoulder, Seth guided her out of the kitchen. "My sister is no chickenshit. I don't believe she's going to start acting like one now."

"And my brother isn't one either. Are we headed back to the station now? I didn't finish the dishes."

"Yes, oh wise one." Seth let his arms drop from her shoulder. "I'll even get on my hands and knees to grovel for his forgiveness."

"Oh, I'm going to get that on camera."

Shoving her playfully, he laughed. "Don't you dare."

They grabbed their jackets from the coat closet and put them on.

Swiping her keys from the hook near the closet door, she giggled. "It's nice to see my brother again. That other asshole can stay away."

"I promised Danny I'd let this Evan shit go. It's going to be hard as hell, but I will."

"It's better this way."

Kat stepped to the door first, Seth right behind her. Opening the door, she jerked and froze. She felt Seth stiffen behind her, his hand touching her waist as if he could somehow whip her behind him and shield her. He wouldn't be able to make one move without someone getting hurt.

Because the gun pointed directly at her chest said nobody would be moving an inch.

19

Danny opened Logan's office door without knocking, and for a moment felt regret for being so rude until he saw Derek's smug face sitting to the left of Logan's desk and decided against it. What did he look so smug about? Maybe he shouldn't act like an asshole, and he could've knocked, but not when Derek looked so full of himself.

"How did it go?"

Arching a brow, Danny honestly wasn't sure how to answer Logan's question. Being direct seemed like the best option. "Seth didn't stop by?"

Logan's frown was answer enough. "How long ago did he leave?"

"I'd say about thirty minutes ago. It didn't take too long to crack Evan. I just got off the phone with Deke."

Walking around his desk, Danny couldn't help but love the eagerness in Logan's eyes. It reminded him of how excited he could get with news. Maybe they had more in common than he first thought. Maybe he had been a little too rude and arrogant than he realized.

"What did he say?"

A wide smile spread across his face. "A lot more than I expected. I'll have to thank Seth for being so persistent his friend was lying because he was. His brother, Wayne, did approach him about a month before Aubrey got away."

"That son of a bitch," Derek exclaimed.

Danny nodded. "I thought the same thing. He said it had nothing to do with Aubrey. Wayne wanted him to run drugs through Lucky."

Logan leaned against the front of his desk as he crossed his arms. "You know, now that I think about it, we did have a small influx of drugs in the area around that time. Evan had a part in that?"

"He says he told him no. Wayne didn't like that answer."

"Wayne always danced to his own tune. That or his father's. I wouldn't be surprised if the old man had a hand in it. I can't imagine he simply took no for an answer," Derek said.

"He wasn't at first," Danny glanced between the two, "until the other guy stepped in. His half-brother, Joshua Barten."

Logan stood up slowly. "I've never heard of him. Did he...did he have something to do with Aubrey's disappearance?"

"I don't know yet, but I will. Apparently, his father had an affair, and I'm assuming the other woman fled town right away. I'm not sure, nor is Evan, how those two met and got into business together. Evan did say Joshua had more power than Wayne because as soon as he told Wayne to leave him alone, he did. They left, and he never saw them again."

"What did Deke say?"

Danny shrugged at Logan's question. "Nothing yet. I gave him the information to run a background check, and he'll call me as soon as he has something. I'd like to find this guy and interview him."

"Thank you, Danny."

One of the friendliest smiles he ever produced for Logan appeared. "I didn't do much. Let's solve this other case."

"Yeah, I'm sure you want to get back home," Derek said a little too eagerly for Danny's tastes.

"I'm in no rush, actually."

For a moment, they stared at each other. That smug look Derek had when he walked into the office slowly disappeared. Derek thought he was ready to leave. That he'd be out of his way to make another move on Kat. Well, he was wrong.

Okay. He walked away from Kat. From all of them earlier. It certainly didn't mean he was ready to walk away from Kat for good. Derek would do well to understand that. He wasn't going anywhere.

"Maybe we should go talk to Mr. Barten. Ask about his other son we had no idea about," Logan said softly, as if he was afraid to break up their stare.

"We could." Danny looked away from Derek and rubbed his jaw. "So...Aubrey's been having nightmares lately."

"Yeah."

"She still maintains it was only Wayne she remembered?"

Logan nodded. "He was the only one to ever step foot in that room. She never heard any other voices. As far as she's concerned, he was the only one. Wayne was a loose cannon. He might've been running drugs with his brother Joshua, but if he wanted to do something on the side by himself, nothing would stop him."

"It's weird, you know. This other brother popping up.

Evan was embarrassed, or ashamed, to admit anything to Seth. I believe him."

"We can charge him with hindering an investigation?" Danny didn't miss the way Logan said it as a question. As if he were asking him what he thought.

Blowing out a breath as he rubbed his jaw once again, he couldn't believe what he was about to say. "You can turn him loose. I'm pretty sure losing his best friend is penance enough."

He saw the understanding glimmer in Logan's eyes. He knew as well as he did that Seth and Evan weren't likely to ever make amends.

A buzzing sound punctured the odd silence. Pulling his phone from his pocket, he unlocked it to check the text from Deke.

"Shit." His heart plummeted as he stared at the photo. "Where's Kat?"

Logan nodded toward the door. "She's out by Charlotte. Why?"

Danny held out his phone. "This is a picture of Joshua Barten. He's the same man who claimed to be Aubrey's neighbor's brother. I ran into him a few days ago. I never knew her neighbor, Jared, had a brother. The guy rubbed me the wrong way."

"So he really wasn't his brother." Logan's features dipped into horror. "Maybe we solved your mystery with mine."

"Yeah, that's what I'm thinking." Danny hit a few buttons on his phone. "I need to call Deke to check on Jared." He looked at the doorway. "Then I need to talk to Kat."

They had a lot to talk about. The case might be close to being solved.

Then he could go home.

But he wasn't ready to leave.

Not yet.

Maybe never.

DEKE KNOCKED ON THE DOOR. Seconds later, he turned to pounding. Sometimes Jared couldn't hear anything when he was absorbed in his music. And it wasn't because his music was terribly loud. It was because he lost himself in the beautiful sound he created.

"I haven't seen him in a few days."

Jumping, his hand went to his firearm on instinct, but then he laughed when he saw Mrs. Bederman standing in her bathrobe, her hair in curlers, and a sweet smile on her face.

"Good afternoon, Mrs. Bederman."

"I didn't scare you, did I, Deke?" The twinkle in her eye said she enjoyed every second she startled him.

"Now, how could a beautiful woman ever scare me?" He gave her one of his signature smiles meant to make a woman swoon.

Mrs. Bederman might be in her eighties, but her cheeks blushed a slight shade of red. He knew once she took out the curlers and fixed her hair, she'd be a gorgeous woman. Age didn't define beauty in his eyes. Her character and the infectious humor she had were what made her so damn beautiful. Her Harold had been a lucky man.

"You can't fool an old woman." Her features dipped as she glanced behind him to Jared's door. "I was actually thinking about calling Danny. I'm worried about Jared. I usually see him at least once every few days, but it's been a while. You know how he can get with his music, but maybe...maybe you should check on him."

"I can do that. I need to talk to him." Deke surmised in his head how long it would take to go find the landlord, plead his case on a wellness check so he didn't have to produce a warrant. He didn't have time for that. Danny was expecting results. Not two hours down the road, but now. Immediate results.

A crafty smile touched Mrs. Bederman's lips as she slipped a key out of her bathrobe pocket. "He gave me a spare for emergencies. This seems like an emergency."

Deke chuckled as he took the key. "Do you have a spare key for every apartment in this building?"

Her laughter filled the hallway. "Don't be silly. I only have one for every apartment on this floor."

Oh, but she was a hoot. He laughed as he turned around to the door, knocked loudly one more time, and when nobody responded, he inserted the key. With a quick glance to Mrs. Bederman, his expression softened into concern. "I have to ask you to wait out here. I think you should go back to your apartment. I'll return your key when I'm finished."

Mrs. Bederman nodded in understanding and hustled back to her apartment.

Deke had a funny feeling. Since the moment Danny called him about Joshua Barten and the man claiming to be Jared's brother, the feeling centered in the pit of his stomach and churned like acid invading his system. His gut feelings were never wrong. Mrs. Bederman must've sensed his concern, or maybe she had the same weird intuition because she didn't argue with him once.

Pulling his weapon out of its holster, he then opened the door and made entry. He swept through the kitchen and living room quickly, noting nothing out of place. The apartment was a disaster, music books piled high on the floor, leftover food sitting on the counters, dirty clothes scattered about. Oddly enough, that was normal for Jared. Simple tasks like picking up after himself always fell to the wayside because of his music.

As soon as he neared the bedroom, that strange feeling burning a hole in his gut intensified to acceptance. The nasty, pungent smell that clogged his nostrils could only signal one thing.

A dead body.

Using as bare of a touch as he could, he twisted the knob and shoved open the door. Jared lay sprawled on the floor on his stomach. Blood pooled around him with several deep wounds coating his back. It looked like he had been stabbed multiple times from behind. They probably wouldn't find any defensive wounds on him because whoever had killed him had surprised him unaware and swiftly taken care of business.

That churning sensation in his gut started to twist and turn until, for the first time at a crime scene, he wanted to get sick.

Turning away from the horrifying sight, he pulled out his phone. Hesitating for a second, he pushed through his worries and hit dial.

"Hey, Danny. We have a problem." A heavy breath released. "Jared's dead. Murdered."

KAT WANTED to grab Seth's hand and hold on to him, gather some strength. She felt like all of her bravado she always maintained was slowly slipping away as they walked deeper and deeper into the woods. The light coating of snow didn't deter their movements, but her feet were starting to freeze from the temperature. She would've killed for her winter boots right now. Trudging through the woods and the snow in her sneakers was not her idea of smart.

After being forced to handcuff herself to Seth, the man with the gun, whom she didn't recognize, told them to get into the trunk of his car. She and Seth had shared a look about trying to overtake him and get the gun, but then he dashed those hopes when he whipped the butt of his gun into the side of her temple. She passed out after that and woke up to the sudden bumps and jarring movements as they drove in the trunk of his car.

The space had been tight, cramped, and very dark. But she heard the relief in Seth's tone when she finally gained consciousness. He told her how he caught her before she fell and put her in the trunk without fighting the guy. Although it had been dark in the trunk, almost claustrophobic dark, she could hear the guilt in his voice. He thought he could've done something to save them. But what? Especially when she was knocked unconscious.

Not long after she woke up, the vehicle stopped, and the man forced them out of the trunk and demanded they start walking.

Here they were, walking into the woods, and no one knew they were missing. Her head hurt. The bile kept rising in her throat every so often. It took more strength than she cared to admit to keep from throwing up. She didn't want to give away how terrible she felt. How weak she was.

If she and Seth had an opportunity to get the gun away, they had to take it, but the man couldn't know how weak she felt.

Because right now, she was the weak link. And being handcuffed to Seth didn't help his odds if he wanted to fight back.

Stumbling on a branch, Seth grabbed her arm with his loose hand.

"Hey, you okay?"

"I'm fine."

Seth's voice lowered. "Seriously, are you okay?"

Shifting her eyes, trying to eye the man behind them, she almost couldn't hide the grimace as a flash of pain tore through her head.

"Kat?"

"My head hurts a little. He hit me hard."

A ragged breath escaped. "You don't have to tell me. I thought..." Seth sucked in a harsh breath. "I thought he killed you when you fell like that."

"I'll be okay."

"Look—"

Kat stumbled and fell to the ground as a strong hand pushed her from behind. The cold snow slapped her brutally in the face. Seth fell right along with her. Her fingers felt like icicles already. Falling down, sinking them into the icy white snow wasn't helping her throbbing head. Each new thing made her feel more and more drained. Oh, to have thought of grabbing her gloves, hat, and scarf. But no, she only grabbed her jacket, as had Seth.

"No more talking."

They both turned to stare at the man towering before them, the gun steady in his hand aimed directly at her.

"Don't make me shoot her. You'll tire very easily if you have to carry her."

Seth swallowed and nodded.

"Now get up and keep moving."

Seth helped Kat up to her feet, holding her steady for a moment as a wave of dizziness attacked her. She tried to play it off as nothing, but a quick glance at the man told her he knew exactly how injured she was. Perhaps that had been his plan from the start.

She nodded at Seth that she was okay, unwilling to test the man's patience, and then they started walking once again.

As they continued to walk deeper into the woods, the surroundings started to look a little familiar. If she wasn't mistaken, they weren't too far from their family cabin. And the direction they were headed was where Aubrey had been held for over three months.

She almost stumbled again as the terror swamped her at being stuck in the deep, black pit as Aubrey had suffered.

Then her mind calmed down when she knew that wasn't possible. Logan had the entrance filled with dirt, the doors removed. If anyone came across the area, they wouldn't even know a hidden bunker, or whatever they wanted to call it, was there.

Where was he taking them, then?

How could they get out of this?

Would Logan and Danny know where to look? And how long would it take them to realize they needed to look for them?

"I won't let him hurt you again, Kat."

Seth's voice was so low, she almost didn't hear him. Not reacting at all, she kept her head straight forward and her stance steady.

"If I have to, I'll kill him. If I get a chance, I'm taking it."

She couldn't argue with that. Even as the pain lingered in her head, echoing from ear to ear, the ringing, the nausea still present, if she saw an opportunity, she'd take it as well.

"We'll fight him together." Her lips barely moved as she responded.

A shot rang out as a sharp pain sliced through her leg.

Kat fell down in a heap, Seth right along with her as he shouted in rage. The frosty snow didn't even penetrate her senses this time as agonizing pain ripped throughout her body.

Glancing at the man, she couldn't help but shiver from the hatred and malice dripping from his gaze. He might frighten her, but she would never cower and show her fear and how much pain she was in.

"I told you to stop talking. I can't hear what you're saying, but I know you said something. Now look what you made me do."

Seth quickly unzipped his jacket and ripped part of his shirt as best as he could to staunch the bleeding in her thigh. She couldn't hold back a rippling scream as he tied it as tightly as he could around the wound. So much for holding her pain inside.

"I'm sorry, Kat. Shit. I'm sorry."

Tears silently coated her cheeks as she looked at Seth. The ache in her head drifted away as the pain in her leg took front and center.

"Get up. Keep walking."

"She—"

"Shut up and get up." The man aimed the gun at her. "Do you want me to shoot her again? If I say something, I mean it. I told you to stop talking."

"Help me up, Seth. I can do this."

His jaw clenched, a muscle ticking like a time bomb, his hands fisted. The rage echoed from corner to corner on every inch of his body.

"Seth..."

He looked away from the man. His features softened as soon as he caught her eyes. "I won't let you die."

"I know. Help me up."

Seth gently helped her to her feet once again, the pain so intense, she moaned. But she refused to scream again. Every time her terror let loose, the man smiled. He was enjoying her torture way too much, and she refused to give him the satisfaction.

Seth couldn't drape his arm around her with his right hand cuffed to her left, but he held onto her as best as he could as they started slowly walking. Each time she took a step forward, the urge to scream in agony rose to the tip of her lips. Each time she forced it back down her throat, her features taut with tension and determination.

She'd survive this. And she'd make this man pay.

20

DANNY DISCONNECTED WITH DEKE, rubbing a hand down his face. The gesture immediately reminded him of Logan. It was a common gesture he loved to do. He noticed right away when he first met him.

"What's wrong?" Logan asked.

"We need someone with Aubrey. Along with Kat." Danny sat down on the couch in Logan's office and sighed. He couldn't believe what was going on. "Jared's dead. He's probably been dead since I ran into Joshua Barten in the hallway."

Without looking up, his eyes trained firmly on the ground, he listened as Logan told Derek to go to Aubrey's school and stay with her until he had a chance to go get her himself. Danny didn't know if Aubrey was in any danger, but with Joshua being brothers with Wayne, he couldn't take the chance. He'd never let his sister get hurt again. Not while he had any breath left in his body.

"We can talk to Kat together."

Danny jerked his gaze to Logan and almost nodded in

agreement but stopped himself. "I'll do it. I need to talk to Kat about a few other things anyway."

Logan looked curious but thankfully didn't ask why. It wasn't something he wanted to talk about with her brother. Hell, he was nervous as shit to talk to her about it.

But there were things he needed to say. Things he should've admitted a few days ago when they surfaced.

Ever since losing Aubrey for three months, the unknown of where she was, of what she was enduring, he didn't like to hold things back. What if he never got the chance to say how he felt if he held back? But sometimes, his fear took a stronger hold than his desire to speak freely.

So yeah, he and Kat had some things they needed to talk about.

"She's sitting up front with Charlotte. I'll go get her for you." Logan headed for the door, his steps slowing before he completely exited. "Are you sure you want to let Evan go?"

"Only if you do as well. I'm not..." Danny exhaled slowly. "I'm not the only one who cares about Aubrey. I honestly don't believe he had anything to do with what happened to her. I respect whatever you think."

Logan nodded. "I've only wanted to make her happy since the moment I met her. I'm sorry if it seems like I'm taking her away from you. I respect what you think as well. I'll cut him loose."

Danny nodded.

Logan walked out.

Weird. They might actually become friends if they kept up with this friendly demeanor. For Aubrey's sake, he was okay with that. Hell, if he officially started to date Kat, he needed to get along with Logan. It wouldn't kill him to be a little nicer.

Less than a minute later, heavy footsteps made their way back to Logan's office. He hadn't moved one inch on the couch. He glanced up in surprise by the tense expression on Logan's face as he walked back into the office.

He slowly stood up. "What's wrong?"

"Kat left with Seth about an hour ago, and Charlotte failed to inform me. Obviously, because she knew it would upset me."

Well, Danny didn't like that idea, but she was with one of her brothers. She should be reasonably safe with Seth. Although, Seth didn't have a background in law enforcement. Could he protect her if he had to? Neither did Kat, but he knew she could hold her own if need be. He had to believe Seth could as well.

But why didn't she tell him she was leaving? That part bothered him more than he cared to admit.

"I trust Seth." Danny shifted on his feet. "Unless you're suddenly not in the trusting mood."

A hand ran down Logan's tired face. "I tried calling Kat and she didn't answer. I also tried Seth." He blew out a breath. "Seth not answering doesn't surprise me, but Kat should've."

Danny's entire body went taut with tension. He wouldn't let panic set in. He wouldn't think the worst simply because Logan was portraying his worry. "What are you saying, Logan?"

"I don't know. But I'd feel better if I knew where they were."

"Where do you think they'd go?"

"Kat can get all mother-hen like. Probably her house."

"Then let's go." Danny grabbed his jacket from the coat rack and headed for the door. "I know you're dying to talk to Seth. Now is a good time."

Logan grabbed his jacket as well and followed him out of the building, both of them walking quickly to Logan's vehicle, although trying not to make it appear as if they were worried.

Kat was fine. There was absolutely nothing wrong.

Danny had no choice but to believe that.

Because if he didn't, he didn't think he'd survive if he lost her.

Especially to a madman.

By the time they arrived at Kat's house, his nerves were so frazzled, he thought he was about to have a coronary. The one thing that calmed part of him down was Derek had called informing them Aubrey was in his eyesight and safe and sound. At least one of the women he loved was accounted for.

God, he loved Kat.

So obvious now. Just the thought of her in harm's way sent him spiraling into the deep netherworlds of hell.

The first sign that something was wrong hit him square in the gut when Logan knocked on the door, no answer, and then turned the knob and it swung open with ease. If the door was unlocked, why didn't anyone answer the door?

They searched the house quickly. Danny saw evidence Kat and Seth had been there, but not anymore. The house was empty. Where were they?

Walking back outside, Logan muttered under his breath, then said, "I wonder where they went."

"The door was unlocked. I don't like it."

Logan shrugged. "Around here, that's not uncommon. We're a small town, Danny. Leaving the door unlocked isn't a big deal." He pointed to Kat's car. "Her car in the driveway with no sign of them is what concerns me."

Danny shook his head, unable to understand how

anyone could leave their house unlocked while they were gone when his eyes saw something on the ground. Walking closer to inspect, his entire body paled as the blood rushed to his head. He almost fainted at the sight in front of him.

Logan was suddenly by his side, a hand on his shoulder to steady him.

He had never fainted in his life. He couldn't believe he almost did.

"We'll find them. We will." Logan's hand increased in pressure. "Are you okay? Do you need—"

"There's blood on the ground."

"What?"

Danny ignored the panic in Logan's tone as he pointed at the spot in front of him. "Blood. It's happening again. First, Aubrey was taken from me. Now, Kat."

Logan shoved him hard. He stumbled, but managed to correct his balance before he fell. Glancing at him with shock, he almost swung a fist at his face. "What the hell, man?"

"Don't stand there and say shit like that. I see the blood, but I refuse to believe my sister and my brother are in danger."

All the sudden anger that had flooded his body because Logan touched him disappeared—vanished as if it never appeared. "I thought that the first time when Aubrey originally went missing. I thought this can't be happening. Three months later, a sheriff from a small town asked for help, it had been real. Real and frightening and the worst three months of my life."

Danny stepped forward, shoving a hand against Logan's chest. "There's blood on the ground that wasn't there when Kat and I left this morning. Don't be an idiot, Logan. Joshua Barten is here, and he has her. He probably has them both."

A slow breath released. "So, Sheriff, where do we start looking? This is your town."

He would turn over every rock, every nook, tear through every building, house, and place in his sight until he had Kat back in his arms. He would not lose her. Not like this.

Logan breathed deeply a few times before running a haggard hand over his face. "I have no clue."

"You better start thinking because he's already killed one person that we know of. I won't let him kill two more."

"I guess we start with Mr. Barten himself. He's a real jackass, and he hates me."

"Good. I like jackasses. I feel like unleashing some anger on one."

He stalked toward the truck, determined more than ever to find Kat. Nobody would stand in his way. Nobody.

He'd find Kat, and when he did, he'd confess his deepest fear.

That he loved her.

KAT'S EYES rounded in disbelief as they neared the spot she had never wanted to see again. A big hole, with mounds of dirt and snow piled around, sat where doors once led down to the pits of hell. Logan might've dismantled and erased the place that gave Aubrey nightmares every night, but this man, whoever he was, had dug it right back up. How? With the temperatures so cold and low? How long had it been this way? Snow coated the mounds of dirt as if suggesting he dug this a while ago.

How far did he dig? To the chamber where she almost died of smoke inhalation?

She didn't want to find out.

Yet, the man with the gun had other plans. She didn't like where this situation was leading.

Seth held onto her as best as he could. The pain in her thigh ached, reaching inside like barbed wire coiling tightly around each and every vein. She wanted to fall to the ground and pass out. The pain didn't just coat her thigh, but everywhere. Every inch of her body, like a million fire ants were eating her alive. She couldn't prevent the tears silently streaming down her face as they trudged through the woods, but she had held back her screams and moans of pain. Giving this asshole the satisfaction of her pain would never happen.

Stopping a few feet from the large hole, Kat could do nothing but stare at it. Seth had other ideas.

"Why are you doing this? Who are you?"

"You know my brother."

At that, Kat twisted her head toward the man and watched as the evil danced in his eyes as he stared at Seth.

"Who's that?"

"Evan."

Seth jerked so hard at that revelation, he made her stumble, which sent a new fresh wave of pain up her thigh and straight to her head. A tiny whimper escaped before she could stop it. The man's laughter burned a hole in her gut.

Seth tried to steady her, a soft apology under his breath as he twisted her slowly so they could look at the man head-on, the big hole now to their backs.

Seth's grip on her arm intensified as he said, "Evan has one brother. His name is Wayne. And you're definitely not Wayne."

The man chuckled, the sound carrying within the trees as if it were a cackle from a witch, brewing a potion to lead them to their deaths. "He has two brothers. I happen to be the other one." The man shrugged casually. "Well, okay, I'm his half-brother, but still, a brother."

"Fine, you're Evan's brother. Does he hate me so much he asked you to do this? To hurt my sister?"

She wanted to tell Seth to back off. To hold in his rage that she knew was seething, waiting to burst free. They couldn't afford to provoke him. The pain in her head hadn't disappeared, or the nausea. Now, a bit of dizziness was setting in. She was losing blood. She couldn't afford to lose any more if this maniac decided to shoot her again because Seth couldn't control his temper.

But how did she say all of that without letting the man hear her?

"Evan is nothing to me. I barely know him." The man stepped toward them, but not close enough for them to reach out and touch him. "Now, Wayne, on the other hand, well, we're close. Very close."

"How close? Did you have something to do with Aubrey's disappearance?" The words were out of her mouth before she could stop herself.

Sick laughter echoed through the woods. "No. I actually had no idea what Wayne was up to concerning her, but I would've been on board. It upsets me he kept it a secret."

Oh, that didn't bode well for them. She didn't like hearing that at all. With the way Seth tensed next to her, he didn't either.

The man took another step forward, the gun hanging by his side. But the murderous rage in his eyes told Kat he'd be ready to aim the gun within a second if they made one wrong move.

"Wayne is behind bars because of you Caldwells. You hurt my brother. I hurt you."

"He kidnapped and tortured and held an innocent

woman captive. He's sick. He deserves to be behind bars." Each word flew out of her mouth with fury. She wanted to jump at him and beat him to a bloody pulp for trying to blame them for something so ridiculous.

Except, the man didn't take kindly to her outburst and stalked to her, raising the gun until he had it pressed firmly against her forehead.

"I see your other brother, the sheriff, closed up this little haven that meant the world to Wayne. So I dug it back up." The gun pressed harder into her skin. "You're about to suffer more than that blonde bitch ever did." He leaned closer. "Did you like the flowers I sent you?"

Her eyes rounded with surprise. *He* sent the flowers with that cryptic message, please forgive me? Why? He obviously wasn't sorry about anything.

"Why are you doing this?"

An evil grin touched his face. "Because I can. Because I want you to suffer. Because I want you to pay for what happened to Wayne. The flowers were just the tip of the iceberg. I should've tortured you with so much more before now. But," he shrugged, "oh, well. You and your brother are going to get in that hole, and then I'm going to close it back up." His eyes glittered with rage. "Then I'm going to kill your other brother in front of Aubrey and take her with me. Wayne thought she was something special, so that means she's special to me."

Kat couldn't control the sob that escaped as he removed the gun from her head. Thousands of tremors coated her entire body. Hiding her fear and panic was impossible, especially with the way he said it. He sounded as if he couldn't wait to kill them. Bury them alive. He sounded as if he enjoyed killing people. That he was going to enjoy getting his hands on Aubrey.

"You'll never get your hands on Aubrey. Logan will destroy you."

"I would watch what you say to me."

"Or what?" Kat snapped, "You'll shoot me again. I thought you wanted to make me suffer and bury me alive."

She didn't like being threatened. The raging bitch in her always flew out without warning. She had loose lips, telling people what she thought, whether they wanted to hear it or not. This man could say what he wanted, but she would not stand here and listen to him say the things he was about Aubrey. He was going to kill them anyway, so what was the point of keeping her thoughts to herself.

The man cocked an amused brow as his hand lifted toward Seth.

He might win and kill them, but not without a fight. She wouldn't stand here without showing him who the hell he was dealing with.

Before his aim connected with Seth, she lunged forward, her right hand going for the gun. Seth must've sensed what she was about to do because he did a crazy move she never knew he could do with his legs, swiping the man to the ground with one swift kick.

The gun went off, the loud shot rang throughout the woods, echoing, signaling how close they were to death.

But not yet, because she would beat this man alive if she had to.

Before she could do anything, Seth was kicking at the man again. The gun flew from his hands. She started to step forward and help somehow, but a sharp pain attacked her leg as she put too much pressure on it. Her stance wobbled, which didn't help Seth, who stopped to steady her. The man took the opportunity to roll away and jump up, ramming into Seth instead of retreating to find the gun.

All three of them fell to the ground. Kat couldn't hold back a terrifying scream as the pain in her leg twisted with fury. She wanted to help Seth, jump into the fray, but she could do nothing but lay there as the pain immobilized her. Grunts and groans shouted in her ear as her arm jerked to and fro as Seth fought with the man.

She felt like an old Raggedy Ann doll, her body jerking this way and that as Seth tried to use both hands to subdue the guy. But he was strong, throwing punches and shielding blows as Seth fought back equally hard.

Her vision started to blur, the trees swaying viciously as if a tornado was descending upon them. Bile rose to her throat once again, but she forced herself to hold it back as she tried to focus and block out the pain everywhere in her body.

She wasn't a quitter. She didn't let people get the best of her. She certainly had no intention of dying in the woods.

Without looking, barely able to concentrate, her vision unstable, she brought her good leg up and kicked as hard as she could. A moment of triumph swamped her as she heard a loud grunt, then a loud thud.

"Nice kick, sis," Seth muttered as she felt him move around her. She didn't have the energy to look at what he was doing. Her eyes drifted close. She hit the right person. She honestly had no clue who she kicked.

"Hey, no, stay with me." A light slap to her cheek made her eyes pop open. A tender smile shined at her. "You kicked him good. He fell into the hole. You knocked him out. I don't want to stick around to find out if he can climb out. Stay with me, and let's get the hell out of here."

She nodded but made no move to get up. "I don't think—"

"You can. I'll help you walk."

Her hand barely moved, but she twitched it enough for him to get the drift how difficult it was for him to help her walk when they were handcuffed together. They had no key. The man could have one in his pocket, but they couldn't go down there and check, especially since the coldness from the snow was starting to seep into her bones and freeze her like an ice sculptor.

She needed to push the pain aside, do what she had to do, which was get her ass up, and get moving.

"Let's get out of here."

"That's my Kat." Seth grinned and slowly stood up, helping her gently to her feet.

Looking around, she tried to figure out where the gun might've landed. She didn't trust the man would stay unconscious and in the hole forever.

"Where's the gun?"

Seth grabbed her as best as he could and started walking, guiding her along. "No clue, but we can't waste time looking for it. Let's head for the cabin and call Logan."

Yes, she liked the sound of that plan.

But would they make it before she completely passed out? Her energy was slowly draining to nothing. Spots danced in front of her eyes, her vision wonky as the trees continued to move as if it were a windy day. And it wasn't.

"I'm losing too much blood, Seth. My vision..."

"You're fine. You're going to be fine, Kat. Do you hear me?"

She kept walking even as she ached to close her eyes and let the pain drift away.

Maybe if Seth told her she'd be fine a few more times, she'd believe it.

Because, as she took another step, the sharp, brutal pain

in her leg from the jarring movement told her she wasn't fine at all.

She felt herself falling before she could shout out a warning.

"Shit! Kat!"

Then she heard nothing else as the aches in her body disappeared, and darkness replaced it.

21

"OKAY. So, Mr. Barten is a real jackass. Like, waiting with a shotgun, kind of jackass."

Danny nodded as Logan pulled into Barten's driveway. "I feel like shooting someone. I'm okay with that."

Despite the terrible situation they were in, Logan chuckled. "I would actually like to see that."

A tiny grin appeared before it vanished as Kat's beautiful face punctured his mind. She had to be okay. She had to be. He couldn't go through another loss like this. Another three torturous months of waiting, wondering, and praying his sister wasn't dead and buried in someone's backyard.

"Do you think he knows anything?"

Logan shrugged as his hand went for the door handle. "If he does, he's not likely to tell us anything."

Danny exited the vehicle and took a spot next to Logan as they walked cautiously toward a man, who, like Logan said, had a shotgun in his hand as he stepped off his porch.

"Git off my property. I got nuttin' to say to you, you sons of bitches."

His hand itched to grab his weapon, but he figured that

would set off the old man even more. Since he didn't know Mr. Barten as well as Logan, he decided to follow his lead.

"I don't want any trouble, Mr. Barten, but if you don't put the shotgun down, we're going to do more than just talk."

Danny would be fine with that. He wanted to rip this man apart if it brought him one step closer to finding Kat. The tension emanating from Logan said just as much.

Mr. Barten spat a huge loogie in their direction as it looked like his grip got tighter on the weapon. "Ain't got nuttin' to say to you, Sheriff. Git off my property."

"Have you seen your son lately?" Logan asked as if he were asking about how nice the weather was today.

"Why would I talk to that pansy-ass boy?"

Right then, Danny knew Evan wasn't lying about anything concerning Aubrey. With the way his father felt about him, why would he lie for these people?

"I wasn't talking about Evan." Logan smiled, an evil-looking smile that Danny found very amusing. "I was talking about Joshua."

No words left his mouth, but by the way he paled, the blood draining from his face, Danny knew Mr. Barten knew exactly who Joshua was.

"You took one boy away from me, and now you planning on taking another. Not today," Mr. Barten yelled as he raised the shotgun.

Danny and Logan didn't hesitate. They both reached for their weapons, aiming more precisely than Mr. Barten's unsteady stance.

"We'll leave peacefully if you tell us where he is. We'll pretend you aren't aiming a weapon at us," Danny said as calmly as he could. His finger felt itchy on the trigger. He wouldn't hesitate to shoot this man like he didn't hesitate to shoot his son Wayne.

"Over my dead body."

Without warning, Logan lowered his weapon. "Okay, Mr. Barten. Have a good day." Logan turned to him as if he didn't have a gun aimed at him by a crazed lunatic. "Let's go, Danny."

"Are you fu—"

"Let's go," Logan said more firmly.

Danny didn't know what the hell he was doing, but he followed Logan to the vehicle, not once turning his back to Mr. Barten or lowering his weapon.

As soon as they closed their doors, Danny let loose his rage.

"What the hell was that? What are you doing?"

Logan started the car as calmly as could be, then backed up. "I'm not into getting shot today. He would've, Danny. There's no doubt in my mind. We can always come back later with reinforcements and lock him up for pulling a gun on us."

The gun rested heavily in his lap as he watched Mr. Barten, who continued to stand with his shotgun aimed in their direction, as Logan turned out of the driveway and onto the road.

"He knows where Joshua is."

"Yeah, and I think I do, too."

Surprised, Danny jerked his gaze toward Logan. "Suddenly, you know. How?"

"Well, I wasn't absolutely sure if Mr. Barten knew about Joshua. But since he does, I'm thinking a good place to start is his hunting cabin. He doesn't let anyone go in there. The only other person he ever let step foot in that place was Wayne. And if he's so protective of Joshua, then I'm thinking maybe he'd let him stay there."

"I hope so. I'd hate to hit you."

Logan chuckled. "You can still hit me if you'd like, but I saved us from a gunfight."

"We're going back there later."

His hands tightened on the steering wheel. "I don't relish that thought, but you're right. We need to at least charge him for pulling that shotgun out."

"How far is this cabin?"

"Not far. It's about five miles or so from our cabin."

Danny nodded, praying they'd find Kat unharmed, and soon. The deep ache in his chest was getting so large, he didn't know how much more he'd survive. The unknown would kill him if he didn't get control of it.

Glancing toward Logan, he noticed how tightly his hands were on the steering wheel.

Well, wasn't he a jackass? Here he was, worried about Kat when he knew Logan had to be going out of his mind for not only Kat, but his brother Seth.

"I'm sorry."

Logan's brow rose. "For what?"

"For...everything. I guess I forgot Kat's your sister and Seth is with her. I've only been thinking about myself."

A breath escaped. "I get it, Danny. I finally know what you had to be going through when Aubrey went missing. It sucks. And..." Logan released another breath, "and I know what Kat means to you. At least, I'm getting a good idea."

Looking out the window, Danny didn't respond. He'd let Logan decipher on his own what he felt for Kat because he wouldn't be pouring his heart out to anyone but her. And he would. He would find her. He wouldn't stop looking until he did.

A sharp ringing pierced the awkward silence. Danny was grateful for the interruption.

With one steady hand on the wheel, Logan dug for his phone.

"Hello?" A slight pause. "How bad?" Another pause. "We'll be right there, Seth. Stay calm and we'll be right there."

Danny jerked his complete attention to Logan when he heard Seth's name. He waited in dreaded silence as he listened to Logan disconnect and make another call to request an ambulance. Why an ambulance? What about Kat? Who was hurt?

Logan threw his phone on the seat as he drove faster. "He took them into the woods, to the same place Aubrey..." His voice cracked. "They got away and managed to make it to our cabin."

"Who needs the ambulance?"

Logan didn't look at him. "Kat. He shot her. She's lost a lot of blood. Seth was barely keeping it together."

Danny stared straight ahead, willing the vehicle faster, even though he knew Logan was driving as fast as he possibly could.

Kat was hurt.

How in the hell was he going to keep it together?

What felt like seconds later, more likely several minutes, they were jerking to a stop in front of the cabin. Danny dashed out of the vehicle, racing for the cabin with Logan a step behind him. He slammed through the door so fast the door hit the cabin wall with a thud. Seth looked up from kneeling near the couch where Kat lay, a look of terror on his face.

Danny wanted to rush to her side, yet he controlled himself, barely, to let Logan go to Kat's side where she lay so deathly still on the couch. He hated to concede control, but

Logan *was* her brother. He was just a guy she slept with. That didn't compare to family.

"How long has she been out?" Logan asked quietly. Yet, to Danny, his words rang loudly in the small confines of the cabin.

"I don't know. She keeps going in and out. She passed out on me as soon as we started walking away. I had no choice but to put her over my shoulder and get her here as fast as I could. I tried to run."

Logan grabbed Seth into a hug. Danny glanced away as Seth embraced him back. He didn't want to see that. He wanted to shove both of them out of the way and go to Kat. His eyes trained on Kat's pale face. Dried blood circled around a deep cut on her forehead. Obviously, she didn't only get shot.

How many injuries did she have? How badly was she injured? Would she survive this?

"What happened?" Logan asked as he pulled a set of keys out of his pocket and undid the handcuffs around Seth and Kat's wrists.

Seth stood up, stretching. "We were leaving to head back to the station. Kat opened the door, and this guy stood there with a gun in our face. He made us handcuff ourselves together and told us to get in the trunk of his car. When we hesitated, he hit Kat in the head." Seth choked on his words. "That was the first time she blacked out on me. Thankfully, she came to in the trunk, but I could tell the whole time she wasn't feeling right. Then he stopped and made us start walking. He said..." His eyes shot to him. "He said some things about Aubrey."

Danny didn't think his heart could hurt any worse. But hearing his sister's name made it beat like a racehorse hell-bent on winning the race. "What?"

"He blames us for Wayne getting arrested. All of us Caldwells, as he put it. He had no idea what Wayne was doing with Aubrey, but he planned on killing us all and... and taking her."

"Nobody else is hurting my sister." Danny would kill anyone who dared to try.

"How did you get away?" Logan asked quietly.

"Kat and I took our chances, even though he had a gun. She kicked him into the hole he dug. We didn't stick around to see how badly he was hurt."

Logan stood up. "There's a four-wheeler in the shed. I'll go find him." He looked at Danny. "Stay with Kat and Seth. I'll bring this bastard in."

Danny wanted to argue so badly. He wanted to find this asshole himself. For killing an innocent man. For threatening his sister. For hurting Kat.

Then his eyes glided to Kat, and he knew he wouldn't be able to leave her side. Not while she was injured.

He nodded but didn't say anything. Nothing he would say would be pleasant.

"I'll go with you."

Logan looked at Seth. "No. You stay here."

"Come on, Logan. Don't argue with me. This guy is crazy. He shot Kat because we were talking while we walked. He didn't have to. He did it because he could. I won't let you go out there alone. I..." His voice cracked as his features turned fierce. "I can't lose my brother. I'm almost afraid I'm losing my sister."

Logan grabbed him by the shoulder. "Kat will be fine. Go grab the gun I have locked up in the bedroom safe. I'll meet you outside." Logan tossed him his keys and started for the door before turning toward him. "She will be fine, Danny. Kat's a fighter. The ambulance should be here any minute."

He still didn't say a word. Although, he had to believe what Logan said was true. He couldn't lose Kat. Not like this.

Logan walked out of the cabin. Seth followed shortly after with a handgun gripped tightly in his hand.

With shaky steps, he walked to Kat's side and knelt down, grabbing her hand. She felt warm to the touch, even as she looked as pale as death. Her thigh was wrapped tightly with what he assumed was Seth's shirt. He didn't like how her forehead was coated with blood, but now that he had her hand in his, he couldn't walk away to find a wash-cloth and wipe it clean.

He heard the dull roar of the four-wheeler, then the noise drifted away.

Leaning closer to Kat, he brushed a hand across her cheek. "Wake up, sweetheart. Show me those beautiful eyes. I can't lose you. Do you hear me, Kat? I can't. I won't."

No response. Although, her eyes fluttered.

He needed her to open her eyes. Just a peek. Just so he knew she was okay.

The sound of the cabin door opening jerked his attention that way. But he had no time to reach for his weapon, as the man who had introduced himself as Jason, Jared's brother, stepped inside.

"Well, well. This is a development I didn't see coming." Joshua Barten laughed as the gun in his hand looked steady, aimed in his direction, even as his appearance looked completely disheveled as if he had worked mighty hard to crawl out of a hole.

"You'll pay for hurting her like this." Danny meant every word. He wasn't a man with a badge right now. He was a man aching for the woman he loved to be okay.

"Or not." Joshua let loose a cackle. "I think I'll kill you now."

22

———

THIS WASN'T the first time Danny stared down a gun. But unlike the time he had to talk down a maniac holding his family hostage, this situation felt a thousand times worse, as if he wouldn't be able to control anything. He had worried he wouldn't get the family out alive, unharmed. Although he did, not one bullet was fired by either party. But right now, right in this moment, his panic level was so high, he thought his heart would burst.

The man before him was crazy, just as Seth said. He had no doubt in his mind he would squeeze the trigger without thought. He'd kill him, then he'd kill Kat, then he'd hurt his sister. No matter what happened to him, he wouldn't allow Joshua to lay one finger on his sister. Or Kat, for that matter.

"You do know reinforcements will be here any second." Danny actually had no clue if backup would accompany the ambulance, but he hoped like hell they did.

"You'll be dead. She'll be dead. And I'll be long gone." Joshua's lips curled into a terrifying grin. "I can't wait to meet your sister. I want you to know that I'll take good care of her."

So many vulgar words teetered on his lips, but he held them back because that's what Joshua wanted. He wanted him to fight back. To revel in his pain. Danny refused to give him the satisfaction.

His grip on Kat's hand tightened when he felt her move. Joshua gave no indication he saw her move, so he didn't want to risk it by looking at her. He had to hope she took his cue by squeezing her hand to stay still and her eyes closed. He wasn't sure how he was going to get them out of this, but he would. Losing Kat wasn't an option, or losing his sister again.

"Nothing more to say, Agent O'Rourke? I'll let you have some last words if you'd like."

The evil pouring from his eyes made Danny shiver. He was crazier than his brother Wayne. Still, Danny said nothing. Laughter almost bubbled up his throat at the way Joshua's veins in his neck bulged. He obviously didn't like the fact Danny wasn't engaging with him. Good. Danny wasn't about to give him what he wanted.

"Okay, I gave you a chance for some last words."

His time was up. Would he be able to reach for his weapon and return fire? Danny didn't know, but he'd take his chances. If he was shot, so be it. But he'd at least try to take down Joshua before he was able to hurt Kat again. He would shield Kat with his body as he reached for his weapon and get one shot off. That's all he would need.

Joshua's eyes narrowed as the gun in his hand took aim.

Danny went for his weapon, pulling it out of its holster and aiming it at Joshua like a gunslinger from the wild west. He didn't hesitate. He didn't think about how it would feel as a bullet tore through his body. He only thought of Kat as he shielded her body and fired his weapon.

Loud shots echoed throughout the cabin.

Danny flinched.

He waited for the pain to consume him.

Then he watched in fascination as Joshua's eyes went round and then he crumbled to the floor. Standing tall, and with a little shock of his own, was Deputy Bolten. Since arriving in town, he hadn't seen the deputy, but he was damn glad to see him now.

"I shot him."

Danny nodded. He couldn't be sure who fired the shot that dropped Joshua, and he didn't really care. He was alive. Kat wasn't in any more danger. Life could go back to normal.

"It's damn good to see you, Deputy Bolten."

"Please, call me Bolt like everyone else." His eyes looked sort of glazed as he said it.

Danny nodded and tried to glance behind him. "Is the ambulance here? I didn't hear any sirens."

"I was visiting with Charlotte when the call came in. I'm off today, you know, easing myself back into work since I got shot. Now, I just shot a man."

Danny could see the shock strengthening in his eyes. He snapped his fingers, trying to get Bolt's attention. "You did what you had to do. You did good, Bolt."

A slow smile gradually appeared. "I did do good." Bolt's eyes went to the floor. "Who is this guy?"

"He's—" Danny jerked his gaze at Kat when he heard a low moan. "Kat, sweetheart."

Her eyes fluttered once again, rapidly, before her gorgeous golden brown eyes looked at him.

"Keep your eyes open. Stay with me."

"I...hurt."

Leaning closer, he brushed a tender hand across her cheek. "I know, sweetheart. Stay with me a little longer. You're going to be fine."

"Seth?"

"He's with Logan. He's fine. You're both fine."

Her eyes started to drift close.

"No, Kat. You can't close your eyes."

As she enjoyed doing, arguing in every way possible, her eyes remained closed. He couldn't sit here and wait for help.

Standing up, he pierced a dangerous glare at Bolt that portrayed he'd better not disagree. "I need the keys to your car. I need to get her to a hospital. What the hell is taking the ambulance so long?"

"Lucky's a small town. The hospital is twenty minutes away, at least."

"I can't wait for it."

Bolt nodded, tossing his keys to him. His hand gestured toward the floor. "What about him?"

"Leave him. Wait for Logan to get back. In fact, try to call him and tell him what's going on. Tell him Joshua Barten is dead."

Danny scooped up Kat as gently as he could, then started for the door. He didn't even glance once at the dead body. He never wanted to see his face again.

As he stepped outside, the low wail of sirens echoed in the distance. His heart started to pound.

"Help is here, Kat. You're going to be fine."

Less than a minute later, relief swept through as the ambulance jerked to a stop in front of him. He would've driven her to the hospital himself, but he was damn glad to see the paramedics burst out of the doors and rush to his side.

He hopped in the back with them, without much arguments on their part, thankfully, and prayed like hell Kat made it in time.

If he lost her, he wouldn't survive.

"HEY."

Danny glanced up and produced a smile for his sister even though he didn't feel like it. He didn't know how well she was holding up since he'd been keeping to himself mostly, but he knew he had to put a brave front on for her just in case.

She sat down next to him. "How are you doing?"

"I should be asking you that question."

"I wasn't in any danger today." The gentle smile on her face almost relaxed him.

But she was.

She simply didn't have any clue.

He wasn't going to tell her what Joshua Barten had planned for her, and he didn't think Seth, Logan, or Kat when she got better, would tell her either. What Aubrey didn't know wouldn't hurt her. She had already been through enough pain.

"I'm okay, Aubs."

Her eyebrow rose skeptically. "Are you? You've been sitting in the hallway more than you've been sitting in the room with Kat. The doctors say she's going to pull through. I never had any doubts. She's so strong and tough."

Danny grabbed her hand and squeezed. "And so are you. I wish I could help you somehow. I don't like knowing you've been struggling lately."

Her grip tightened. "Don't dodge the conversation. We weren't talking about me. Why don't you come to Kat's room with me?"

Extracting his hand slowly, his gaze drifted to the floor. He couldn't go in there. He couldn't watch and wait for her to wake up. Every time he looked at her, his gut twisted with rage, his heart ached with torment.

He couldn't save his sister from a madman.

Apparently, he didn't learn from his mistakes.

He couldn't save Kat either.

She should've never gotten hurt. Joshua Barten should've never had the opportunity to get that close to her. He stood in front of that man, spoke to him, and didn't do a damn thing.

He couldn't do anything right, apparently. He couldn't keep his sister safe, or Kat. He couldn't help his sister through her pain. He felt useless.

"Danny...you do help me. All the time."

It's as if she heard his thoughts. Or maybe he said that out loud.

He looked up. "I don't live here. We barely talk on the phone, and when we do, it's short. How is that helping?"

Her smile, like an angel floating on heaven's clouds, almost soothed his weary heart. Almost, but not quite. "Every time I hear your voice it helps. Your love helps. It might not seem like it, but it all helps. Just you being you."

"I can't stay, Aubs."

The words just blurted out. He had no idea where that came from or why he even voiced it. He knew he couldn't stay. He would miss Kat. His heart would probably never love another woman like her, but he couldn't stay.

He couldn't even wrap his mind around the fact his sister thought he helped her in any way. He didn't do shit. The few times he did call her, he didn't say meaningful things. Hell, she carried most of the weight of the conversations. That wasn't helping. Just...useless.

He might love Kat. He might've wanted to tell her. But he

couldn't. Not anymore. He should've saved her from all of this pain, and he didn't. He didn't deserve her.

Her eyes glistened. "What about Kat?"

He averted his eyes once more. "I don't want to hurt you, Aubs, but it was never anything serious between us."

Jerking from the sudden slap against the back of his head, a lame chuckle escaped as he looked at her. "What the hell was that for?"

"For lying to me. For lying to yourself. If you can't man up, then maybe Kat is better off without you." Aubrey stood up and slipped back into the room where Kat lay recovering from her injuries.

He couldn't dispute her words. Kat was better off without him. He couldn't save her from harm this time. What made him think he could in the future?

"She packs quite a slap." Seth chuckled as he walked closer with two cups in his hand. He handed him one of the cups. "You looked like you could use a coffee when I left. Aubrey hollered at me the other night. So glad she didn't slap me like that."

Danny grinned despite feeling like complete shit about everything. "Don't worry, keep up the attitude you got, and she'll dub you with one of her signature slaps."

"So it's a sign of love? I should work my way toward one?"

Shrugging, Danny let a laugh escape. "You could call it that." He took a sip of coffee. "Pretty sure she loves all of you already."

Seth nodded. "I love her back. She's a nice addition to the family. Are you...did you sleep with Kat?"

"What kind of question is that?"

"The kind a concerned brother asks. What can I say? Neither of you noticed me standing there so I heard most of the conversation. Aubrey's right. You haven't been in Kat's room a lot."

Danny kept his eyes trained to the floor. This wasn't a talk he wanted to have, especially with Seth, one of Kat's brothers. "She's your sister. I'm giving you guys space."

"Or you're scared as shit. My sister doesn't let many people in. I'd hate to think she trusted the wrong person."

He looked up, assessing Seth. "How are you feeling? Most people don't go through what you went through."

A shiver rippled through, his coffee almost spilling over the edge of the cup. "I'm fine. Honestly, I don't know what I'm feeling right now. But, overall, I'm fine. Why the change of subject? Are you that scared of my sister?"

Hell, yeah, he was scared of Kat. She made him feel things he had never felt before. That was scary as hell. He wasn't afraid to admit that. Well, to himself. He would never admit that out loud.

He also knew his limitations. If he couldn't protect her from Joshua, how could he protect her from further harm?

"It's a lot to process. If you ever need to talk, I'm here."

Seth stood up. "I can see where Aubrey gets some of her traits. She can be as stubborn as you're being. I can't even say why I'm trying to push you toward Kat. I barely had time to process you two were an item before a gun was thrown in my face. Staring a gun down really makes a man reevaluate things about his life. I guess it doesn't affect you like it did me."

With his eyes still boring laser beams into the floor, he shrugged. That's the most he was willing to give. He wouldn't be spilling his guts today, if ever. What could he say to make it right? No eloquent words came to mind.

"If that's how you feel, maybe you should leave now before she wakes up."

Danny finally looked at him. "Hey, Seth, mind your own damn business."

He wasn't about to get advice from some punk ass kid who would hit his own brother. And he wasn't about to leave Kat until she woke up and at least gave her the decency of a goodbye.

"Yeah, I'm never good at that. Sorry to disappoint you. I suggest you stay out of the room while I'm around." Seth walked inside her room, the door shutting with a loud click. He didn't quite slam it shut, but he didn't close it quietly either.

Danny didn't respond to threats very well. Jerking to his feet, he opened the door and stepped inside, his heart hammering like a nail gun gone haywire. With a few steps, making sure they didn't look as tentative as they felt, he took a seat near the end of the bed.

A quick glance at Seth made him feel like a fool. He was played like an idiot because the crafty smirk on his face said he didn't care if Danny came in the room. In fact, it said Danny did exactly what Seth wanted.

Averting his gaze, he looked at Kat. She still looked deathly pale to him, but oh so beautiful. Seeing her alive and well was a beautiful sight.

How would he leave her? How would he survive?

Fortifying his resolve, he knew how.

Like he did everything else. He'd push his emotions aside and pretend like nothing was wrong.

He'd survive because he had no choice.

23

Logan shut his door quietly, although he knew Mr. Barten heard the truck pull into his driveway. He saw the cranky old bastard peek through the curtains in the front bay window. He'd be stepping outside onto his porch soon with his shotgun in hand, ready to threaten them once again. Well, he and Danny wouldn't be leaving until he was in handcuffs.

He let Mr. Barten get away with too many things, mostly because he kept to himself. But pulling a gun on him and Danny was unacceptable. If he didn't throw some charges at him now, he'd continue to exert his dominance over them until he actually pulled the trigger one of these times.

As he met Danny in front of his vehicle, he worried Mr. Barten would pull the trigger today. His son was dead. He wouldn't be happy about that. They hadn't been by to inform him of the news yet, but he figured Mr. Barten found out somehow. It was a small town, news spread fast, even if Mr. Barten barely left his residence.

"How do you think this will go?" Danny asked as they made their way to the front door.

"Not good. We killed his son. We locked up the other one. He didn't like me before all that happened."

"Maybe you shouldn't be here."

Logan ran a hand down his face. "Why is that?"

Danny paused in his steps, the creaking sound of the door opening in the distance. "Because if he does fire a shot, I'd rather you went home to my sister. She needs you."

He slapped a hand to Danny's shoulder as he met Mr. Barten's stern gaze. "She needs both of us. We aren't getting shot today, Danny. Not today."

Mr. Barten stood on the edge of his porch, shotgun in hand and a disgusted look on his face. "Git off my property."

"Lower your weapon and put your hands behind your back. Come peacefully to the back of my vehicle. You're under arrest, Mr. Barten," Logan said calmly, his hands itching to grab his weapon, but he made no move to do so. The slightest movement could make Mr. Barten's trigger finger touchy.

"Leave. I will shoot."

"You're threatening an officer of the law. I suggest you comply." Logan felt Danny tense next to him, but thankfully, he didn't add anything.

"What you gonna do, Sheriff? Uh? I'll shoot you before you can even pull your weapon out. Git. Off. My. Property." Mr. Barten's stance didn't wobble as he raised his shotgun a little higher.

A brief glimpse of his sister lying in the hospital recovering from a gunshot wound flashed across his mind. He didn't want to be lying next to her recovering from one as well. Nor put Aubrey in a panicked state. Obviously, that's what Danny had been thinking when he suggested he shouldn't be here. Aubrey wouldn't take it well at all if he got shot. Although Danny failed to realize, even if it didn't seem like it to him, Aubrey wouldn't take it well if Danny got shot, too. She loved them both.

He didn't want to get shot. He didn't want Danny to get shot. Nobody would be getting hurt today. Not even Mr. Barten himself, even though he was tempted to show him some pain.

Which was why he came prepared this time for Mr. Barten to resist.

"If you do not lower your weapon, Mr. Barten, my deputies will be prepared to use lethal force."

At that statement, Derek and Bolt both stepped around the corners of the porch, flanking Mr. Barten, their weapons high, and aimed perfectly at him.

Mr. Barten's gaze darted back and forth, a bit of hesitation forming in the crazy depths of his eyes. "This ain't right! You harassing me. My boys!" His grip on his weapon started to loosen.

"I will only ask you one more time to lower your weapon and put it gently on the ground." That's all Logan was willing to say. He wasn't about to engage in an argument about the kind of men his boys were. They were nothing but trouble and deserved everything they got.

Logan had talked to Bolt somewhat about how he was feeling about shooting Joshua. Bolt appeared to be okay, although a little shaken up. Or maybe he was internalizing everything. He hadn't been too vocal when he was shot himself a few months ago.

Right now, Bolt's gun looked steady in his hand, ready for anything. That's all that mattered to him. As soon as Kat was released from the hospital, as soon as everything felt like normal around here, he'd pressure Bolt a little more to talk to him. He needed to know his deputy was good to go to stay on the job.

Mr. Barten glanced one more time back and forth from Derek to Bolt. Finally, after what felt like ages, but only mere seconds, he lowered his weapon, setting the shotgun on the porch. Mr. Barten's nasty gaze met his calm eyes. "You'll regret this one day, Sheriff. You just wait."

Walking up the few steps, he pulled his handcuffs out and grabbed Mr. Barten's grimy hands. "I regret nothing. I suggest you remain silent before you dig yourself deeper into a hole you won't be able to climb out of."

After handcuffing him, he let Derek lead Mr. Barten to his vehicle, happy to have the old man walking away from him. Not because he was close to losing his patience, but because he also smelled terrible. Of course, that didn't surprise him, especially how dirty and greasy he looked from head to toe every time he saw the old man. Dirty, oily hair that always peaked out underneath a scraggly old base-ball cap. Wrinkled, smelly clothes that probably hadn't seen a washer in weeks. Being locked up would be a good thing. Maybe he'd actually smell nice for once after a shower.

Danny cracked a grin as he looked at him. "That was intense."

Logan couldn't stop a chuckle. "It went better than I imagined." He nodded toward his truck. "Come on. Let's book him, then head back to the hospital."

A frown coated his face as Danny nodded, but didn't look too happy about that prospect.

Why the melancholy look?

Well, he could probably answer that fairly easily.

Danny wasn't planning on sticking around. The thought made him sad. For Aubrey. For his sister.

But they were both tough and strong. They'd survive it like they survived everything else.

Especially his sister.

KAT SAT in the wheelchair as Logan gathered her belongings and then nodded to the nurse he was ready. A few minutes later, they were out of the hospital and in Logan's truck heading home. Her home, thankfully. Logan tried to insist she stay with him and Aubrey for a while, but she wanted to be alone.

Completely alone.

Danny left yesterday claiming he had to get back to Florida because his latest case he was working on hit a lead. The case he thought might've had something to do with her, but it turned out another psycho wanted to hurt her.

Joshua Barten.

His name alone gave her the heebie-jeebies. But no matter how hard she tried, she couldn't shut her mind off everything that happened. She couldn't erase his name from her memories.

Her head hurt as everything swirled around her mind. Resting her head gently against the window, she closed her eyes and tried to forget about it all. It was useless.

She could still see the pain in Danny's eyes as he told her he had to leave. She also didn't miss the longing, the tiny flame of desire. When he stood close to her bed, she had hoped he'd cave in to that small craving and kiss her good-bye. Anything. Maybe even grab her hand and give her some sort of comfort.

He didn't do anything. He barely said a word.

Kat always knew it wouldn't last. But she never expected when the time came, it would hurt so badly as if someone had taken a knife and gutted her from head to toe.

She wanted to hate him and curse him straight to hell,

yet she couldn't. She understood why he left, why he didn't even profess any sort of feelings.

The guilt.

She saw it in his eyes the few times everyone talked about Joshua Barten. He thought he should've saved her. He thought he could've prevented it. She didn't need to hear him say that to know it was true.

He put too much responsibility on his shoulders, thinking he had to be the savior for everyone he cared about. He still couldn't forgive himself for Aubrey getting hurt.

The truck slowly stopped.

"I'll help you inside. Maybe Aubrey and I—"

"I'll be fine, Logan." She lifted her head and turned his way and attempted to give him a smile that portrayed she was fine when she felt nothing but a big churning funnel of turmoil. "I can manage just fine with crutches. And I want to be alone. I want to relax and chill out on the couch with some movies."

Logan's eyes crinkled with concern, but then he nodded. "Can I at least help you to the door?"

"Fine. Bring my bags to the door."

A tender smile brightened his face. She wanted to prove she could handle everything on her own, even walking to her door.

But really, she wanted to prove she was fine Danny left. She figured that was why everyone wanted to smother her. If there was one thing she hated the most, it was being smothered with attention.

Getting out of the vehicle slowly, she tried not to roll her eyes at the way Logan stood almost bouncing back and forth on his feet as if he wanted to step forward and help her out but resisted because he knew she didn't want his help.

She wouldn't say she wasn't nervous to walk with the crutches, especially with the snow on the ground, but it also wasn't going to deter her from her goal. Proving she didn't need help.

Holding onto the door with one hand, ignoring the slight pain tingling in her leg, she grabbed one crutch at a time from the backseat. She made it to her front door easily, getting the hang of using crutches without much issue. She couldn't wait to toss them in the garbage and get back to her normal self. Maybe another week or two before her leg felt healthy enough to walk on. At the moment, anytime she put any amount of pressure on it, it felt like a thousand tiny daggers were twisting in her leg with rage. Getting shot really sucked.

Unlocking the door, she stepped inside and offered another smile as Logan deposited her things on the floor in the foyer.

"I could probably start a load of laundry. And if you're hungry, I can—"

"I'll be fine." She smiled, a big warm smile, hopefully to portray how much she would be okay by herself. "Honestly, I will be okay."

"Maybe, but it doesn't mean you can't accept some help. I hate it when you push people away like this. I'm sorry that Dan—"

"It's okay he left."

Logan's expression softened. "Is it? I know you care about him." He hesitated. "I know he cares about you."

Glancing away, she shrugged. "It was never going to work. It was...a little bit of fun."

A strong pair of arms wrapped around her. She didn't resist his brotherly hug, even as she itched to do so.

"Maybe Danny needs to know who he's messing with."

"Logan, don't do anything stupid. Aubrey would be upset at you."

He squeezed her tighter. "I wasn't talking about me." He stepped back, winked, and left before she could find a good comeback to that.

Wow. If she didn't know any better, Logan insinuated she should fight for Danny. That she should—Oh, dear, she had a hard time even thinking about it.

When did she ever back down from anything? She didn't.

And surprisingly, she had Logan's complete blessing.

She made a swift decision.

She would fight for Danny.

She would admit she loved him.

But first, she had to recuperate and get rid of these crutches. Then she would settle this business between her and Danny because the way he left, nothing was settled.

Because, damn it, the least she deserved was a goodbye kiss.

24

A LIGHT KNOCK SOUNDED on his door. Danny thought about ignoring it, but he knew it would be a futile effort. Deke wouldn't care one bit if he ignored a dozen knocks.

"What's up?"

Deke poked his head into his office and grinned. "Well, it's always a good morning when there are doughnuts in the break room, and my best friend actually looks approachable."

Danny couldn't resist rolling his eyes. He might feel like he was slowly dying inside as each new day passed, leaving Kat behind, but he worked hard at not displaying his pain.

"And where's my doughnut?"

Chuckling, Deke took a seat across from him. "Sorry, dude, I grabbed the last one." His eyes glided to the photos sprawled across his desk. "Why are you still looking at these photos? We got our guy."

Thank goodness, too. Three dead bodies by the hand of this killer had been enough. He was good, but not that good. The trace evidence found on the third victim hadn't panned out to be anything, but a witness seeing a strange man leaving the building and snapping a picture because they couldn't resist, helped lead them to their killer. Just a random citizen who had a funny feeling stopped a madman from an even larger killing spree. The killer, a thirty-two-year-old single man, who could never keep a girlfriend, with a violent temper, and multiple arrests for domestic calls, finally took his rage to another level. He liked all kinds of women, and they had yet to determine why he picked all women whose last name started with a C, or sent his creepy little gifts of chocolate. So far, he wasn't being cooperative in sharing anything or confessing.

Danny glanced down at the photos lying across his desk. They might not have his confession, but they had a witness. They were also combing through every aspect of his life and trying to place him in the vicinity of each murder. So far, everything was falling into place. He'd be prosecuted without much issue.

"Danny?"

Looking up, he shrugged. "I wanted to take one more look. I'm glad this one is solved."

"Me too." Deke shifted in his seat, then quietly coughed. "So...have you talked to her?"

That didn't take a genius to know whom he was referring to. Deke had told him numerous times over the past two and a half weeks how much of an idiot he was for leaving Minnesota without declaring some sort of feelings for Kat.

Maybe he was an idiot.

Maybe he'd go insane one of these days missing her the way he was.

But it was for the best.

"Stop ignoring me."

"No, Deke, I haven't talked to her. I have no reason to."

"No reason at all?"

Danny looked away. "What do you want me to say?"

"The truth. You miss her." Deke stood up. "You're the biggest idiot there is."

"As if you haven't already said that. Goodbye, Deke."

He started for the door, stopping short of leaving. "When are you going to finish packing up Aubrey's apartment? I can help."

He hated when Deke brought up Kat, and he also hated when he mentioned Aubrey's apartment. Everything was packed and ready to go. It had been basically finished before he and Kat left for Minnesota. Over the past two and a half weeks, he debated many times about going over there and taking everything to the donation center, and shipping the few things Aubrey wanted. Each time, he couldn't find the strength to do it. It would make it official. His sister wasn't coming back.

"Danny? I keep losing you. You keep getting this far away look in your eyes."

He shrugged. "I'm not ready to empty the apartment." But maybe it was time he got it over with.

"Maybe it won't be as bad as you think. Check your email. Just think about it before you say no."

Before he could question Deke, he walked out of his office with a wily grin on his face. Hesitating, he wasn't sure he wanted to know what Deke had done. Giving in, he opened his inbox and scanned the contents until he saw an email that made his eyes bulge.

Request For Transfer

What did he do?

Nerves, as thick as molasses, attacked his hand as the

cursor hovered over the email. He clicked with haste, wanting to get it over with. He read the entire email quickly, then drew in a deep breath reading it over one more time with care.

Deke was certifiable.

And maybe the smartest man alive.

Not only did he ask about Danny transferring to Minnesota, but he added himself in the mix. He told their supervisor, if Danny went, he wanted to go, too.

Did he want to transfer to Minnesota?

Yeah, he'd be closer to his sister. He actually loved that idea. He missed her like crazy way too often. Phone calls here and there weren't cutting it anymore.

But what about Kat? Could he handle seeing her all the time without pulling her into his arms? Would she even allow him near her anymore? He left without saying much of anything. He left without even kissing her one last time.

Could he bring potential danger closer to his sister and Kat? His job could do that. He dealt with cruel and evil individuals day in and day out. He couldn't positively say nothing bad would ever follow him home.

He couldn't save his sister from a lunatic.

He couldn't save Kat either.

Transferring closer to them wouldn't help his anxiety.

But he missed them both so much.

His finger hovered over the reply button, the indecision of what to do, eating him alive, slowly, painfully.

There was only one thing he could do.

He clicked reply and wrote the fastest email he had ever written in his life.

KAT FROZE, the box heavy in her arms, as the lock on the door twisted. The door swung open.

"What the hell do you think you're doing?"

She almost smiled at the horror on Danny's face and the panic in his tone of voice as he rushed to her side and grabbed the box from her.

"Are you insane? You're still recovering. You shouldn't be lifting heavy things."

"I feel better." Which was mostly true. Her leg still gave her moments of pain, but she was off the crutches, so there was that accomplishment at least.

Danny set the box on the ground. "What are you doing here?"

"What does it look like I'm doing? I'm finishing the task I should've finished before I left."

His eyes narrowed. "How long have you been here?"

"I just got here today. About an hour ago."

"Why didn't...why didn't you call me? I would've picked you up from the airport."

A smile graced her face. She thought about it, but then the thought of seeing him scared her. She needed time to prepare what she wanted to say, not that she didn't have two and a half weeks to think about it. But actually having the opportunity to speak to him again made her nerves jump forth with ease.

Then something occurred to her. "What are you doing here?"

He cocked a brow. "It's my sister's apartment. I have every right to be here."

She tossed a hand to her hip. "You know what I mean. I guess..." She hesitated. "I didn't expect to see you here."

"I figured it was time I finished packing and clearing everything out." He took a step closer. "Kat...I'm sorry."

She swallowed, her smile dying some. Sorry about what? That he didn't love her. That nothing would ever work between them. "What for? I didn't call you because I didn't want to bother you while you were working. I can handle this."

"You're not handling any of this. I will. You need to be at home relaxing." He took another step closer. "And I'm sorry for leaving the way I did."

"You had a break in a case. I understand."

Another step and he was close enough to touch her, which he did. A warm hand caressed her cheek as the other wrapped around her waist and pulled her closer. "You're not supposed to be understanding."

She chuckled as she soaked up his soft touch. "And how am I supposed to react?"

"Argue with me. Yell at me. Demand I never do that again."

"Why would I do that? It's not as if—"

His hand tightened around her waist when she stopped speaking. "As if, what?"

"As if I have a claim over you."

"And if I wanted you to, what would you say?"

Her heart started to beat erratically. She had no idea why he was doing this. Pushing at his chest lightly, she stepped out of his embrace and walked across the living room to put some distance between them. Why did she do that?

This was why she came here. To tell Danny how she felt. But to hear him voice it first surprised her. It scared her. But why?

She wanted him. She wanted his love as much as she wanted to give him love. So why did hearing he might want that, too, frighten her so much she wanted to run back home to Minnesota?

Actually, it pissed her off. Why didn't he tell her how he felt before he left? How dare he make her wonder and worry and go out of her mind whether she should come to Florida and confront him.

"Kat, I'm..." He cleared his throat. "I'm terrified."

Jerking her eyes to his, her anger dissipated at the fear reflected deep in the depths of his eyes. "I—"

"Not about us. Don't get me wrong," he said as he took a few steps toward her, "I'm terrified I won't be able to keep you safe. I already failed once. I failed you and Aubrey. That fear keeps making me push you away. That's why I'm sorry I left the way I did. I didn't have to leave. I chose to."

The pounding of her heart, which had been bouncing up and down like a pogo stick, started to simmer down to a low drum roll. "You can't save us from everything. It's not your fault. None of it is."

"Maybe not, but I should've. I talked to Joshua outside this apartment. Right in the damn hallway," he hollered as he whipped his hand toward the door. "I could have done something right then, but I didn't."

"You didn't know who he was. You can't blame yourself like this." She brushed away her anxiety and walked back to him. He didn't hesitate to wrap his arms around her once again. "I won't let you blame yourself. So stop it. How's that for arguing?"

A dangerous grin, one that had her wishing he'd whisk her to a bedroom, punctured his lips. "I love arguing with you. You're so beautiful when you're angry. I'm glad to see you again, but you're not doing anything in this apartment."

She grabbed the front of his shirt and squeezed, the

tension quickly filling up in her veins. She could do this. "I didn't come to finish the apartment."

"Then why'd you come?"

"To tell a boneheaded man how mad I am at him for leaving without kissing me goodbye."

"So you are mad at me?" The silky, devilish grin on his face made her want to laugh. Then his lips met hers, lightly, softly. "I am sorry."

"Sorry because you'll never...love me?" Her grip tightened on his shirt, then she shoved away from him. "I love you, Danny. Every obnoxious thing about you. And you just left. I'm probably making myself look like a fool right now, but there it is. I love you."

His expression fell blank as she backed away a few more steps. That look told her enough. He didn't love her. He probably didn't even know what to say.

"You can go, Danny. I won't touch one box, but please leave."

Eyebrows dipping low, the annoyance filled his face instantly. He stalked to her in three long strides, grabbing her by the shoulders. "I'm not leaving again quite so easily because I love you, too, Kat. Every aggravating thing about you." His grip softened, then his hands slid down her arms and linked fingers with her. "I have no idea how this will work."

"It doesn't matter if you want it to work."

A gradual smile lit up his handsome face. "Oh, I want it to work. I might be an idiot once, but never twice. I'm not leaving you again."

"Well, this was easier than I thought. I figured I'd have to knock some sense into you."

He kissed her sweetly, his tongue taking its time to make

entrance and entice her for more things to come. "I like that you weren't going to take no for an answer."

"So..."

Cocking a brow, his silky smile deepened. "So, what?"

"I mean, we should talk some sort of logistics here. I've never imagined moving away from my family, but—"

Tender lips met hers once again. He kissed her as if he'd never get to kiss her again. "I like interrupting you. I'm going to do that every time I hear something crazy come out of your mouth."

"What's so crazy about talking where we're going to live? I'm not doing a long-distance thing wit—"

This kiss was urgent and a little frenzied when he interrupted her once more. If his kisses continued on this path, she might think of ways to get him to interrupt her. She missed him so much.

"We're not having any discussion about moving. My transfer to Minnesota went through this morning. As of next week, I'll be heading there to live. The commute from Lucky might suck, but for you, I'm willing to suffer."

Her mouth dropped as she let his words sink in. Here she had all this worry and madness floating around her stomach, almost on the verge of getting sick every time she thought about what she'd say to him, and he had made plans to come to her.

"I hope you don't mind Deke's tagging along, too. I guess he liked Minnesota as much as me." His cheeks started to tint a light shade of red. "I should be honest. He put in the transfer for me without my knowledge. I was planning to wallow in self-pity. I thought I was doing the right thing by staying away from you. He made me see how dumb that was. I'm still scared of losing you. If anything ever happens to—"

This time she cut off his words with a delectable kiss of her own. It might take her a while to convince him he couldn't save her from everything. She looked forward to each moment.

"I'll be fine. Aubrey will be fine. You're not responsible for everyone."

"I love you, which means I will protect you every day of my life. Prepare to be smothered by me."

She giggled, already imagining his hovering and protectiveness. "I'm an independent woman that takes no shit from anyone. Prepare to be put in your place every single time."

Letting go of her hands, he grabbed her around the waist and lifted her. She screamed in delight as she wrapped her legs around his waist. A slight tinge of pain hit her thigh, but she ignored it because she loved being this close to him. He walked down the hallway to her old bedroom she slept in the last time she was here.

Laying her gently on the bed, he kissed her softly. "I look forward to every moment, in anger, in frustration, in worry, in love, with you. There's never a time that's dull with you, and I wouldn't have it any other way. Now, I'm going to show you how much I truly love you. I'm going to show my forgiveness in every way I can."

She smiled as his lips started at her neck and then went downward.

He showed her what kind of love she had been waiting for her entire life.

The perfect kind of love. Fierce. Loyal. Exciting. And absolutely breathtaking.

EPILOGUE

Grabbing another box from the back of the van, Seth chuckled. "Dude, you have way too much crap. Aubrey had, like, three boxes."

Danny rolled his eyes as he grabbed another box and followed him. "Yeah, she didn't want half of her stuff. I do."

"This isn't all going to fit in Kat's house. What are you, a hoarder, or something?"

"I don't like to part with stuff."

Seth laughed again as they set their boxes next to the pile already stacked in Kat's living room. He couldn't resist smiling as he glanced at the Christmas tree sitting in the corner of the room he put up for Kat last night before she arrived in town with Danny.

Kat loved Christmas, as did the rest of the family. He loved the holiday, but he could take or leave the decorations. He appreciated the company and food on Christmas Day more than anything else.

With everything that had happened, she never put up her tree. He was still trying to make it up in any way possible for the way he acted with everyone, so he figured decorating her house for the holidays, since Christmas was only a week away, would help in his favor.

It had. Kat's beautiful smile when she walked into the house to see her tree lit up and her decorations situated around the house as she liked it, had been worth every moment of digging through her attic for all her Christmas decorations. And she had a lot of crap.

The only thing he didn't quite finish yet was the lights on the outside of the house. He planned to do that later today, as soon as they finished unpacking the moving van.

He followed Danny out of the house to grab more boxes.

"Have you talked to Evan lately?"

The question threw him so off-balance he almost tripped going down the two porch stairs. "What for? I'm never talking to him again."

Danny stopped and turned toward him. "He's your best friend."

"He's an asshole, and this subject is officially dropped."

He walked around Danny, ignoring the concern in his eyes. What did Danny care if he talked to the asshole who lied to him for over two months? If he would've confessed sooner about Joshua Barten, his half-brother, maybe that psycho would've never hurt his sister. He wanted so badly to confront him that he barely got any sleep at night.

Hell, most nights he roamed his single-story house from one end of the hallway to the other. It was a damn small house with only two bedrooms, a small kitchen attached with a dining room that was barely a room, and a living room. He swore he could see his footsteps etched in the floor, he paced so much the last few weeks.

But he promised Danny he'd leave it alone, and he wasn't known for breaking his promises.

He wasn't in the mood to forgive Evan. If ever. He didn't

deserve his forgiveness, not after Kat got shot and almost died.

A hand touched his shoulder. He swiped it away as he turned around and then cringed when he saw who stood there. "Shit, Aubrey, I'm sorry. I thought you were Danny."

She smiled warmly at him as Danny walked beside him and slapped the back of his head. "Watch how you touch my sister."

"Stop, Danny. You obviously upset Seth. It's okay if you don't want to talk about Evan, but eventually you should." Another sweet smile punctured her gorgeous face as she grabbed a box and walked away.

Seth glared at Danny. "So you hit the back of my head. Does this make me your brother now? A sign of affection?"

Chuckling, Danny shrugged. "I guess. Eventually we'll be brothers. It's weird to think about, so let's actually not think about it."

They both grabbed another box and headed for the house. Seth agreed. It was weird to think about. Logan was going to marry Aubrey, who was Danny's sister. And Danny was going to marry Kat, who was Logan's sister. Although, he hadn't asked Kat yet.

"When are you going to give Kat a ring?"

Danny's box dropped with a loud thunk to the floor. "We just decided to make a go of things. I'm moving in. One thing at a time."

"Are you afraid of marriage?"

"Are you afraid of dealing with your problems?"

Seth's eyes narrowed, tempted to hit Danny for bringing the subject of Evan back up.

Danny grinned, slapped him on the shoulder, and guided him out of the house. "I'm sorry, Seth. I'll drop it. And don't worry, Kat and I have talked about marriage, especially since we had all the time in the world when we drove the moving truck from Florida to Minnesota. It'll happen someday, but right now, we're going to enjoy what we have. We're in no rush."

Seth nodded, accepting that without question. Kat never rushed into things. He found it surprising she was moving in with Danny so quickly, but he figured it was only because Danny was moving out of state to be with her. Where would he live otherwise? It simply made sense.

"Danny, can you help me move the dresser in my room? Logan keeps giving me daggers every time I try to take one end," Kat hollered from the front door.

The expression on Danny's face said he couldn't believe she even attempted to help Logan. "You better not be moving that thing. You were specifically told not to touch anything."

"I'm not useless. I can help with some things."

"You're still limping. Until you're completely healed, you touch nothing."

Kat's eyes narrowed, then she squealed in happy delight when Danny grabbed her around the waist and picked her up, kissing her madly on the lips. They disappeared from Seth's sight.

The sweet gesture made him smile. It was nice to see his sister happy. He wouldn't lie and say it wasn't surprising to find out Danny was the man who made her happy because it was. He would've never guessed that in a million years. But, after you got to know the guy, he was decent. He couldn't fault the choice she made.

As he reached for another box, his phone buzzed in his pocket. Pulling it out, his hand tightened so hard around the device, he swore he could've crushed it to pieces.

Why the hell was Evan calling him?

A tender hand touched his shoulder. "I think you should answer it."

Another box disappeared as Aubrey walked away, her simple words ringing in his ear.

Should he? What did the asshole have to say?

Swiping his finger across the screen, he didn't say hello.

"I'm surprised you answered, but grateful. I'm sorry, Seth." A moment of silence. "Want to grab a beer and talk?"

No, he didn't. He never wanted to see Evan's face again. Well, maybe one more time to tell him exactly how he felt having a gun in his face, watching his sister fall in agony as a bullet tore through her leg, watching as she passed out on him and he had to carry her for what felt like miles and miles until he could call for help. So, yeah, maybe he did want to grab a beer and talk.

"Yeah, let's do that."

Then he could move on with his life. Without his best friend.

———

DON'T MISS the next book in this exciting romantic suspense series!

STOLEN MEMORIES

For Seth & Pepper's story
Stolen Memories
A Lucky Town Novel, #3

Some secrets are worth killing for...

Seth Caldwell has always been the family troublemaker, but he's ready for a change—starting with his best friend Evan. But before he can talk to him, Evan goes missing and his boss turns up dead. Despite the lies between them and Evan being the prime suspect, Seth knows he's no killer. Now, in order to find him, Seth is forced to turn to feisty new deputy Pepper Wilson for help.

With her razor-sharp instincts and ability to unnerve him like no other, Pepper quickly becomes a temptation he can't resist. But Seth senses she's hiding her own secrets behind that alluring smile. As the danger grows closer and they spiral deeper into a twisted web of deception, one truth becomes clear—some will go to brutal lengths to exact revenge.

Grab this enthralling thrill ride that will leave you gasping for more today!

For Bolt & Cherry's story
Forgotten Memories
A Lucky Town Novel, #5

She isn't looking for trouble...

Despite being a city girl, Cherry Chapman could get used to the small-town life. Not that she's welcome in Lucky. She only wants to meet her half-sister, Pepper, and get to know her, not stir up a hornet's nest. So far, the only person welcoming her is Deputy Bolten, and at times, she feels even he doesn't trust her. The way things are going, she's going to need more than just his kindness. She's going to need his help. But if he doesn't trust her, how can she trust him with the problems that followed her to town?

While the past year has been a rough one, Bolt is trying to move forward. When Cherry comes crashing into their town with her sweet and innocent nature, he can't help but be wary—and attracted to her. The more he gets to know her, the more he wants to help her. He knows something is going on, but no matter how hard he tries, she won't confide in him. He's failed before—getting shot is proof of that—but he vows not to fail again. He'll protect Cherry at all costs, even if that means being on the opposite side of his friends.

*With high tension, suspense, and smoldering romance, dive into the danger and desire with the final book in the **Lucky Town series** today.*

ABOUT THE AUTHOR

I'm a *USA Today* Bestselling Author that loves to write contemporary romance and romantic suspense novels, although I am partial to romantic suspense. I even dabble in paranormal. Honestly, I love anything that has to do with romance. As long as there's a happy ending, I'm a happy camper. And insta-love...yes, please! I love baseball (Go Twins!) and creating awesome crafts. I graduated with a Bachelor's Degree in Criminal Justice, working in that field for several years before I became a stay-at-home mom. I have a few more amazing stories in the works. If you would like to learn more about me and my books, head to my website by scanning the QR code. Thanks for reading!

Scan me